A SOLDIER *of the* COMPANY

LIFE OF AN INDIAN ENSIGN 1833-43

CAPTAIN ALBERT HERVEY

EDITED AND INTRODUCED BY

CHARLES ALLEN

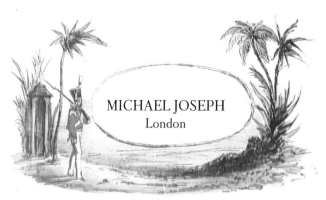

MICHAEL JOSEPH
London

Published in association with the National Army Museum

MICHAEL JOSEPH LTD
Published in Association with the
National Army Museum,
Royal Hospital Road, London SW3 4HT

Published by the Penguin Group
27 Wrights Lane, London W8 5TZ, England
Viking Penguin Inc., 40 West 23rd Street, New York, New York 10010,
USA
Penguin Books Australia Ltd, Ringwood, Victoria, Australia
Penguin Books Canada Ltd, 2801 John Street, Markham, Ontario, Canada
L3R 1B4
Penguin Books (NZ) Ltd, 182–190 Wairau Road, Auckland 10,
New Zealand

Penguin Books Ltd, Registered Offices: Harmondsworth, Middlesex,
England

First published in this abridged edition in 1988

A CIP catalogue record for this book is available from the British Library

ISBN 0 7181 3121 5

Typeset in Fournier by Goodfellow & Egan Photosetting Ltd, Cambridge

Printed and bound in Great Britain by Hazell, Watson and Viney

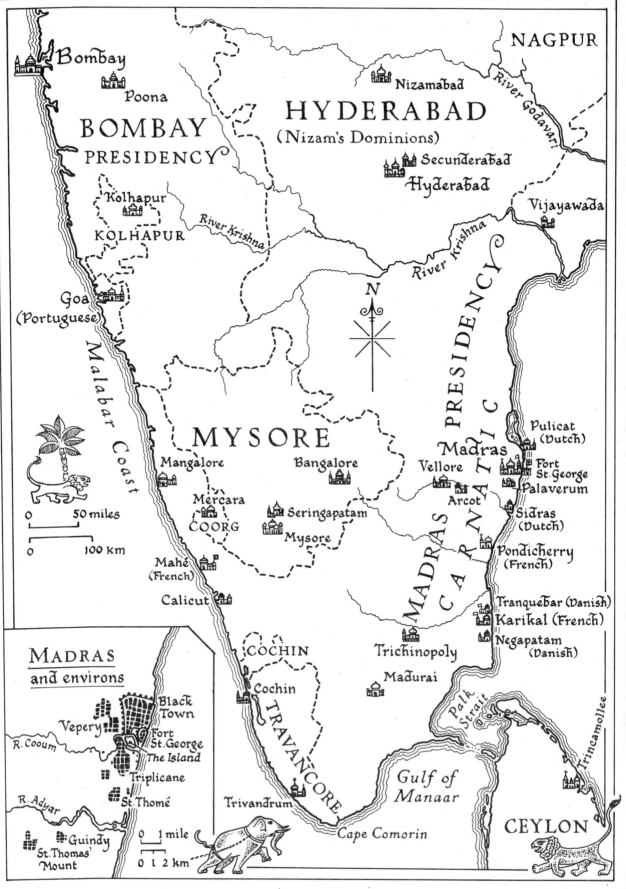

$25

NAGPUR

Bombay

Poona

BOMBAY
PRESIDENCY

Nizamabad

HYDERABAD
(Nizam's Dominions)

River Godavari

Kolhapur

KOLHAPUR

River Krishna

Secunderabad
Hyderabad

Vijayawada

River Krishna

Goa
(Portuguese)

Malabar Coast

50 miles

100 km

MYSORE

Mangalore

Bangalore

Mercara
COORG

Seringapatam
Mysore

Mahé
(French)

Calicut

COCHIN

MADRAS
and environs

Vepery

R. Cooum

Black
Town

Fort
St. George
The Island

Triplicane

St. Thomé

R. Adyar

Guindy
St. Thomas'
Mount

0   1 mile

0 1 2 km

PRESIDENCY

MADRAS

Madras
Vellore

Arcot

Fort
St. George
Palaverum

Sidras
(Dutch)

Pondicherry
(French)

Tranquebar (Danish)
Karikal (French)

Negapatam
(Danish)

Trichinopoly

Madurai

Cochin

TRAVANCORE

Trivandrum

Cape Comorin

Palk
Strait

Gulf of
Manaar

Pulicat
(Dutch)

CARNATIC

Trincamallee

CEYLON

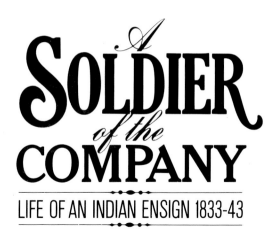

A SOLDIER
of the
COMPANY

LIFE OF AN INDIAN ENSIGN 1833-43

CONTENTS

A Cadet of the Madras Army; a watercolour portrait of Cadet Thomas Gillespie c. 1850

THE INDIA OF
CAPTAIN ALBERT HERVEY

IT HAS BEEN SAID that India was to Britain what the Frontier was to America – a land of limitless opportunity, a testing-ground, a place of romance and adventure. What is certain is that India in the nineteenth century provided a jobs market for the British upper and middle classes. Young gentlemen who sought employment with the civil or military services in British India could expect to live a little dangerously – but like gentlemen. A tradition was soon established whereby sons followed fathers over several generations, and in this respect the Hervey family was no exception.

The Herveys were a typical Indian – as they then called themselves – family. The connection begins with two illegitimate brothers packed off to India in the 1800s, one to the Bengal Army, the other to the Bombay Army. The first prospers and ends his days in retirement in Darjeeling as a much-decorated general. The other is less fortunate: he marries and fathers four children but his wife dies young and then he himself is drowned off the coast of Coromandel in 1824. His orphaned daughter and three sons become the wards of a wealthy and well-connected aristocrat, the Hon. Hugh Lindsay, a director of the East India Company. After being repatriated the boys are placed first in a private school in Hampstead and then sent on to the East India Company's military college at Addiscombe. All three are put down for cadetships in the Company's military service: the eldest in the Madras Army; the second in the Bombay Army; the youngest in the Bengal Army. One – the middle brother – is invalided home early in his career but both his brothers rise to the rank of major-general. Of the next generation one member, at least, conforms to family custom by going into the Indian Army.

Albert Henry Andrew Hervey was the oldest of the three brothers. He received his cadetship from his guardian as an eighteen-year-old on Christmas Day in 1832 and was gazetted an ensign in the Madras Native

Infantry (MNI) within a few days of landing at Fort St George, Madras, in June of the following year. His first year and a half in India was spent as an unattached 'doing-duty *wallah*' with the 5th Regiment MNI, newly-returned from the Malay Archipelago. On 27 October 1834 Hervey was posted to his regiment, the 40th MNI, on whose roll he would remain for the next forty years.

To Albert Hervey's enormous regret his years with the 40th were quite remarkably uneventful. Neither he nor his gallant sepoys were given the opportunity to put their fighting mettle to the test. The unlucky 40th slips through the annals of military history with scarcely a mention or a footnote. Its one memorial is Hervey's memoir, *Ten Years in India or The Life of a Young Officer*, published in 1850. 'Alas!' laments the writer, 'mine has not been a service of hard-fought battles; of lengthened sieges; or of dangers dire by flood and field.'

Hervey was writing of the India of the 1840s, which was dominated by the extraordinary ruling power that went by the grandiose title of 'The Honourable the East India Company' (HEICo), known more familiarly to its subjects as 'John Company' or '*Kampani Bahadur*' (heroic company). The HEICo had come to govern large tracts of India partly by chance, partly by deliberate intent on the part of a few ambitious officers who seized opportunities whenever they were presented. Over a period of some eighty years it had acquired a handsome empire for itself that required a large civil service to administer and sustain, and an even larger army to hold – an army that was to grow into the largest volunteer force ever known.

During Hervey's early years as an army officer the Company's wars of pacification and annexation rolled on more or less without a break from one campaign to the next – but always in the theatres of North and Western India: the forgotten Shekhawattee and Goomsoor expeditions of 1834–5 and 1836; the catastrophic invasion of Afghanistan of 1838–42; the conquest of Sind in 1843 and the Gwalior Campaign in the same year; the First and Second Sikh Wars of 1845–6 and 1848–9. In the South, meanwhile, Madras remained enveloped in the calm of the *Pax Britannica*, seemingly intent on justifying the title of the 'benighted Presidency', where no man stirred and nothing of consequence occurred.

Peace had come to South India with the climactic destruction of the 'Tiger of Mysore', Tippoo Sultan, in his island-fortress of Seringapatam in 1799. With its enemies obliterated and its princely allies firmly under its thumb the HEICo was content to let the South settle down to enjoy the longest period of civil order in its history. Much of the land continued to be governed in traditional style by local rulers while the rest came under the authority of the Madras Presidency, divided into districts and divisions where Collectors governed with the support of local garrisons of native infantry. Here and there at strategic points were quartered full army brigades made up of two Company regiments of native infantry and one King's regiment of British infantry, plus a cavalry regiment and artillery. Bangalore and Secunderabad, two little pockets of British territory set within the princely domains of Mysore and Hyderabad, also had their brigades, while a full division of troops were quartered at the Headquarters of the Madras Army at Guindy, on the plains outside Madras Town. The backbone of this army was its fifty-two battalions of native infantry, each with its small complement of British officers.

In the thirty years before young Hervey's arrival in Madras only one slight hiccough had disturbed the Southern lassitude. In 1806 sepoys stationed at Vellore mutinied and massacred British officers and troops in the local fort. This was followed by an equally savage counter-massacre when the fort was recaptured. Brief as it was, the horror of this event still lingered in officers' minds many years later.

The other blot in the South's otherwise pacific record took place in Hervey's time. In 1833 the unfortunate Rajah of Coorg, a small mountain

The final assault on Seringapatam by the 76th regiment, 1799; watercolour by R. Simkin

principality in the Western Ghats, failed to heed the Company's local Political Agent. The consequence was a short, sharp campaign that ended in the annexation of his territory. A contingent of Hervey's 40th MNI did manage to get involved in the fighting – but not Hervey himself. Hopes were again raised in 1837 when the King of Burmah was deposed by his brother and threats were made against the British. In April 1838 the 40th were moved across the Bay of Bengal to Moulmein, on the estuary of the Salween river. However, the crisis blew over and four years later the 40th was back in Madras, ready to pick up the familiar patterns of turn and turn about at one station or another within the Presidency.

Although it was the seniormost of the three HEICo Presidencies, Madras had long since lost the initiative to Bengal. Calcutta was now the seat of power in India, an ideal jumping-off point for the British expansion into the Indian interior and an ideally-suited market place. Madras, by contrast, was in a hopeless position – a relic of the days when European traders in the Indies thought themselves lucky to be granted so much as a toe-hold on the shores of the sub-continent. Even in Hervey's day Madras remained irredeemably provincial, a beach backed by a façade of fine buildings clustered round Fort St George but with an empty plain behind, unable even to provide safe anchorage for several months of the year. Hervey is only one of many commentators who found Madras 'society' dull, caste-ridden and snobbish.

Fortunately for our young officer, military society was very different. Hervey revelled in the comradeship of the mess and the *esprit de corps* of the regiment, and his affectionate portrayal of this military world is his memoir's best feature. Though he was not to know it then, this sepoy army that he had entered in 1834 was well into the autumn of its days. Yet it was still recognisably the same institution that had been hammered into being in the days of Coote Bahadur and Stringer Lawrence three-quarters of a century earlier. Regiments still moved across the land like plagues of locusts, with vast baggage-trains in tow and an attendant army of camp-followers; the sepoys themselves still dressed, drilled and went into battle in the manner of their grandfathers – often under the command of men old enough to be their grandfathers; officers still bought their way into certain plum posts and, in desperation, clubbed together to buy out older officers in the regiment who blocked the promotion ladder.

The Madras Army quickly became Hervey's life. Like so many British officers before and since, he became utterly devoted to his regiment. Not that he turned a blind eye to the many faults of the army and of those who served in it. Indeed, the most remarkable aspect of Hervey's memoir is the amount of space he gives over to criticisms and instances of bad soldiering. This was a very brave – or very foolish – act on the part of a young captain with only ten years of service behind him and hopes of advancement before him. Hervey saw much that was wrong with the system and went to great pains to say so, even though he hedged every criticism about with polite apologies.

Hervey disliked much of the behaviour of his fellow-officers. He hated the excessive drinking that was so characteristic of the British male in India at that time. He took strong exception to the more blatant forms of what we would now call racism that were starting to become accepted behaviour among his generation – although this does not prevent him from having views about 'Blackie' and his faults that are enough to make modern readers squirm. The fact is that Albert Hervey was much more a child of the times than he may have realised.

The British in India of the 1830s and 1840s had come a long way. They had become mightily proud of themselves. Time and again British forces had trounced local armies many times their size; mighty kingdoms and confederacies had been overthrown; the Company's standard and the Union Jack flew side by side over practically every corner of the sub-continent. All this had been accomplished by a few thousand Britons who saw themselves increasingly as a superior people set by providence over an inferior people. A handful of enlightened individuals took an interest in Indian customs and Indian ideas but the great majority cared not a fig for a race and a culture that seemed to have sunk into the mire. Hervey shared this prejudice. He took not the slightest notice of his Indian surroundings – unless something happened to shock him into taking an interest – and he lumped all Indians together as deceitful, drunken, degenerate – and heathen to boot. Even his beloved sepoys suffer from being too Indian for their own good.

Just at the time that Ensign Hervey was starting to learn the duties of an officer on the parade grounds of Palaveram, T.B. Macaulay was putting the finishing touches to his notorious *Minute on Education*, presented to the Governor-General of India in February 1835. Macaulay spoke for most of his fellow-countrymen in India when he wrote of Indians 'sunk in the lowest depths of slavery and superstition' and when he dismissed Indian culture as 'history abounding in kings thirty feet high, and reigns thirty thousand years long, and geography made up of seas of treacle and oceans of butter'. Instead of teaching Indians their own classical languages – 'barren of useful knowledge' – in schools, he proposed that English be taught instead, so as to create 'a class of persons, Indian in blood and colour, but English in taste, in opinions, in morals and in intellect'. The effects of this doctrine were to be profound.

Another threat to Indian custom that was beginning to make itself felt at this time was the growth of Evangelical Christianity. In its early days the HEICo had banned all missionary activity within its territories. In 1813 this ban was lifted and church missions were encouraged to come out and set up schools and colleges. As Hervey himself illustrates, the British in India in the 1830s were still a particularly godless lot – but this was something that changed dramatically as the Victorian era set in. The devout family man of the late 1840s who sits down and writes his memoirs is very different from the careless young subaltern of the 1830s.

Changing attitudes like these on the part of the British in India conspired to drive an ever-thickening wedge between rulers and ruled. Hervey has a fascinating opposite number in the person of Sepoy Sita Ram, a soldier in the Bengal Army whose memoirs were translated and published in 1873 under the title of *From Sepoy to Subedar*. Sita Ram joined the army twenty years before Hervey, at a time when 'the sahibs could speak our language much better than they can now, and mixed more with us'. By Hervey's time a change for the worse had taken place: 'The sahibs speak to their men only when obliged, and show that it is irksome to them, and try to get rid of them as soon as possible.' Hervey, it must be said, was well aware of this change but, blinded as he was by Victorian notions of moral and religious superiority, he could not see where it would lead to.

Victorian morality also prevents Hervey from being frank about some of the other habits of his countrymen that Sita Ram touches on, such as the keeping of native *bibis* or mistresses, which was still a common enough practice in Hervey's time. After describing a brief romance as a griffin (the Anglo-Indian term for a newcomer to India) that ends in tears, Hervey steers clear of sex altogether. Even his own marriage to the daughter of an artillery major in Burma is only referred to in passing. Perhaps he was planning to tell us more about this second phase of his army career in a sequel. Hervey refers to a planned second book when skimming over his four years in Burma, but if he ever did sit down and write such a book it was certainly never published.

In 1843, Captain Hervey and his wife returned to Britain on furlough and it seems probable that his reminiscences were set down in some form during this first three-year leave. In 1846 he was back with his regiment in Secunderabad, probably fretting away at the slowness of promotion and adding all the afterthoughts and sermonising that made it necessary to put out his book in three volumes. *Ten Years in India* was eventually published in London in 1850 while Hervey was still in India, with its author being identified on the title-page as 'Captain Hubert Hervey, Late of the 40th Madras Infantry'.

How *Ten Years in India* was received by the reading public is not known but its critical content can hardly have gone down well in the upper echelons of the Madras Army or the HEICo. Captain Hervey himself came home for a second leave in 1852 but if he had had thoughts of resigning he evidently changed his mind, since he was back in India again in 1856, stationed this time in the isolated military cantonment of Kampti, in the very heart of the Indian Deccan. Here he and his regiment spent the next two years while the terrible events of the 1857 Mutiny played themselves out in Bengal and Upper Hindustan. One wonders whether Hervey, in his lonely outpost, found any satisfaction in knowing that he had done his best to warn the authorities of the likely consequences of pushing the sepoys too far.

The rebellion of 1857–8 finished off the old John Company. The Bengal Army was destroyed, with nearly all its infantry regiments being disbanded. In the Madras Army, however, there had been no mutiny – despite all the provocations. The war in the north had been none of their concern, so the fifty-two battalions of infantry of the line had stood firm.

In 1860 Albert Hervey moved with his regiment to Singapore and three years later when they returned to Madras he became the regiment's Colonel-Commandant, continuing to hold that post until his final promotion to Major-General in 1874. His last appearance in the Madras List is in 1877, when he appears as 'on furlough'. He died on 27 October of that same year in Edinburgh; by coincidence, the forty-third anniversary of his joining the 40th MNI.

Perhaps it was just as well that Hervey did not live to see his beloved regiment disbanded in 1882 as a consequence of the foolish dogma propounded by Lord Roberts, then Commander-in-Chief in Madras, that some Indians made good soldiers because they belonged to 'martial races', while others – notably the Madrassis – made bad soldiers because they had lost their 'ancient fighting spirit'. How the old sepoy general would have bristled to the very roots of his regulation military mutton chops to hear such nonsense, knowing as he did that there could be 'no soldiers more faithful, more brave, or more strongly attached to their colours and officers, than those of the Madras Army'. Fortunately, Hervey's youthful tribute to the Madras soldier and the men who led him lived on. Neglected and long-forgotten it may have been these many years, but as an evocation of a lost society on the verge of dissolution this memoir surely deserves a place among the classics of Indian military history.

In abridging Captain Hervey's original three volumes down to one I have tried always to keep the narrative flow that holds Hervey's book together. Much of Hervey's very original punctuation remains as it was. A great deal of what he had to say was repetitious or unnecessarily long-winded. He also held strong views and offered plenty of advice at great length. Much of this has had to go but enough has been retained to show how strongly Hervey felt on such subjects as the problems faced by sepoys – and to illustrate that the author was not intent simply on writing a book of reminiscences. I have retained what are surely the original's best features: the details of military life and day-to-day proceedings. Less important, perhaps, but just as engaging is the character of the writer himself as it develops on the page. Albert Hervey took himself seriously as a professional soldier – perhaps rather too seriously. He comes across as a bit of a prig, and there is something almost Pooterish in the way he makes dramas out of little mishaps and unfortunate encounters. One gets the impression that some of Hervey's more hearty companions must have thought him an awful wet blanket – and yet for all that he was a man with an open heart who wrote very much from the heart. This abridged version of his original text is as much a memorial to a decent young man as it is to the regiment he loved and the times in which he served.

CHARLES ALLEN
September 1988

A SOLDIER

of the

COMPANY

LIFE OF AN
INDIAN ENSIGN
1833-43

CAPTAIN ALBERT HERVEY

INTRODUCTION

Iɴᴅɪᴀ! Iɴᴅɪᴀ! Iɴᴅɪᴀ! is now all the vogue. That land of the sun, with her swarthy millions, now occupies the attention of our own country, and attracts the eyes of the whole civilized world. Year after year witnesses the sons of Britain land on its burning shores, to join the ranks and follow the banners of her gallant armies, and many a tear of parting sorrow is shed, as some member quits the bosom of his family, the much-loved and cherished home of his childhood, and parts from all that is most dear to him on this earth.

Many and various are the circumstances under which the sons of our best and wealthiest families leave England to enter the Indian Army, and lucky, indeed, is the youth who can now-a-days secure an appointment from the Court of Directors, which obtains for him a commission in so honourable a profession, and a consequent provision for life.

The wretched widow, whose husband, probably, breathed his last on the bloody field of battle, in the performance of his duty, sends forth her only son to follow the glorious career of his father, and pours forth her parting benediction as he tears himself from her fond embrace. The wealthy citizen, fortunate in the acquaintance of a Director, prepares the Cadet for a military appointment, and embarks him for one of the Presidencies.

The nobleman, also, turns his haughty eye towards the East, and deigns to enlist his youngest into the ranks of an army, which once he had looked upon with disdain, but which he now considers as worthy of receiving a member of his family.

Thus the East has become the stage upon which the children of the most respectable, and the most ancient families of our native land perform a prominent part in the histrionic page of Queen Victoria's reign, giving free scope to that spirit of enterprise so peculiar to the English, to journey eastward in quest of a livelihood, so difficult to be obtained in their own country.

Recent occurrences, partly adding lustre to the arms of our country, and partly deteriorating therefrom, have combined to render our interest in India greater than heretofore. The Bengal and Bombay Presidencies are those on which the attention of Europe has been fixed, as playing the most distinguished part in the tragical drama which has been lately enacted, whilst the sister Presidency of Madras has apparently sunk into insignificance, and been termed, by the would-be-witty, the *benighted Presidency* (whether justly so or not, is another thing). But the Madras Army has been, as it were, resting and looking on at the deeds enacted in the north-west; burning with a desire to join their more fortunate comrades in arms, in the glories of the field, and hoping that they may still be called upon to take their share. They have already conquered, and are ready to conquer again and again.

Give them the opportunity, and they are second to none in the deadly charge, the skirmish, or the escalade; and it is because these brave troops have been left in the background, that the other two armies have been brought conspicuously before the world, that the former glorious deeds of the *benighted* are thrown into the shade, as of secondary consideration, leaving our good folks at home to imagine that we are a mere civil police, kept up more for the purposes of gathering the revenue, and of holding the peasantry of the country in check, than for actual service.

But no! such is not the case. Military ardour and heroic chivalry are at the present period as bright in the breasts of our noble *sepahees* as they were wont to be in the days of Clive and our other heroes. There is no Army in the whole of Europe in which military discipline is better maintained. There are no troops better clad and appointed; there are no soldiers more faithful, more brave, or more strongly attached to their colours and officers, than are those of the Madras Army.

I have the honour to belong to this Army, and I am proud of it! I have served in the ranks of one of its regiments, and have had opportunities of judging and appreciating the characters of the men who compose our soldiery; and I can safely say, that a more manly set of fellows I never could desire to command. The grand secret is, to treat them as men should be treated, and a more tractable race of beings I would never wish to see.

But of this I will make mention hereafter, begging the reader to follow me in my reminiscences of a service with these said Madrassees of upwards of ten years from the date of my first entry to that of my return home on furlough.

But, reader, mine has not been a service of hard-fought battles; of lengthened sieges; or of dangers dire by flood and field. Alas, no! The star of my fortune has not shone either in the one or in the other. I have had no such good luck. It has been my misfortune, and not my fault; though the day may come, when we may smell powder in real earnest, hear bullets whizzing about, and very likely have a taste of one of them. All I can say is, that I heartily envy my brethren in arms who have partaken of such pleasures, and hope when my turn comes I shall have enough to make up for lost time.

My object in publishing the present Work is, to be useful to my fellow soldiers – if I can; and more particularly to such of them as may hereafter wend their way to those sunny climes in which their lot may be cast. This book is intended to instruct, advise and amuse; and I trust it may be found useful to young officers of every branch of the service, be they in her Majesty's or in the Honourable Company's army. People go out to Madras, as well as to Calcutta and Bombay; and, although the scenes and occurrences about to be narrated lie in the former, and the humble author of these pages is in every sense of the word a *Mull* (that is, a Madrassee), he sees no reason why he should not attempt to make himself useful to the *Qui Hais* and *Ducks* as well as to those of his own immediate Presidency.

With these preliminary remarks, and with an apology on my part for having so long detained my reader on the threshold of my narrative, I will at once make a commencement, trusting that the intention which inspires my feeble efforts will be appreciated; that my failings will be treated with an indulgent forbearance; and that my errors, whatever they may be, will receive forgiveness, the more particularly so when I here declare that it is principally from the stores of that strong and faithful ally – my memory – that I am about to supply the substance contained in the following chapters, which I now place before those who may favour them with a perusal.

THE AUTHOR

I T WAS EARLY in the year 1833, that, bidding farewell to England, I shook hands with my two brothers, piped my eye a little, and, with ten shillings in my pocket, embarked at the Tower Stairs on board a steam-boat going to Gravesend, where lay the ship which was destined to convey my precious little body to India.

I say '*little body*', for I was a very little fellow indeed; so little, that people looked on me with wonder and surprise, and some exclaimed, 'Is that child going to be an officer?'; so little, that my guardians would not trust me with any larger sum of money than the ten shillings alluded to, but gave ten pounds instead to the skipper to take care of for me!

I was indeed little, but who cared? I did not. I must be little, thought I, before I am big, and there was every chance of my growing; so, I snapped my fingers at them all, and thought myself of some consequence, notwithstanding my smallness.

I joined the ship; her name was the *Warren Hastings*, 1000 tons burthen, belonging to the East India Company, or rather one of their '*chartered vessels*', commanded by the gallant Captain T —— S ——, a good fellow in his way – most extraordinary in a propensity for anything connected with fox hounds, and a bit of a wag – fond of jolly companions, though a perfect gentleman nevertheless, and moreover in every way prepared to be kind and friendly to me.

My friends had secured me an excellent cabin in the poop of the ship, and I had with me, as companion, a young writer fresh from Haileybury, who thought of nothing morning, noon and night, but hunting, riding, shooting and dissipation; and who considered it very manly and very fine to swear and curse, and to go to bed in a state of inebriety.

Such being the individual I had for my '*chum*', the reader may imagine that I was not particularly comfortable; indeed, it was quite the contrary. I never was so miserable in all my life, and longed for the voyage to terminate (though it had not yet commenced), when I should be rid of my noisy friend, and be once more independent.

And here let me give a little advice in writing, which I have ever given *verbatim* to many young people whom I have met since my return to England. Never take a cabin in partnership with another, not even if he be an intimate friend; for there is no knowing the misery and discomfort you entail upon yourself by having such a companion.

I look back to those four months on board the *Warren Hastings* with feelings of horror, nor would I undergo a similar ordeal for worlds! I suffered severely from sea sickness, so much so that for the greater part of the voyage, and more particularly in very rough cold weather, I was confined to my cot. During this dreadful sickness, my fellow traveller would enter, bring company into the cabin, play at cards and make such a noise, that I was in no very enviable situation. Speaking to them was out of the question. I was only laughed at, and the din and shouting were worse than before.

I remember one night; there was a jollification in the cuddy; my friend had taken a great quantity of wine, and became very much intoxicated. He came to the cabin, and turned into my bed whilst I was on the poop. He was sick, of course, and made my sleeping things in such a condition, that I was obliged to give them away to the sailors, for I could never use them again myself. I cannot bear to think of the horrors of that night.

We had recruits on board, eighty in number, commanded by a Bengal subaltern, rather an aged one, too, nothing very particularly bright, and a sorry specimen of one of that Presidency. The other passengers were king's officers (though I ought now to say '*queen's*' instead of '*king's*'), all huddled together in the large stern cabin down below, where they had it all their own way; but as the regions in which they vegetated were too hot for them when the stern ports and dead lights were closed during the rough weather, they used to come up into our cabin, and a precious disturbance they used to make, too!

They were, however, a jolly set of care-for-nothing young fellows, and proved themselves everything that was amusing and agreeable to those who could bear them; but sea sickness, and other evils combined, rendered their society neither desirable nor pleasant to me.

We were detained three weeks at Spithead in consequence of contrary winds. A very large fleet of ships lay there, amongst them line of battles and several of our thundering East Indiamen, which vessels, being manned and armed as men-of-war, gave them more that appearance than of ships for carrying tea, cotton and other cargoes.

When at length we did get away, we had a narrow escape of running foul of the *Thames*, a 1400-ton ship, caused by the obstinate stupidity of the pilot; and, had it not been for the timely interference of the captain, who immediately took command, we should most certainly have bumped against her, and the damage would have been considerable.

It came on to blow when passing the Needles; there was a seventy-four, the old *S——*, going out with us, and '*reef topsails*' was the order. Through some clumsiness or oversight the gallant *S——*s lowered their topsails without letting go the top-gallant sheets: the consequence was that they all snapped like whipcord, and the sails fluttered in the breeze, making a noise like thunder. This accident delayed her, whilst the Indiamen reefed, hoisted, and sheeted home; and one of them, the *Herefordshire*, bending beautifully to the squall, sailed round the seventy-four, then at a stand-still. As they sailed close by us we could hear the gallant fellows '*splice the main brace*', their skipper having given them a treat for their smartness in beating a seventy-four in reefing top-sails.

But I will not trouble the reader with a lengthened account of a voyage to India. We had dreadful weather in the Bay of Biscay, and I was as sick as possible, could not eat, drink, or even get out of my bed, notwithstanding that I made several ineffectual attempts to do so; the captain was very kind to me, tried various methods to cure me, but all was to no purpose. I really thought I should have died.

In this state I continued until we nearly reached the Line, where the weather was fine, and I contrived to crawl upon deck, but so emaciated and reduced that my fellow passengers scarcely knew me. In crossing the Line, the usual ceremonies of shaving and ducking were gone through. I was exempted from the dirty ordeal, in consequence of having crossed before on my way to England as a child; though I paid Neptune five shillings by way of a fee.

Our voyage was a dull, uninteresting one. There were courts-martial innumerable amongst the recruits, several floggings, and one death. Off the Cape we had very severe weather. I shall never forget one night; I happened to be on the poop, sitting against one of the hen-coops, muffled up in my cloak. The ship was on her course, and the wind blowing very smartly, while the sea was running mast-head high. Suddenly we heard a crash, and a report above head, and found that one of our sails had given way.

Hands were sent aloft to secure the sail and stow it on the top; during this operation one of the topmen, a fine lad, unfortunately fell overboard. I saw the poor fellow fall into the water, and as I was seated on the tafferel I could observe him swimming nobly through the waves; he called out most lustily to 'lower away the boat'. I was on the point of cutting the lashings of the life buoy, when the captain, who had that moment come on deck, touched me on the shoulder and told me to stand fast.

In the meantime the quarter boat's crew were piped aft, the ship's sails thrown aback, and every thing cleared away for lowering the starboard cutter, when the coxswain of her came up to the captain, touched his hat, and said:–

'We are ready to go, sir; but do you think the boat will live in such a sea as this now running?'

I remember the captain's answer as he gave it.

'You are right, my lad. Pipe belay there! and secure the boats again. Square away the yards, and lay the ship on her course. It is impossible to save him; and it is better to lose one man than a whole boat's crew.'

The boats were secured, and the ship put on her course. Oh, what a moment was that! We could hear the agonized shriek of the drowning man as he cried to us –

'Lower away the boat! – lower – away!' the voice getting less audible in the distance: I ran up the mizzen rigging, and could see the poor man swimming beautifully, sometimes on the crest of a mountain wave, sometimes in a valley below; the phosphoric light showing whereabouts he was. I almost fainted as I came on the deck; the thoughts of a human being perishing within sight of apparent rescue were indeed terrible.

It so happened that the coxswain who had spoken to the captain was the brother of the unfortunate lad, and when he heard who it was that had been lost the effect upon the poor man was indescribable.

This was not the only man who fell overboard; there was another, but we succeeded in saving him. The day on which he contrived to tumble into the sea happened to be his birthday: his messmates had given the fellow their grog, and, when he went aloft in the evening to rig in the larboard fore-top-mast-sternsail-boom, he was so totty, that, over-balancing him-self on the footrope, he turned a summerset on the yard, and fell into the water.

Fortunately we were going slowly at the time. The punt astern was lowered, and he was saved. The first words he uttered when he touched his hat on coming on deck were a dreadful oath, and an expression of satisfaction on being once more in the old tub of a ship!

Our passengers used to amuse themselves in various ways; they were however generally very idle. Cards, and consequently gambling, were the favourite occupations, and at the end of the voyage some of them found themselves woefully out of pocket. I passed my time in studying the Hindustanee grammar, which I found, when I began with a *Moonshee*, of the greatest service to me.

Of course I was considered a great '*spoon*' for my pains, but that did not hurt me much; and I strongly advise my young friends to adopt a similar mode of employment: it is of great assistance hereafter, and I think 'board-a-ship' just the place for such sort of amusement. I have known many a young man lay a foundation for the lamentable propensity to gambling merely by playing during the voyage; and I could name several now no more, who, from beginning with small stakes, have gone on and got themselves dreadfully involved. Some, to drown care, have taken to the bottle, and others have been dismissed the service; whilst others, again, have been carried off by the consequences of debauchery, brought on by playing, late hours, and drink.

Shun those amusements, therefore, while on board. You have many other ways of killing time: read, write, draw, keep a journal, work the ship's course, take the latitude and longitude, the lunars, keep the time of the ship's chronometers, and, above all – a word in your ear, my young friend – remember what you have been taught by your 'mothers' in regard to your duty to God – spend a portion of your day in thinking of, and praying to Him – and forget not what our blessed Lord's behest was, 'Watch and pray, lest ye enter into temptation!'

Off the Cape we were visited by the birds peculiar to that part of the world; and, as usual, the guns of the passengers were at play upon the poor creatures all day. I was foolish enough to unpack my guns but scarcely fired out of them myself, being, as I before observed, much afflicted by sea sickness, and consequently scarcely able to do any thing. I lent them instead to one of the young men, like a greenhorn that I was.

Our cabin was turned into a kind of shamble or slaughter-house, where these things were brought; the stench was horrible! There were albatrosses, Cape pigeons, and other birds, placed in every corner of the room; the *spolia opima* of my chum, who must needs have them skinned and stuffed – the pepper, powder, and other preparations used for curing the skins, nearly stifled me; indeed I could not bear to enter my cabin; and,

Shooting albatross on the outward voyage; lithograph from Views of India

had it not been for the kindness of one or two of the officers of the ship, I do not know how I should have got on, for I used to take refuge in one of their apartments for the greater part of the day, preferring that to the abominable stench of my own, to say nothing of the noise and hubbub – such firing of guns, such shouting, such swearing!

Our lads used to amuse themselves in unsoldering their uniform cases and swords to show them off. I had no uniforms, but my sword was unpacked one fine day while I was asleep in the doctor's cabin, and the consequence was, that it got rusted and spoilt. The poor griffins, while on board, think it a very fine thing to show each other their kits. They therefore open their boxes, put on their uniforms, and run about the ship, to the great amusement of the officers and crew, and the detriment of their wardrobe.

I remember one young cavalry officer, just let loose from his dear mamma's apron strings, who, before he had been a month away, unpacked his cases, put on his full dress uniform, helmet, sabre-tache and all, not omitting his spurs, and went aloft! The sailors, determined to enjoy the fun, ran up after him, and catching him in the topmast rigging, made a beautiful '*spread-eagle*' of the trooper, to the great amusement of the spectators, to his great annoyance, and to the irreparable ruin of his beautiful new coat (which had cost his poor mother many a pound, and which she probably could ill afford to pay), it having become covered with pitch, tar, and other marine abomination.

We touched nowhere on our voyage, and only fell in with one homeward-bound ship, by which we sent letters making mention of our welfare – *very* agreeable intelligence doubtless to those who are interested in the parties from whom such letters come; but considered generally '*a bore*' by the good folks at home, who, in some cases, look upon those they are sending out to India as a good riddance of bad rubbish, and the less they hear from them the better. There *are* however exceptions.

In due course of time we made the Madras coast, where we found that several of the Indiamen which had sailed at the same time and after us, had already arrived in the roads; this was owing to their superior qualities, the *Warren Hastings* being after all nothing better than a huge tub, in every sense of the word.

We were instantly surrounded, of course, from stem to stern by *Massulah* boats and catamarans, laden with fruit and *rascals*; the latter crowding the ship, and the former the stomachs of all the raw inexperienced hands in her. I abstained from the fruit, not only from knowing the danger of indulging in it, but from the bad quality brought for sale; and I would advise all newcomers to follow my example. I recollect several of

A massulah *boat crossing ehe Madras surf; watercolour by Lt. Robert Thompson of the 43rd MNI c. 1850*

our lads were laid up with severe attacks of dysentery from eating the fruit on first arrival, and they were a long time getting over their complaints.

The number of natives who came on board caused a great confusion. Several of them addressed me, but, as I had been in India before, and knew their characters, I made use of such few sentences in Hindustanee as I could call to my recollection, and I was not pestered by them. These poor fellows came on board to seek for employment, and if they are fortunate enough to secure some *dreadful* griffin, they stick to him like a leech, and demean themselves in such a plausible manner, that their employers are duped into the belief that they have obtained a really honest servant.

One of these candidates for service generally begins as follows:–

'How you do, Sar? Hope Sar, master is vell. My name, Sar, Ramaswamy. I dubashee! I glad see master. Master look ver vell – hansom, rose cheek got – good calor – good yealth – nice country Yenglan. I glad do master sarvice. I very hanest man, Sar. Plenty cractur got – spose master's hanors plase I show em. Master istranger gentlemans, come to Madras – know nothing – I know yebry thing. Spose, Sar, you yemplay the me, I be very good servant for master! I die for master! Spose master want shoes, I make em from my roan ishkeen! And master want to drink, I give my roan blood! I foor man, Sar, but I hanest man too, Sar,' &c. and so forth, and would go on without ceasing, if not stopped.

Well, after such an idiomatic speech, the cunning would-be employé makes a series of obeisances and salaams, fumbles in his pocket for characters (all borrowed for the occasion at perhaps one rupee each from the many servants at Madras), and at the same time talking most vehemently, and with such apparent candour and innocence, making the green-horn believe every word he says. He alludes to his letters of introduction, asks his name, and then says:–

'Shall Ramaswamy look after master's buggage? How many trunk master got? I take plenty care, master neber pear. I very hanest man, Sar! Master nothing to do – I got boat for master all ready – my roan boat – nothing to pay for landing, I take master free to the shore.'

These sort of speeches very often terminate in the person so making them being engaged, and then commences a train of cheatery and rascality too long for me to enter into. Woe betide the purse of the green-horn, or his nice kit of clothes! The simple-spoken honest *dubashee* takes care of the former, and keeps the keys of the trunks containing the latter! For every sovereign that he changes a deduction is made by him of perhaps two rupees, a payment of four shillings in the pound! And out of every dozen articles of clothing, probably a fourth is appropriated by this trust-worthy menial, and make their way into the '*thieving bazaar*', where all stolen articles are vended, and find numerous purchasers.

Ramaswamy does everything for his master; he tries all in his power to please him; as a matter of course is always at hand; stays outside the door of his room; sleeps there, and will not allow a soul to come near or have anything to do with him; and, should it so happen that a discovery is made by the servant that any one is trying to cheat master, he becomes so infuriated with the unfortunate individual detected, that he strikes, kicks, buffets without mercy, and adds thereto such a volley of abusive language, that the hearer is perfectly astonished, and gives the zealous *dubash* the credit of being, at all events, an honest man, and one faithfully attached to his master!

Thus far so good – all is as it should be – the servant is all attention, devotion, fidelity, and honesty; while the master is all trust and confidence; everything goes smoothly on. The young griffin ventures to boast to his companions, and even writes home to his friends in his first letter, that he has been *so* fortunate as to pick up *such* an honest, faithful servant!

This continues for some time, according to circumstances. If Ramaswamy sees he benefits aught by staying in his master's service, the knavery will be carried on for some months, and even years; but if Ramaswamy sees that his master is a little more keen and alive to his interests than the generality of griffins; why the farce is concluded by the

The griffin besieged on landing; lithograph from F.J. Bellew's Memoirs of a Griffin, *1843*

faithful, honest *dubash* making himself scarce with a good supply of master's things, including gold or silver watch, spoons, and forks, in fact, everything that is valuable, and most easily converted into money. Ramaswamy is off! and nobody knows where he is gone to! As for poor griffin, he is minus this, that, and everything else!

Beware of these silvery-tongued, smoothfaced *dubashes*; they are the veriest rogues in Madras; they will cheat you with the greatest coolness possible, and think no more of telling a downright lie, than if they were going to a meal! In nine cases out of ten, servants taken on board ship are invariably thieves. Have nothing to say to them if you value your kit, or your purse.

Wait patiently until you meet a friend, who can put you in the way of procuring such as will be useful to you, and who are known to the parties recommending them, and then you are comparatively safe; employ a *dubash*, and you are robbed to a certainty.

Amongst those who boarded our ship on coming to an anchor, was an European sergeant in full dress, who brought a despatch to the captain. This was to hand over to the sergeant such cadets as were passengers in his ship. I being the only individual bearing that exalted rank, the sergeant (a thundering grenadier) touched his cap (at which I was very much pleased), and told me that he had brought a boat for me to go on shore in, and hoped I would show him my luggage.

I felt quite delighted when the boat pushed off from the sides of the huge Indiaman, vowing I would never again share a cabin with another man, and hoping that I might never again put foot on board of a vessel in which I had spent so many unhappy days.

Everybody has heard or read of the famous Madras surf, that tremendous barrier which guards the shores of the coast, so replete with danger to the uninitiated; and those dreadful sharks which swarm outside ready to pounce upon any unfortunate victim who may fall into the water. In crossing the surf some degree of skill is necessary to strand the boats in safety, and the boatmen usually demand a present for a job, for which they are already well paid; but griffins are *so* kind and *so* liberal, and these boatmen are *such* acute judges of physiognomy, that they can tell at a

glance, whether there is a probability of success or not. If refused, they sometimes bring their boats broadside on to the surf; the consequence is a good ducking, if not an upset altogether into the briny element; this is by way of revenge.

The person who most deserves a present, if any, is the poor *catamaran jack*, who follows each boat in his frail bark, ready to pick up any body in case of an upset; and I have invariably given these poor fellows half a rupee (one shilling), as a present, merely for being ready, in case of necessity.

I remember an instance of a boat crossing the surf without the attendance of one of these men. The surf was very high, the boat was upset; the crew all escaped by swimming, but one poor old soldier, going as a passenger to one of the ships, not being able to swim, was seen to sink, and rose no more: he must either have been drowned or carried off by a ground shark.

We crossed the dreaded surf and landed in safety. Passengers are either carried out of the way of the water in a chair or on the backs of the boatmen. Upon gaining a footing, I was instantly surrounded by a multitude of naked looking savages, all jabbering away in broken English and Malabar, asking me to take a *palankeen*, and some actually seized hold of me, and were about to lift me into one; however, I asked the sergeant, who was with me, for his cane, which being obtained, I laid about me right and left, and soon cleared myself of the crowd.

The sergeant took charge of my traps and we walked on to the fort, which, by the way, was a very foolish trick on my part, for, though the day was fair, and a cool breeze blowing, I found the sun much warmer than I had ever felt it in Old England. I recommend my friends to be more careful than I was; I consider walking in the sun ten times worse than eating fruit, particularly without a covering to the head. I have known a young man struck down by a *coup de soleil* on first landing, merely from walking as I did; it is indeed a most foolish trick.

Passing through the north gate into the fort, the sergeant took me direct to the adjutant-general's and town-major's offices, where I reported myself in due form. I was then conducted to the cadets' quarters, where I was told I should have to reside until further orders.

Behold me now, gentle reader, safely arrived at Madras, the scene of my future career. Verily was I like a young bear, with all my troubles before me; I was, however, as happy as possible.

I found several old Addiscombe friends already arrived at the cadets' quarters, all griffs, as young and inexperienced as your humble servant. There was a mess kept for us, three meals a day, for which we had to pay most dreadfully; everything to be had was bad, and knavery and cheating in most glaring colours reigned supreme in this asylum; a place kept on purpose by government, to give the poor inexperienced cadet a home on first arrival, superintended by an officer who was of no use whatsoever, and frequented by the greatest thieves and vagabonds in Madras, from the villain butler to the sweeper!

The butler was paramount in authority, and I could compare him to nothing but the bull in the crockery shop; for he had it all his own way, and a more consequential, over-fed Pariah rascal I never saw. The fellow, I recollect, had the insolence to show me his portrait (such as it was) as much as to say, 'If I were not an honest man, do you think I would have had my likeness taken?' I greatly exasperated the old thief by telling him that I thought the picture more like a *baboon* than a human being, and certainly very much resembling his butlership.

I had brought out a letter or two to some of the residents, and I was

View of Fort St George, Madras; coloured aquatint from Voyage to Madras and China

determined to deliver them as soon as I could conveniently do so. The day after my arrival I jumped into a *palankeen*, and, armed with my letters, went in quest of those for whom they were intended. One of the gentlemen was kind enough to invite me to put up at his house, which invitation I gladly accepted, as I was already disgusted with my quarters and longed to be away from them.

The reception I met with from my friend was hospitable, and the next day found me settled in his house, where I was kindly treated, and lived upon the clover of a staff appointment.

I remember a young man arriving at Madras armed with strong letters of recommendation to the commander-in-chief, who it appeared was acquainted with his parents, as well as several members of his family. He made sure of a room at the chief's, and was certain of being appointed at least an aide-de-camp. Poor boy! he was much surprised when he was told to go and learn his duty with a corps several hundred miles up country.

Letters to great folks at the outset do more harm than good in my opinion. A young man should be away from the Presidency as fast as he possibly can, get over his drill, learn his duty as an officer and a soldier, become acquainted with the language, and then think of preferment; but, before these objects are attained, letters of introduction had better be left alone.

I landed in India on the 7th June, 1833. About a week after we saw our names in orders, as being admitted on the establishment, promoted to the enviable rank of ensigns, leaving the dates of our commissions to be settled hereafter. In the same Gazette I saw myself with others posted to do duty until further orders with the —— Regiment of Native Infantry, stationed at Palaveram, a military cantonment about thirteen miles from Madras. We were directed to join and report ourselves to the officer commanding that corps forthwith, giving us time, however, to prepare our uniforms and other things.

My friend with whom I resided, procured for me the requisites for a sub; to wit, a camp cot with mattress and pillows, mosquito curtains, and water holders for the legs of the bedstead, the former to guard against those nightly abominations so well known in all tropical climates; and the latter, against the visits of the little red ant, which, without those articles, will swarm a poor man's bed, get into his hair, and bite like so many little fiends! I do not know which is the worst, the sting of a mosquito, or the bite of an ant; both are bad enough, and to avoid which, all newcomers particularly should be prepared with those appendages, without which they must never expect a night's rest.

Besides the above, I had a folding camp-table, and a large chair, a queer looking article, still strong and serviceable. I also purchased a brass basin on a tripod stand, very useful in marching, and a well-known accompaniment to every officer's kit.

As a bit of horseflesh is indispensable to a sub's '*turn-out*', my friend bought me a stout Pegu pony, with a saddle and bridle. I knew nothing about riding, and as to a knowledge of the qualifications of a horse I was as ignorant as a babe. I gave two hundred and fifty rupees for my pony, saddle and bridle, and thought myself fortunate in getting the animal and his trappings so cheap.

An ensign has no business to give more than three hundred rupees for a horse, and that sum, in my opinion, is just one hundred and fifty or two hundred rupees too much. There are many good, strong, useful hacks to be had from one hundred to two hundred rupees, which will answer the purpose admirably well.

The best way is to wait for a general sale by auction, and then you will have an opportunity of picking and choosing. I have seen horses sold at these sales for two rupees – four shillings! It is not only very foolish in young men giving a large sum and purchasing a really valuable horse, but it is running a great risk having such a one in his stables; because, ignorance of the treatment of a horse will make them liable to all sorts of mishaps, thereby endangering their lives, and the hard work, which a sub's nag is subject to, will very soon knock up one of that description.

Now, if the griffin have a horse of a small value, and should anything happen to him in any way; should he be carried off by the gripes, or have '*a stroke of the land-wind*', or should he fall down a hundred times, there is not much lost, and the money that is saved by buying such an animal, will enable him to procure another in case of any accident. A cheap horse, therefore, for a griffin is the best in my humble opinion. None of your fine animals will ever do.

In making any purchases at first, it is better to consult some experienced hand, and the newcomers will always find many ready and willing to put them in the way of obtaining the articles they want in a more economical manner, than they themselves could possibly manage. Some young fellows, with a good supply of cash, start in first-rate style, by keeping two horses, a buggy, and other extravagances, but these only last as long as the coin does, and that is not long; for money in the hands of a griffin, is generally like two ships in a storm, they very soon part company – and the end of it is that the reckless individuals only get laughed at.

I JOINED THE —— Regiment NI about the latter end of June, being taken to Palaveram in my friend's carriage. He was kind enough to accompany me thither, and we went to the house of an acquaintance of his, the quarter-master of the regiment, who received me most warmly. I was asked to reside with him as a temporary arrangement, until I could get myself a bungalow in the Cantonment; an invitation I gladly accepted.

The next morning I was roused out my bed very early indeed, and had to put on my uniform for the first time: my new friend T——n telling me I must accompany him to the parade ground to meet the commanding officer, and to be introduced to the adjutant, who was ready to make a soldier of me. I buckled on my sword (an immense long one, too, it was; I had selected the largest in the outfitter's shop, as I said I should be big enough in time for it) and sallied forth to the barracks and parade, where I saw a most dignified looking personage, with a very healthy looking countenance, sitting on horseback, and another officer, also mounted, conversing with him. They were looking at a body of soldiers in white coats drilling. We went up to these officers and touched our caps, and I was introduced to them as Ensign Hervey, recently posted to do duty, and come to report myself as joined.

'Well, Mr Hervey,' says the dignified looking personage; 'I am glad to see you; welcome to the ——th. You'll do very well, I have no doubt, under my adjutant there. Mack——, allow me to introduce a young aspirant to military fame. Take him in hand, and teach him his duty!'

The adjutant came up, shook hands with me, and said,

'I am happy to see you with us; we will teach you the *proper business*, though, I suppose, you are quite an adept at *balance step, without gaining ground, &c. &c*; and I dare say you know how to show *the advantage of shifting the leg*, eh? You know that business well, I suppose?'

'Yes, sir,' said I, 'I have good cause not to forget all I learned at Addiscombe. We had plenty of drill there.'

'Well, then, suppose we try now,' said the adjutant. 'We shall soon see what you are made of.'

Then calling the drill *havildar*, he said something to him in Hindustanee, and the man touched his cap to me, and smiled a most military smile.

A squad of recruits was brought up, and I was ordered to fall in. We went through all the facings and marchings. The major and adjutant both expressed themselves much pleased with my display. This was my first *debut* as a soldier; and, after further conversation, the major permitted us to retire.

My good friend T——n asked the two to come and take a cup of coffee, which they did; and I was happy to find that my new brother officers were all on excellent terms with each other; that the rigidity of the commanding officer was put on one side in the private gentleman; and that all whom I saw were disposed most kindly towards me. How fortunate did I consider myself at being at once so comfortable and happy, and amongst such a quiet set of officers!

I did not go in quest of quarters for myself at all, as T——n very goodnaturedly told me that it would be better for me to reside where I was, as I should then have the benefit of his advice and experience. He had me posted to his own company, and I became completely under his authority, a fortunate thing for me, as I learned my duty the quicker, for he was one of the smartest officers in the regiment.

I must here mention that the regiment to which I had become thus attached, had but recently returned to Madras, from three or four years *foreign service*, in the Straits of Malacca, where it had been actively employed against some insurgent Malays in the interior. They had suffered severely from the effects of climate; had lost many men; and had returned in a very reduced state, both as regarded officers as well as privates. Several had been killed and wounded; amongst the latter were T——n and his chum W——t.

Palaveram is well known. It is a hot station, evincing but scanty proof of the skill in selecting ground, on the part of him who constituted it a military cantonment. Situated at the foot of a range of hills, it is as grilling as it well could be; the said hills completely shutting out the delicious sea-breeze so much prized by Indians.

Palaveram has barracks for four regiments. The officers' houses are neat and comfortable, and laid out in regular streets; those nearest the hills being appropriated to the field officers and captains, as being the hottest, I suppose, and they being better able to bear the heat than the younger subalterns, whose quarters were furthest from the hills, and consequently the coolest. There are one or two bungalows situated outside the cantonment, and it was in one of these that my friend, his chum, and I resided during our stay at Palaveram.

We had hard work of it at the drill, morning and evening, though it did not last long. We were dismissed in about three weeks as fit for duty, and then only had we time to look about us a little.

My friend T——n regularly took me in hand, and made me keep the books and accounts of his company. This I at first objected to, but he showed me a paragraph in the *Standing Orders* which induced me to obey him; and I found it to be of the greatest benefit to me afterwards; as it not only gave me an insight into regimental matters, but brought me into contact with the men, by which means I became acquainted with their names, and their characters, as well as the peculiarities of their castes, religions and manners.

Let me urge on all young officers the necessity, the great necessity, of attending to this duty; not that I claim any merit for myself, as it is all due to my worthy friend, and I owe much to him for insisting on my compliance.

In addition to writing the books and keeping the accounts, I used to pay the men, visit their barracks and huts in the lines, as well as the sick in hospital; hear their complaints, and investigate their quarrels and dis-agreements, &c.; all this I did, not for my own pleasure, but because I was obliged by the desire of my company's superior. I had therefore no alternative but to obey. I had also to make my reports to him.

At the same time, and in order that I might understand what was said, I fagged hard with the *Moonshee*, who used to come to me every day for four hours. I held conversations with my teacher in English; every sentence uttered was put down on paper in Hindustanee, and the next day what I had written down in Hindustanee, was brought to me fresh written by the *Moonshee*, and these sentences I re-translated into English, so that I not only gained a knowledge of words, but was able to read the common writing, which was of the greatest assistance.

I fagged thus hard for three months, working away without relaxation, except for meals and a *siesta* in the heat of the day (a very bad habit by the way, and one which ought never to be indulged in); and occasionally receiving a visit from some of my neighbours.

A young fellow is often laughed out of the good intention of studying the language, by being told that it is all stuff and nonsense; that there is no necessity for it; that a man can get on well enough without putting himself to such trouble; that all he has to do is, to say '*Achha*' (Very good) to everything that may be told or reported to him.

Now, it so happened to one of our doing-duty ensigns that he was orderly officer of the day on the occasion of a fire in the regimental lines; it was his particular duty to be present on the spot, and to assist in putting the fire out. The bugles sounded *the alarm*, the drums beat *the long roll*, guards and pickets turned out, and the men flocked to the place. The officers were also present doing all they could to extinguish the flames.

Everybody was on the spot, excepting the one of all others who should have been there, viz. the officer of the day, who was nowhere to be found; not at his post, at all events. He was seated in his bungalow, in deshabille, smoking a cigar, taking it coolly, as people say. He had heard the bugles, but he did not know one *call* from another; and as for the drums, he imagined them to be someone practising! Presently in rushed a *havildar* breathless with running, '*Sahib! sahib, line ko rĭngār lŭggyā!*' (Sir! sir, the lines are on fire!) The young officer responded to the intelligence by saying, '*Achha!*' The *havildar* retired.

Shortly after in came a *naigur* (corporal), repeating the same fact. '*Achha*' was the answer he got, and he retreated also. I happened to gallop through the man's compound, on my way to the lines, and called out to him, but he heeded me not.

'Where is the officer of the day?' inquired the major; 'Send and call him! Send an orderly immediately!'

An orderly came and found my gentleman seated as before!

'Major *sahib bolātā hai – sahib!*' (The major calls you, sir) exclaimed the orderly, and quitted the bungalow; but '*Achha*' was the answer he received; another orderly came, and received the same reply. At last in galloped the adjutant.

'Hallo! Is Mr —— at home?'

Up jumped the unfortunate griffin, puffing his cigar, with a glass of brandy pawney in his hand, and went out.

'Do you want me? What is the matter?'

'Matter, sir?' asked the adjutant. 'Don't you know that the lines are on fire and that you should be there? The major has sent twice for you, and you are not moving! You have got yourself into a precious scrape! Make haste and put on your things, and hurry down to the barracks!'

Poor lad! He made as much haste as he could, and presented himself long after the fire had been put out. He got a terrible rap over his knuckles for his '*Achha*,' and never committed himself in a similar manner again.

At the end of the three months, I passed a regimental examination in Hindustanee, and the major (who was always kind to me) placed me in the entire command of the company to which I was attached. This gave me an immediate increase to my pay, and placed me in an independent situation, which the other cadets, some of them my seniors, did not enjoy.

I was also the first to mount main guard. This I did as a supernumerary to learn my duty. I remember that day well. My superior was an officer of another corps, and he very kindly (rather *unkindly*, for so it was), allowed me in the night to take off my clothes and go to bed. At about twelve o'clock, the field officer visited the guard, and upon its turning out, inquired where the supernumerary subaltern was?

The answer was, 'In bed. I told him, sir, he had no occasion to get up.'

An orderly came up into the room and gave me a poke on the ribs, and told me that the *field officer sahib* wanted me. Bah! What a fright I was in! The perspiration poured from me: visions of courts-martial and all kinds of punishments flitted before me. I was so confused that I did not know what to do, or which way to turn. However, I at length presented myself, apologizing for keeping him waiting in the damp cold night. Poor Captain M—— gave me a good wigging, telling me that I was very wrong.

'Let this be a lesson to you, sir, never to take off your things while on guard. An officer on duty should ever be on the alert. He and his sword should never part company. I hope, sir, this will never occur again.'

I felt myself quite ashamed to be thus reprimanded, resolving that if I mounted guard a thousand times a month, my uniform, sword and sash, should never be separated from my body. It is the worst thing an officer can do, and sets a bad example to the men, who are ever ready to follow such whenever they have an opportunity. 'The officers do it,' say they, 'and why should we not?' Picture to yourself your position before an enemy; the officer without his clothes on; the post attacked, and no one ready!

I contrived to have a good gallop morning and evening, after drill, every day, and that was excellent exercise. My pony turned out to be a *brute*. He was as stubborn as a jackass, had a mouth like iron, and shied most dreadfully; I falling off on one side, while he would jerk away to the other. I am only surprised that I had not my neck broken, for I had many a severe fall, one of which hurt me so much, that I was laid up for some time on the sick list, with leeches, &c.

The pony and I could not get on at all together. I therefore resolved on parting with him, which I did shortly after to a native, who gave me my money for him. Besides riding out, I used to go into the brushwood and jungle in the neighbourhood of Palaveram, popping away at all descriptions of the feathered tribe, now and then getting a shot at a stray partridge or hare. I was astonished with my success as a sportsman, and was old enough at last to venture upon snipe, getting better and better the more I practised.

I will allow that I often took a *pot shot* at an unfortunate paddy bird standing on one leg, or at a *Brahminy kite*, seated shrieking on a Palmira tree; but that was not very often. However, pigeons, and occasionally ducks and hens, used to feel the effects of my fire.

I one day let fly into a flock of geese, killing one and wounding another. They turned out to be the poor brigadier's! I was obliged to give the affrighted keeper a couple of rupees to silence him. The killed and wounded were taken home, and furnished two capital dishes for our next day's tiffen.

A few months after joining the ——th, our gallant major gave a pic-nic party, on the strength of his promotion. Tents were sent out, also large supplies of beer and soda-water, (principal ingredients, without which nothing can be done), to say nothing of other drinkables as well as eatables. I took both my guns – indeed I had three – and an enormous quantity of powder and shot. To have seen my ammunition, one would have thought that I was going to attack a fort; and I was nicely laughed at.

We formed a merry party. I think there were some twelve of us, and the place of rendezvous (well known to all Madrassees) Vendalore, or Smith's Choultry, capital ground for snipe and other small game. I rode out on the Pegu, affording my companions much amusement, for he shied at every stone or leaf on the road, keeping me in constant dread of an upset. There was a great deal of damage done, hundreds of snipe slaughtered, to which I added my quota of two brace and half; one paddy bird, one kite, and a guana! We had snipe at table in every shape; snipe-à-la-mode, snipe curry, snipe pie, snipe stew, and snipe devils. There was plenty of beer drank, and some of the party were very merry, as is generally the case on these occasions.

This was the first thing of the sort I had witnessed; I had therefore a good opportunity to watch and see how matters were conducted. I observed that those who had done least in the way of sport, ate and drank most, and were more intoxicated than those who had borne the heat of the day. There was not, however, any disturbance, excepting plenty of singing, roaring, and laughing.

Those who did not go shooting remained in the camp, attended to the cooking, &c., played at cards, and baited jackalls; the latter a cruel amusement, I thought, though I could not but help admiring the hardy courage of those poor animals as they stood at bay against five or six English bull-terriers; it was a piteous sight, and I was sorry to see English gentlemen indulging in such sport.

The third day that I was out, I had a very narrow escape. The sportsmen had all separated in different directions, and I was walking over a swamp by myself, when suddenly a shot was fired and I was peppered most beautifully. The shot stung me on the face, but they did not hurt; had I been nearer it might have been a serious business. However, excepting a regular peeling of the skin off my face, I escaped unhurt. Snipe-shooting is dangerous sport at all times, but to none more so than to a newcomer. I have known several either carried off or crippled for life with rheumatism for indulging in it too soon. But the more I went out the more fascinated I became with it. I have often been day after day, up to my knees in mud, with a hot burning sun over head, fagging about for five or six hours without ceasing, and returning with only one bird, or perhaps none at all!

The ——th had a capital mess, which was reopened upon our joining. S——n was the secretary, and being a first-rate *bon-vivant*, as his size indicated, all that was to be had in the shape of eating and drinking was of the very best. There was a beautiful billiard table, which was a source of amusement to us after our dinner. We were voted in as honorary members – this entitled us to call for whatever we wanted, though not allowed a voice in the affairs or management of the mess.

A mess well regulated serves to keep up the respectability of the body of officers; they assemble at a certain hour of the day in a quiet manner, and partake of a meal; when the strictness and rigidity of military discipline is in a measure put off, and all set down as private individuals of one family. Gentlemanly feelings and habits are thus engendered and kept up; agreeable conversation on the general topics of the day are discussed, and a degree of friendly familiarity prevails.

Young men are, some of them, very fond of staying in their bungalows, and of giving tiffen parties, grog parties, and *other* parties, thereby incurring all sorts of unnecessary expenses, keeping up an establishment they can ill afford, and living far beyond their means. The having to go to mess keeps them from acquiring habits of staying at home, generally speaking in a state of indolence, when they get into all sorts of bad practices, drinking, smoking, gambling, and so forth, which, in the other case, are avoided. An officer carries with him an air of gentility (if I may say so) and, by associating with his comrades, obtains a degree of

polish, so ornamental in the circles of society, and so creditable to the rank he holds. At a mess, an officer sits down to his dinner properly dressed, and takes his meal with his comrades, so that it is at all events a clean as well as a social one. At home, he is generally by himself, and there he eats in his shirt-sleeves, and long drawers, slip-shod, and otherwise uncomfortable.

The drinking at mess depends entirely on the members of it, and those who compose the party at table. There is generally some sort of wine placed upon the table, called *public wine*. Those who partake of it pay their shares, and those who do not have nothing to pay at all. If a man takes his bottle of beer and his share of wine, it is sufficient in all conscience. But I do not think that an ensign has any business to take *both*. An ensign's pay is only 181 rupees 5 annas a month, out of which he has to pay his house rent, messing, servants, and household expenses; so that, if he indulges in beer and wine both, he will find very little, if any, left to answer the other demands on his purse.

A mess in a regiment has its disadvantages more from the fact of its being *mismanaged*, than any thing else. The way in which it is kept up, as regards supplies, is very liable to cause extravagance, thereby giving an opening to young men to partake of such things as are inconsistent with their means. The very circumstance of their indulging in expensive articles, wines, &c., renders it very probable that they run themselves into debt; and in most messes a sufficient *check* is not placed on the young men by the seniors, to regulate their bills in conformity to the totals of their monthly salary.

A mess also gives an opening to dissipation. A set of young fellows assemble together; they call for this and that, never thinking of the expense. And it also sometimes happens that one or two or three go home reeling. Is it or is it not the case? I do not say that this is a matter of *every day* occurrence. No; but it does happen; though, if a salutary check were enforced upon the appetites of the young men, and a good example set by the seniors present, I think that such would not take place at all.

Then there are the public, or guest days, once a week; a large party assembles on such occasions, and the expenditure of wines and other high priced articles, is enormous. Everything is public, and each has to pay so many shares, according to the number of guests he invites, whether the things charged are partaken of or not.

After the dinner is over, the greater part of the guests indulge in the pleasures of the *hookha*, or cheroot; tables are placed either in the open air or in the verandah; bottles of brandy and gin, tumblers and water, and bundles of cheroots, &c., are ranged up and down, and then the business of the evening commences.

Some of the party take a ride, by way of a little fresh air, after the eating and drinking, but return to the scene of dissipation, and all meet again. Smoking, drinking, and singing, are kept up till a very late hour, when the whole adjourn to a hot supper, composed of devilled bones, mulligatawny, and hot stews, beer and other drinks being matters of course. They eat and they drink, and adjourn a second time to the grog table, where the same thing is carried on, till the lateness of the night warns the more sober to retreat, while those who are in the other state, are either carried home by their servants, or remain there until broad daylight; in fact, to quote the old song, 'till daylight does appear'.

What do the sentries in the mess guard room, and the orderlies and servants, think of us, when they see us getting drunk, fighting and squabbling amongst ourselves? What an opinion do they form of us, and what an example is it to them of sobriety, temperance, friendly feeling, and gentlemanly conduct?

Billiards and quoits are sources of amusement at the mess house, but the billiard-table is a favourite lounge for the idle. Young men resort to the table immediately after breakfast, and there they stay for the greater portion of the day (neglecting their indoor duties and employments),

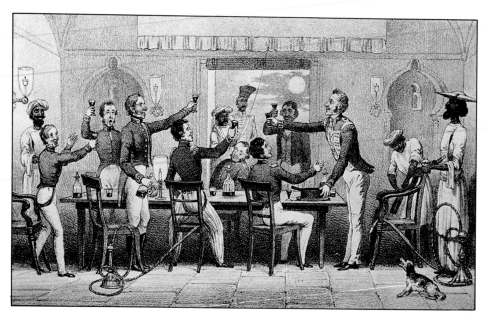

A toast at the mess table; from Memoirs of a Griffin

playing, smoking, and drinking. Then they must have something to eat, they cannot do without that. Cold meat, beef-steaks, or mutton chops, are ordered; and, as a matter of course, they must have some drink as well, to wash the eatables down. Wine or beer is called for, after which they play again.

I have known men go home, rather the worse for drink, from the tiffen table, take a nap, and then throw some *chatties* (earthen pots) of cold water over themselves, dress, and come to mess again to dinner! Eating is out of the question, but drink, drink, drink, is the thing, until they go home again half-seas over; thus becoming in that truly disgraceful state *twice* in one day!

A cigar and a glass of grog are both agreeable companions to those who like them, and oftentimes they serve to beguile an hour or two of a dull evening in the jungles, on a line of march or during the monsoon rains. But young men generally cannot discriminate between moderation and excess. They are not content with *one* cigar and *one* glass of grog of an evening, but they must needs have more of each, beginning immediately after breakfast, and continuing until late at night, with but short intervals of respite from their labours of self-destruction. Instead of one cigar so smoked, ten, twenty, and even thirty are expended, and in lieu of one glass of brandy or gin and water, a whole bottle is drunk, and a man thus becomes an habitual drunkard, to the detriment of his health, the disgrace of himself and family, and the ruin of his character as an officer and a gentleman. At first, the glass of *brandy pawney* (brandy and water) is weak; by degrees, the mixture assumes a darker and *darker* hue, until at length, it is almost *raw* brandy, or *raw* gin! – rank poison, which very soon carries off the unfortunate victim by *delirium tremens*, or, what is worse, the dreadful and unmanly act of suicide.

Poor S—— was a very excellent fellow, much liked by all who knew him. He was a very quiet, steady, young man, zealous in the performance of his duty, always at his books, and studying hard.

Poor S—— had a violent nervous temper in argument, that would affect him so much as to render him agitated to a painful degree, making him shake sometimes like an aspen leaf. He was very fond of his cigar; smoking from the first thing in the morning to the last thing at night; but he never drank anything, and he would say that, as long as he did the one without the other, there could be no harm.

It is a well known fact that smoking generally produces an excessive flow of saliva, and a consequent constant expectoration, which as a matter of course is very likely to produce a dryness, and that must be moistened

The scene in an officers mess; drawn by Lt. H.C. Kensible of the 3rd European Bengal Cavalry

by some sort of liquid or another. In due course of time, S—— used to take a pint of porter with his cigar, with gin and water in the evening. The little harmless pint became a quart, from which it went on to two or three quarts a day.

In addition to the cigar, he would smoke a *hookha* (the contents of his *chillamchee*, or pipe-bowl, being some horrid trash bearing the undeserved designation of *godawk*, made by his rascally servant), the gin or brandy still increasing in strength, with little or no water in the potation.

From a fine, healthy, good-looking young man, he became fat and bloated. His whole body broke out in blains and blotches. He shunned the society of his brother officers, and became dreadfully in debt, so much so that his mess supplies were stopped; but, to indulge his cravings for drink, he would actually get arrack from the bazaar in addition to his porter, brandy and gin, which he would procure from Madras. Poor fellow! The change was truly awful, and really when we called to mind what he had been and what he was, it was quite distressing to see him. He became confined to his house with disease, and a very short time terminated his existence by an attack of *delirium tremens* in the General Hospital; without a friend, or relation, to smooth his pillow, or to soothe his dying moments; no religious consolation to his departing soul.

Alas! alas! how truly heart-rending. Who can tell how secretly and insidiously that mischievous couple, that *sapper* smoke and that *miner* drink, work hand in hand? They approach most stealthily, and before you are aware of it you are in their power. Shun the cigar as you would a serpent, and the bottle as you would poison. I mention this because it reminds me of something which I think I cannot do better than record in this place.

There was a grand dinner at the mess on one occasion, when many guests, as well as the brigadier, were present. I had been out all day in the sun, shooting snipe, and returned home just in time to dress for dinner. The exposure to the sun and fatigue of walking many miles up to my knees in mud, made me very thirsty, and when I sat down at table I began drinking a quantity of claret, which had been beautifully cooled for the feast. I think I must have taken nearly a bottle without eating anything. There was also champagne on the table exquisitely cooled, and of this I took two or three glasses in addition.

By this time I became very loquacious and talked loudly, much more so than was my custom. I recollect well addressing a gentleman who was seated opposite to me; I told him that I had always taken him for a military character, and as such had admired him, but that now I found I was mistaken, he was no more than a civilian, and I did not care a pin for him; or some speech of that import. This observation of mine attracted the attention of the major, who looked volumes at the adjutant. They exchanged signs, and a little after the latter came behind my chair and expressed a wish to speak to me.

I accompanied the adjutant into the back verandah, and he then very kindly told me that I had better go home, that the excitement and the heat of the room might affect me more, and that it would be better for me to walk it off. I took the hint, said that I was obliged to him, put on my cap and quitted the place; I pulled my handkerchief out of my pocket, and, giving one end of it to my servant, desired him to lead the way, as the night was dark, and he had brought no lantern. I had about a couple of miles to walk before I reached home.

The cool air, instead of doing me good, acted in a contrary way, for when I gained my bedroom I felt as sick as possible. When in bed, the room and everything in it seemed to turn round and round, and the sensation I experienced at that time was dreadful. The whole affair was anything but agreeable, and I felt as I had never felt before. In a short time,

I fell into a feverish restless sleep, and dreamt a variety of horrid dreams.

Next morning, as usual, I got up for parade. Oh, how ill I was! It taught me a lesson for the future. It was the first time I had ever exceeded, and I do not think that anybody in this world can say that I have ever been guilty of such a thing a second. That night at Palaveram was enough. I can scarcely bear the smell of wine, such a thing seldom crosses my lips from the end of one month to another; and as for that sour trash, claret, I really do not think I have drunk a whole bottle altogether since that occasion, now upwards of twelve years ago.

3

THE BRIGADIER commanding the station lived on the top of one of the hills, where he had a delightful house, large and commodious. He was an old soldier, and a rigid disciplinarian; had seen plenty of service, and was looked upon as a smart officer. He was very particular in all duty-matters, and in none more so than those connected with the main guard, upon which he always kept a sharp look out by means of a spy-glass, which was ever bearing upon that post.

We 'doing-duty ensigns' were very much the objects of the brigadier's attention and solicitude. He looked out after us as a cat would after a mouse, and kept us ever on the alert against any mistakes on duty matters.

I remember a trick I played the old gentleman one day that I was on guard. In order to observe a kind of counter *reconnaissance* upon his lofty perch, I always took my spy-glass to guard with me. On the occasion I allude to, I happened to be taking a peep up the hill, and saw the brigadier on the point of doing the same at me.

I instantly shut the window of the guard-room, and, taking a sheet of foolscap, daubed the following words in large letters, with a paint brush in ink:– 'Pray what are you looking at!' This I thrust out of the venetians of the window, looking through my glass to see the effect it had upon the brigadier. He looked long through his glass, evidently trying to decipher the writing on the paper, in which he at last succeeded, for he left the stand suddenly with a smile on his face, and with a shake of his fist at me, entered the house. About five minutes after, I saw an orderly coming down the hill, with a note in his hand, which in course of time reached me. It was to my address, and contained, to my astonishment, the following words, as nearly as I can recollect them:

'How dare you, you young whelp of an ensign, to stick up such an impertinent question on paper? But I'll pay you off; come up and dine to-morrow. You know the hour. Yours, in great wrath, &c. &c. &c. Dated the Rock.' He called his habitation 'the Rock'.

The day following found me up at the brigadier's, when I received a thundering wigging in a very jocose manner. I told him I thought it might have been worse, but I hoped it would be a lesson to him for the future, to place more confidence in the officers under his command while on duty. The old brigadier received this rebuff very good humouredly, but he never again took sly peeps at me on main guard – at least, I never saw him.

The British soldier is a paragon of excellence as a soldier; he is a very type of an Englishman in his military spirit; he is as brave as a lion before the enemy, and has a heart, with energy as indomitable as the country from whence he sprang.

But the sepoy is a brave man, too; he has been proved so, not only in former days, but in all the recent harassing campaigns in which our sepoy regiments have been employed, from the early period of our sway in the East to the present glorious and memorable victories over the several enemies against whom they have been engaged; and I think I am not far wrong in saying, that he is in point of moral courage second to none in the world.

Behold the sepoy in the field, on the line of march, in the siege, on board a ship! – in any position, he is still the soldier. How patient under privations! How enduring of fatigue! How meek and submissive under control, or correction! How fiery in action! How bold in enterprise! How zealous in the performance of his duty! How faithful in his trust! How devotedly attached to his officers and colours!

The more I saw of the sepoys the more I liked them: those of the ——th particularly; they were a fine body of men and seemed to be very fond of their officers. Such smart fellows, so well dressed and set up, and so handy with their weapons!

The rifle company was then commanded by an officer of another regiment, though my friend W——t properly belonged to them; he had not, however, done any duty of late, owing to his severe wound, from the effects of which he had not recovered. One ball had broken his leg and another penetrated his shoulder; and, when before the enemy, he narrowly escaped being taken by them. Had it not been for the daring bravery of one of his men, he would most certainly have been cut to pieces, situated as he was, lying on the ground in his helpless state and our troops retreating. It could not have been otherwise, except for the gallant conduct of this single sepoy, who defended him. The sepoy was a very young man, but recently enlisted, a Moslem of good family, and I believe a favourite among the officers who had known him from his childhood. His name was Meer Emaum Ally.

A sepoy of the Madras Native Infantry fixing his bayonet; coloured lithograph c. 1850

I have a reason for making mention of this individual, as I shall have to write more of him hereafter. His daring conduct saved his officer's life, for he stood over his body, and kept the enemy at bay with his rifle, killing or disabling a man at each shot. His unerring aim and his manly bearing, as he stood with his breast to the assailants, checked their advance; and the ringing of his solitary rifle through the jungles told those in camp that assistance was required; the retreating party was reinforced, and the enemy driven back.

W——t was saved, and the noble Meer Emaum Ally promoted to the rank of *havildar*. The officers of the regiment, ever ready to reward deeds of heroism, presented him with a beautiful gold medal, on one side of which was inscribed in English, and on the other in Hindustanee, the cause of its having been conferred upon him. Of this, as a matter of course, the young *havildar* was not a little proud; and the reader may imagine that poor W——t was not a little grateful to the humble individual who had saved him from the hands of the enemy. He showed his gratitude in many acts of kindness to himself and family, acts of kindness which are, in my opinion, never thrown away upon the natives of India.

The *havildar* was made much of by everybody, by the brigadier up the hill particularly, who would have him to his house whenever he had a party, in order that his guests might see and converse with so gallant a soldier. The brigadier went so far as to have the man's portrait taken, and recommended that he should be promoted to the rank of *jemadar*, though the recommendation was not attended to. Little did the poor brigadier think of what awaited him at the time he was making so much of this man!

The native soldiers of our armies are much attached to their service, and have proved themselves worthy of the regard and esteem of their European officers. But I regret much to say that it is too often the case that our European officers, and more particularly those in the junior ranks of the army, do not treat them as they should be treated. People come out to India with but very indifferent ideas regarding the natives. They think that because a man is black he is to be despised. And thus we find young officers, on first commencing their military career, talk about '*those horrible black nigger sepoys*', or some such expressions. They look down upon them as brute beasts; they make use of opprobrious language towards them; and lower themselves so far even as to curse and swear at them!

The grand mistake on the part of our officers is their ignorance of, and their indifference to, the feelings of their men. As long as they look upon them with prejudiced eyes, that want of regard will continue to exist, and the poor soldier will be maltreated until his meek and humble spirit becomes roused, his pride hurt, and the consequences are attended with fearful results. Treat the sepoys well: attend to their wants and complaints; be patient and, at the same time, determined with them; never lose sight of your rank as an officer; be the same with them in every situation; show that you have confidence in them; lead them well, and prove to them that you look upon them as brave men and faithful soldiers, and they will die for you.

But adopt a different line of conduct – abuse them; ill-treat them; neglect them; place no confidence in them; show an indifference to their wants, or comforts – and they are very devils!

Let me entreat my younger readers to mark well what I say. You will never get on well with your men unless you divest yourself of all nonsensical, boyish and would-be-fine ideas regarding these '*black fellows*'. The blood which flows in their veins is as good as ours. They are our fellow-creatures, men as well as ourselves; and as such should be treated accordingly.

There was a young spark amongst the batch of cadets doing duty with the ——th, who was very fond of using abusive language towards the men on parade; for instance, when dressing his company he would come out with such expressions as the following, interlarded with many oaths:– 'Dress up, you black brute' – 'Do you hear me, you nigger?' finishing with epithets that must not pollute our page. This was not a

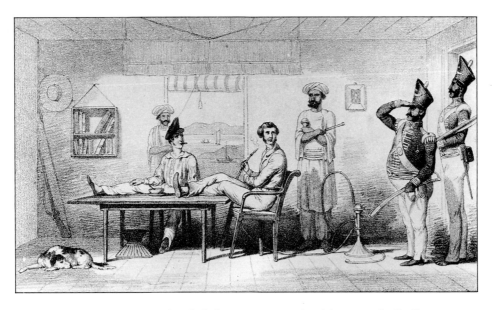

A subaltern receives the subedar's morning report; from Memoirs of a Griffin

matter to be passed over unobserved, so the young man received a reprimand, with a threat that a repetition would be attended with severe measures.

I will mention one more case of harsh treatment which occurred about the same time. The band, drums and fifes of the regiment make a practice of visiting the officers' houses as *waits* during Christmas, for the purpose of wishing 'the officers' honours a merry Christmas and long life, &c. &c.' On these occasions, it is generally customary to present the poor fellows with either money or a bottle or two of spirits, a kind of taxation which has been made on the generosity of the officers every year from time immemorial.

There happened to be three or four griffs residing in our bungalow, all nice gentlemanly fellows and agreeable companions. The band struck up in their compound to the tune of the 'British Grenadiers', which being finished, they marched into the hall of the mansion, headed by the band-serjeant, drum and fife major; here, seated in oriental dishabille, they saw our heroes drinking coffee and smoking cigars! The usual salutation over, the spokesman said that they had come to pay the gentlemen's honours all the compliments of the season, and hoped that the officers would give them something to drink their honours' healths with.

All this was very civil and orderly surely, yet one youngster told them to go to the d——l and wish his Satanic majesty a merry Christmas; the rest set up a loud laugh, and one of them threw a cup of coffee into the band-serjeant's face. Of course, it finally came before the commanding officer, who took the matter up seriously; and, had it not been that the offenders were young in the service, there would have been a pretty business of it, ending perhaps in some severe punishment by sentence of a court-martial.

I liked the native officers very much. These men attain the commissioned ranks after a long and arduous service, rising from private soldiers up to *jemadars* and *subadars* without reference to caste, though they are divided as much as possible between the Hindoos and Moslems, so as to admit of a fair proportion of each. The *subadar* of the company I had charge of was a superannuated old man, and held the exalted rank of *subadar* major. Each regiment has one of that rank, being generally selected from the senior of that grade. This officer and I got on very well. I saw much of him, and he gave me every assistance in carrying on the duty.

The *subadars* and *jemadars* are very useful to their European officers, but they require looking after as well as the rest of them as, however respectable and well behaved, still I do not think they are to be trusted

Eurasian boy drummer and fifers; watercolour by an unknown artist c.1800

entirely without wholesome restraint. They are very apt to introduce many objectionable methods in their conduct towards the men, which require checking. They are likely also to exercise too much influence over those under them, to the detriment of the service and the ruin of military discipline.

We led a very happy life at Palaveram; there was plenty to do, and much amusement. I remember on the morning of Christmas Day in the year 1833, I rose early, took my gun, and, mounting my pony, sallied forth, as was frequently my custom, to have a ramble amongst the jungle and brushwood in the neighbourhood, in hopes of picking up something for my breakfast. At times, I was lucky in bagging a hare, or brace of partridge; at others, I would come home with some wood-pigeon; sometimes, I would pounce upon a few teal on a tank, and at others, I would catch a shot at some stray snipe; my success, therefore, was varied but altogether indifferent. But early rising is an excellent thing in India, and I could never be in bed after the morning gun was fired.

However, I was out of bed and dressed before daylight on the morning I am more particularly alluding to, and wended my way towards a part of the country which I had never before visited in my rambles. I had proceeded about a couple of miles from the cantonment when I found myself in a *tope* (or grove) of palmira trees, surrounded by paddy-fields, the road passing through the middle of them. I had with me my servant carrying my gun; and my horse-keeper, who always follows his master when riding.

When in the very centre as it were of this *tope*, I saw some men at a short distance before me. Who and what they were I could not tell. However, I observed they carried something on their heads, and I also saw that they suddenly separated, and were running along the banks of the paddy-fields.

From this, I immediately conjectured that they must be thieves, or something like them. I therefore gave chase; there were six or seven of them, perfectly naked. I dashed into the middle of one of these watery fields, and then sprang off the pony's back, for the brute shied, and I came plump into the mud and water. However, jumping up, I was instantly after these fellows as hard as I could run; three of them threw down their bundles, and hid themselves in the long grass. These I secured by pointing my gun (unloaded) at them, but the others continued their retreat along the road, though we finally succeeded in capturing two more of the rascals.

I forthwith opened their bundles, fancying all sorts of things, and found that each contained – salt! I made my servant ask the cause of their running away, and what they were doing with the salt, and where they had got it from. They told him that they had smuggled the salt from Covelong (a place down the coast), and were taking it to sell at Madras; that seeing me and taking me for a civilian, they imagined that I had come out on purpose to catch them, they had therefore become alarmed, and tried to escape.

I thought that I should be doing wrong in allowing them to go, so resolved upon returning to the cantonment. I took the rope, which my horse-keeper always carried to hold the horse with, and, tying them one in front of the other in a kind of chain, I made them march before me, and thus took them to the Cutwaul's Choultry (or civil police station), where I handed them over, glad to get rid of them – for, truth to say, I was beginning to fear that I had done something wrong in taking them at all.

I came home in a sad plight, covered with mud, and thus ended my adventure, such as it was, on a Christmas morning, not a very proper way of spending that or any other holy day, but I never gave the impropriety a thought – a proof that I did not pay much attention to religious duties.

And now let me say a few words on this all important subject – a subject, alas! but little thought of; one which should be ever uppermost in all our actions. How often did I go to church while I was at Palaveram? How often did I kneel in humble prayer to my God? Indeed, how often did I even think of Him from whom all blessings flow? Did I ever read my Bible – that sacred volume which should have been a lantern to my path? Did I ever look into a religious book? Did I walk in the fear of the Lord all the day long? No! is the answer to all these questions.

I am ashamed to acknowledge my neglect of those things which I ought to have done; but I do acknowledge it that I may hold myself out to my readers as one instance out of thousands who lead the same life, as a warning to others not to follow in my footsteps.

There is a church about three miles from Palaveram, at St Thomas's Mount, the principal artillery station. Nothing prevented my going to it, and yet I never went. I could mount my horse and ride double the distance, and walk twice as far in quest of a solitary snipe; or, I could urge my beast at his utmost speed for the sake of a gallop, and yet I could not take the trouble to ride three miles to go to church on a Sunday. Our excuse was, 'Oh, the sun is so hot at eleven o'clock it would be dangerous to ride all that way and back'; and yet I could ride and walk in the sun for hours and hours together, shooting, without finding any inconvenience!

All I can say is, that inexperienced as I was, I became easily led away by the force of example daily set before me by those with whom I was associated. I really do not think that more than two or three of the whole number of officers in the regiment ever went to church. Our Sundays were spent in a very different manner to what they ought to have been.

There were no 'new lights' (as they are called) in the ——th, excepting one of the captains, by the way, and he was considered by the rest as a madman. We know of a certain little book which is to be found in the library of every military man – that book is entitled *The Articles of War*. The first article in that little book directs, 'All officers, non-commissioned officers and soldiers, not having just impediment, that is, being sick or on duty, &c. shall *diligently* frequent divine worship; such as *wilfully* absent themselves, or, being present, behave indecently or irreverently, shall, if a commissioned officer, be brought before a court-martial, &c.'

This proves clearly that officers are compelled by martial law (leaving God's holy law out of the question) to attend divine service, a breach of the said law rendering them liable to punishment by sentence of a court-martial; and yet is this article of war attended to? No! Officers are brought forward and severely punished for far more trivial offences, even with the loss of their commissions; but no notice is taken of a breach of one of the most important which a man can commit.

I have often heard the natives make remarks in regard to our religion, 'You call yourselves Christians,' they say, 'you profess temperance, soberness, and chastity, you preach against idolatry; do you show by your lives that you act up to these professions? Your belly is your God; vanity and self indulgence are your worship; and your religion is nothing!'

If it should so happen that any natives are converted, they are so to answer their own purposes, and become worse than they were before. Can there be a greater set of rascals, drunkards, thieves and reprobates than the generality of native Christians? They are looked upon by their fellow countrymen as the most degraded of all castes. The worst characters in our regiments are Christians! And it is no uncommon thing to have some such remark as the following made, 'He is a great blackguard, he is a *parriah Christian!*' A servant presents himself for employment, and is asked what caste he is? The reply is 'I master's caste, I Christian, sar.' He is not taken, because all Christians, with but few exceptions, are looked upon as great vagabonds.

I think it was in December, 1833, that preparations were made for a visit from the general commanding the division. We therefore had drills morning and evening, with ball-practice, sword-exercise and marching parades without cessation. The major commanding seemed determined to

A young officer in a buggy; pencil sketch attributed to the Countess of Powis c. 1800

have everything in proper order, so all hands were hard at work. The whole of December, and the early part of January 1834 passed in this manner, the routine of duty varying but little from every-day repetition.

The general resided at a place called Guindy, a short distance from St Thomas's Mount on the Madras side, and close to the Race Course. He was a very old officer, and had been in India without once returning to England for upwards of fifty years – a long period certainly. But the general was an eccentric old man, devotedly attached to the pleasures of the turf, which was the cause of his never having been able to return to his native land, in consequence of the enormous expenses of his stud, and his losses in racing.

He was an Irishman, but I believe brought up entirely in Scotland, if we may judge from his accent, which was peculiarly broad and Scottish. His whole thoughts were concentrated on two things, viz. horse-racing and jockeyism. His house had a considerable piece of ground attached to it, the whole extent of which was taken up in stables and sheds, where he kept his horses. He had them in all directions, in the open air, under trees; in fact, it was a difficult matter to approach his mansion on account of the number that blocked up the way.

I should say, upon a rough calculation, he must have had upwards of one hundred and fifty of these animals in his possession; and the number of men required to look after them, together with the necessary expenses of feeding, shoeing, &c. &c., must have cost the old man the greater portion of his monthly salary. Indeed, this was the only way in which he spent his money.

He was very fond of getting hold of young officers of light weight, and making them ride, or look at his stud, and if any of them knew anything about racing, he would be friends with them immediately. Many a young man has been brought on by the general just because he would take a fancy to him on account of his knowledge in the mysteries of jockeyism.

I remember meeting him at the race-stand one morning; I had gone there to see the horses training. He asked me if I could ride:–

'For,' said he, 'ye seem capital jockey weight.'

'I am but an indifferent hand on horseback,' replied I, 'and have only ridden one race, which I lost by being thrown against a tree.'

'But I dare say ye'll do vera weel, in time. Have ye yet got a horse?'

'No, sir, I have not,' I replied, 'nothing but an old Pegu pony, which throws me off every time I mount him. He shies so dreadfully, that riding him is neither safe nor agreeable.'

'Get rid o' him, my boy, for he'll brake your neck one o' these days! Get rid o' the brute, and I'll suit ye wi one out of my ain stables. Come down here tomorrow morning, and take some *mullaka* (i.e. mulligatawny, – the general always called that dish as I have spelt it) wi me, and a dish o' tea, and then I'll be wi' ye to the stables, where we can pick ye out a fine little nag, which will answer yer purpose much better than that shying beast o' yours.'

Light cavalry exercising on Choultry Plain; from a sketchbook of watercolours of Madras c. 1800

'I will do so with great pleasure, general,' said I, 'and I feel much obliged for your kindness.'

The next day, I went down to Guindy, had my dish of tea and the *mullaka*, which I swallowed in a hurry, thinking all the while of greys, bays, chestnuts, whites, blacks, duns, and pie-balds.

'I shall take an iron-gray,' thought I, 'that's a nice colour.'

We went to the stables, and saw all the horses.

'What colour wad ye like, mon?' inquired the general.

'Oh! I should prefer an iron-gray, if you please,' said I.

'Well then, just look at this fine little animal here, he'll suit you exactly. D'ye like him?'

'Yes, sir; very much indeed,' replied I. 'I am extremely obliged to you, general, for your kindness; really you are too good!'

'Not at all, not at all, my boy; don't mention a word about that. Ye will not rob me in any way. The horse cost me upwards of eight hundred rupees, and he is worth that now; but I'll make him a present to ye, an ye promise to take care o' him, and learn weel how to ride him.'

'Thank you, general,' I replied; 'I shall try all I can to make myself deserving of your goodness – such unheard of kindness!'

'Aweel then, boy, dinna say anything mair on the subject. When ye get home, ye can send me down an order on your agents for three hundred and fifty rupees, and I'll send ye the horse at once.'

How I started! Here was a pretty business.

'Then,' thought I, 'he does not intend, after all, to make me a downright present of the horse! What a mistake I have made! Three hundred and fifty rupees! I have them not!'

So the grey was sent back into his stable, and I wished the general a good morning. I galloped home as fast as the old Pegu would go, and laid my case before my friends, who had a good laugh at me for being such a griffin as to suppose that anyone would make me a present of a valuable horse!

ABOUT THE FIRST week in January of the following year, the general came up to inspect the 9th regiment. He saw us in *heavy marching order*. The first morning, and while passing down the ranks of the company I commanded, he stopped very abruptly and looked hard at me, as if he were going to speak.

'Oh!' thought I. 'Here's the iron-gray business, I suppose; what shall I do or say?'

But no, such was not the case; he turned round to the brigadier and observed –

'What an excellent jockey that lad wad make! Can he ride at all?'

'But indifferently,' replied the brigadier. 'He is more of an infantry than a cavalry man.'

And the general passed on. The inspection for that morning over; he gave orders for the whole brigade to be out that evening at the practice ground to fire before him; each man to be furnished with six rounds of ball ammunition. I beg to observe that I mention these particulars as they are the forerunners of an event which occurred on that evening, and which created a great sensation throughout the whole of the Presidency.

The brigade consisted that day of two complete regiments, and a detachment of two companies of native infantry. We were drawn up in line, our corps being on the right. The Rifles, under Lieutenant K——, were on the extreme left of our line. The firing commenced, and was carried on as is usual on such occasions, rather slowly, in order to show the mode, the range, and the average of fire.

By the time the fourth round was nearly fired out, the evening began to grow dark, and the general gave the order to fire off the two remaining rounds, one by subdivisions and the last by companies, – from right to left of battalions. The darkness and the distance caused this firing to be irregular, and the brigadier galloped up and down apparently much annoyed, desiring the officers to keep the men steady, and to aim better.

In the meantime, there was something wrong amongst the Rifles on the left. Their firing was anything but satisfactory, and K—— found fault with the young *havildar*, Meer Emaum Ally (already mentioned), who was particularly unsteady and careless on that occasion, so different to his general behaviour. He was such a capital shot, that he was ever trying his best, and generally managed to beat every one; but, somehow or other, he fired very indifferently on this evening; and when K—— observed it to him, he gave that officer an insolent reply. His demeanour was mutinous, and K—— reported him to the major as he rode up to that flank of the line. The major directed the man to be brought to him the next day at orderly-hour.

The firing over, the brigade was broken into *columns of sections*, it being so late that the brigadier did not direct the usual precautionary measures being taken, of discharging the loaded muskets previously to returning home. The general drove away in his carriage, and the brigadier directed officers to mount and the column to *march at ease*. He was

Word of command: 'Ram down cartridge'; from Analytical View of the Manual and Platoon Exercises *by Capt. A. James, 1811*

himself on horseback, standing at an angle of the road, where the troops wheeled on towards the cantonments, the *pivot* of each *section*, as it came up, resting at the point where he stood.

As we passed him, T——n asked the brigadier if he would come to mess and take a glass of cold claret, which would do him good after all his exertions and the heat of the day. He excused himself, saying, 'I have already dined, thank you, before coming down the hill, so should not be able to stand another dinner.'

As I was riding by at the head of my company, he called out to me in a very angry tone of voice to *change flank*, as officers mounted had no business on the *pivots*. I was therefore just going over to the other side, when suddenly a shot was fired. I thought it was accidental, but upon looking round saw the brigadier staggering and falling off his horse. He had been struck by the ball. Then there were a scuffle and confusion, men vociferating and officers giving words of command.

Then there was a noise amongst the Rifles, and several persons shouted out 'Hold him fast!' – 'Take his sword from him!' – 'Secure the villain!' – and so forth. I saw the adjutant rush up to where the brigadier had fallen, and raise him up in his arms.

The whole brigade was presently halted, and there was no knowing what was to be done; some calling out to move on, and others to stand fast.

I shortly after heard someone mention the Havildar Meer Emaum Ally. I went up to where the confusion was, and to my great horror beheld the said *havildar* seized hold of and pinioned by some riflemen, and marched off by a section of the Light Company under its captain towards the main-guard.

Presently the major rode up, and I asked him what it was all about? He told me that the *havildar* had shot the brigadier. Upon being informed who it was that had shot him, the brigadier exclaimed, 'Good God! what harm have I ever done him that he should murder me?'

The medical men examined his wound. The ball had struck the bottom button of his coat, entered the stomach, and had gone out at his spine, making a frightful hole on each side. The wound was of course mortal; he survived in great agony for about five minutes, and then expired. Thus was a smart officer removed from the army by the hands of an assassin, who had experienced so much kindness from the very individual whose life he had so unjustly taken.

In the meantime, the murderer was conveyed to the main guard and there put in irons, with strict orders to the officer in command relative to his safe keeping. When arrived in the cell, he behaved in the most frantic manner possible, throwing himself on the ground, gnashing his teeth, and beating his head against the wall. He worked himself up to such a fearful state of frenzy, that any interference was considered dangerous, as he was a very powerful man. The doors of the cell were therefore closed upon him, and he was left alone.

The cause of this dreadful crime was not immediately known. Truth to say, the unfortunate man was at the time, and for the whole of that day, in a state of excitement from the effects of opium, to which (like most Moslems) he was much addicted, and having been amongst the Malays, who indulge in smoking that drug to a great extent, he had acquired the same habit.

I remember having seen him at a wedding in the Lines the night before he perpetrated the foul deed, when he appeared to me to be much excited, with that peculiar look which men have when under the influence of opium; his eyes shining brightly, and his whole demeanour so different from what it generally appeared. Thus this man must have been quite intoxicated during the whole of the day following, which added to the exposure to the sun, the firing, and above all the reprimand he had received from a strange officer (which K—— was), must have worked him up to the point of madness, and I verily believe that at the moment he discharged the fatal shot he could not possibly have been aware of what he was doing, or whom he was firing at.

The day after the poor brigadier's remains were conveyed to Madras and buried with military honours, everybody attending out of respect not only to his rank, but for his many good and amiable qualities. I happened to be on main-guard that day, and was frequently in the presence of the unfortunate criminal, visiting him every time his food was brought to him.

We were obliged to adopt this precautionary measure, as it was supposed that, being of a good family, some of his relations would make an attempt to rob justice of its victim, by poison, or offering an inducement to commit suicide, to prevent the disgrace of a public execution; the officers on guard therefore had to be ever on the alert. On one occasion, I entered into conversation with the prisoner, in order to investigate the cause of his crime.

'Now tell me, Emaum Ally,' said I; 'you know me well. Why did you shoot the poor brigadier? He was always your friend, was he not so?'

'He always was, sir,' replied the man. 'I never intended to shoot him; I mistook him for someone else – you know who I mean.'

'But,' said I, 'do you not think it was a cowardly act to do at all times?'

'Yes, sir,' answered he, 'it might be considered so; but it was written in the book of my fate to shoot somebody that night, and I might have drawn my rifle at that doing-duty officer who reprimanded and reported me, but, not seeing my man, I fired at the first person I could get hold of, and he happened to be the brigadier. However,' added he, brightening up, 'when I meet him in Paradise, I shall throw myself at his feet and implore his pardon, and I am certain he will readily forgive me.'

Late that evening, an officer came up to the guard-house, and wished to see me. He was the one whose life the prisoner had saved, as I have already mentioned. He asked me to allow him to see the prisoner.

The meeting between these two was most affecting. I shall never forget it. But I must mention that I was the first to convey the dreadful intelligence to W——t of the atrocious deed. He was in the mess-room, waiting for the rest of the officers to sit down to dinner. Little thinking of the consequences, I ran up to him open-mouthed, and told him what had taken place.

He would not believe me! He was thunder-struck. The effect the intelligence had upon him was terrible. He turned pale – staggered – and sank into a chair. Poor W——t! It was a blow he little expected to receive.

The scene in the cell was indeed a most melancholy one. There stood the maimed officer in front of the quondam hero of Naning, now a manacled prisoner; formerly the bold soldier of the bloody field, now the wretched criminal of a foul and atrocious murder! He who had stood the brunt of the battle, and had perilled his life in the defence of that of his officer, was now crouching on the ground before the very individual whose life he had preserved, not daring even, through excessive shame and a sense of degradation, to lift his eyes towards him.

Behold the officer – what were his feelings? He had known him as a child, had had him in his service, had made a man of him, had made a soldier of him! He had been with him in the garrison, in the field, on the march, in the battle; they had fought side by side, and the soldier had stood by him when he lay wounded on the ground, and when all else had deserted him. He had defended him against a host of the enemy coming to mutilate his already mangled body, he had exposed his own life to save his officer, and he had saved him. He had watched by his bedside, had tended him, had dressed his wounds, had proved himself to be not only a brave soldier, but a faithful friend. And now? The officer saw before him Meer Emaum Ally – not the hero of former days, but a vile murderer of yesterday! Alas, what a change!

The poor prisoner on seeing W——t threw himself upon the floor of

Madras Native Infantry sepoy presenting arms on parade; coloured lithograph from Costumes of the Madras Army, *1841*

the cell, took hold of his feet and kissed them, crying like a child, and addressing him in the most heart-rending terms. Even the stern and rugged *sepahees* on sentry were affected to tears; as, for myself, I sobbed aloud. I never in all my life witnessed such a scene.

There was a silence of some moments; at last, W——t broke it.

'What is this,' said he, 'that you have done? Tell me what has caused you to disgrace yourself by so foul an act?'

'Alas, sir,' replied the wretched man, 'it was my fate! I can give you no other cause. I was like a madman! The deed I have committed is a proof that I did a madman's act. I did not wish to shoot the brigadier. I might have shot that young officer there (pointing to me), for he was close by at the time. What excuse can I make? The deed is done, and cannot be undone. I am prepared to stand the consequences, and you shall see when the day comes that I am not afraid of death.'

At this moment, his eye caught sight of his gold medal lying near him among other things.

'Ah!' he exclaimed, 'look at that bright ornament, once the badge of my honour! Now! It shall not be disgraced by having me for its owner! Let it perish with mine honour!'

So saying, and before he could be prevented, he snatched it up and broke it into pieces as if it were made of wood. W——t, seeing that the man was becoming excited, and that he could evidently glean nothing

British and Indian officers conducting a court-martial; from Memoirs of a Griffin

satisfactory from him, quitted the cell, previously to which the prisoner once more threw himself at his feet, and begged *he* would pardon him the crime he had committed.

'If I have *your* forgiveness,' exclaimed he, 'I am content; pardon me, sir, and I shall die satisfied.'

W——t left the cell unable to speak a word, and telling the prisoner to compose himself to sleep, I locked the door and went upstairs. That night the unhappy officer slept in the guard-room, it being too late for him to return home.

In the course of the trial, the prisoner showed great obduracy; and, had a feeling of pity existed in the breasts of any of the members, or the faintest wish to lean to the side of leniency, all that was done away with by his conduct. On the contrary, he assumed that species of bravado so peculiar to natives; and, instead of attempting to excite the commiseration of the tribunal before which he was arraigned, or of showing by his subsequent behaviour that the act he had committed had been done in a moment of excitement, under the influence of a powerful drug to which he was addicted, he seemed to glory in his deed; and thus the man-murderer made himself appear in the eyes of all present, worse than the brute beasts that perish!

The prisoner was found *guilty*, and sentenced 'to be hanged by the neck until he be dead, in such place and in such manner as the officer confirming the proceedings may deem fit to direct' – so it was expressed.

An occurrence of this description, fraught with everything that is capable of striking horror and disgust into the heart, required promptness as well as firmness of decision, in order that the severity of punishment might act as a salutary example, and sink into the minds of the native soldiery while the deed was fresh in their recollection. The proceedings of the court-martial were therefore not long delayed, and after having been carefully perused were confirmed by the commander-in-chief of the army, and the execution was ordered to take place in front of the whole brigade to be drawn out for that purpose. The place of execution was to be the ball-practice ground, and after death the body was to be taken down and suspended in chains upon the top of one of the smaller hills contiguous to the spot where the brigadier had fallen.

I was again on guard the day before the execution, and consequently present in the cell that fatal morning.

Just as the *reveillée* drum had ceased to roll its rumbling on the ears of the sleepers in cantonments, a mounted officer, followed by an orderly trooper, came up to the guard and desired to speak to me. I went down and was informed by him that he had come to read the crime, finding, and sentence, to the prisoner.

The wretched man was asleep on his carpet when I entered, and it took me some time to rouse him from his slumber, so soundly did he repose! And so calm and undisturbed his handsome manly countenance!

Upon being roused, he said to me, 'I know, sir, what you are come for, so early. I was fast asleep, so sound that even the drum did not disturb me. But I am now awake; my next sleep will be a longer one, for something tells me that this is the last, the very last morning I shall ever see the sun rise! Is it not so, sir?'

'I cannot tell, Emaum,' replied I; 'there is no knowing what it is that brings the staff-officer here. You know him well; he is Captain P——, of your own regiment.'

'Ah! Is it so!' exclaimed he. 'How can I see him? He is an officer whom I have known from my childhood. But I must be a man! Wait, sir, a moment until I make myself tidy, and tie on my turban – Now, sir, I am ready!'

Presently, Captain P—— came in, and I stood outside, though I heard what took place in the cell.

'Now listen, Meer Emaum Ally,' said the adjutant-general (for Captain P—— held the situation in that division of the army); 'I have come to read to you the crime, finding and sentence of the court-martial by which you were tried the other day.'

'Read on, sir!' replied the prisoner; 'I shall listen attentively.'

The adjutant-general then read all that was necessary, and, having concluded, said to him:–

'Do you perfectly comprehend all that has been just read to you?'

'Perfectly, sir,' said he, 'but what is the death I am to suffer? I hope it is to be that of a man and a soldier, and not that of a dog! I hope I shall be shot, or blown away from the mouth of a cannon!'

'No!' replied the captain. 'You are to be hanged! and after your death your body is to be suspended in an iron cage on the top of the hill near which you committed your cowardly act, to be held out as a warning to others.'

'Alas, sir!' said the poor criminal, 'I am sorry indeed that I am to be hanged! But this I can say – whatever be the mode of death, I am not afraid to die. Death has nothing in it to terrify me! Put your hand here, to my heart, and see if it beats less strongly now than it ever did? Feel my breast, is it less warm now than it was when I exposed it to the fire of the enemy?'

Captain P—— put his hand to the heart of the prisoner; its beating was calm and regular, his breast was warm, and everything about him betokened perfect self-possession and equanimity. I never saw a man so cool and collected.

The prisoner's father came shortly after, to take a last look at his unhappy son. And here I may observe, that I do not think there is a strong feeling of regard or affection, or respect, on the part of the Moslem natives generally towards their parents. No sooner had the father entered the cell, than the son began abusing the poor old man in a most uncalled-for manner, speaking to him as if he were addressing a dog; while the wretched parent continued collecting his son's things, walking about the room, crying and pulling his beard and then throwing himself upon the ground and making use of the most heart-rending terms of lamentation and woe! His grief was truly touching, while the coolness so apparent in the conduct of the son presented a striking contrast between parental affection and filial indifference.

During the short space of time that the father was in the room, the prisoner was preparing himself by dressing, shaving, and washing, and finally saying his prayers. He demeaned himself as if he were going to a marriage-feast, instead of to the gallows. I do not think I ever saw before or since such a handsome fellow. He was a perfect model of a man – a study for a sculptor! He carefully kept his neck bare, observing to me, 'I do this, sir, in order that the fatal noose should not meet with any impediment in doing its duty.'

In the interim, the whole brigade was drawn up on the ground near the main guard. An escort, or guard of Riflemen, under a *havildar*, came for the prisoner. On his being handed over to the guard, the prisoner went up to the *havildar* in command, and embraced him, with apparent warmth of affection; – 'You!' exclaimed he, 'are amongst the few in the company who have been friends to me! And now you are come to perform a last act by taking me to the gallows! Very well. Such indeed is fate!'

He then turned round to me and said –

'Farewell, sir! You have been three times on guard here since I have been a prisoner, and you have ever proved yourself a kind friend to me. Accept a dying man's best thanks for all you have done. And now, lead on! – I am ready.'

Turning towards the men composing my guard, he gave them all the parting salute, and placing himself in the midst of his escort, the word '*quick-march*' was given, and he left the guard-house; what next took place, I could see and hear from the verandah.

On approaching the brigade and marching up, the prisoner commenced talking, becoming more and more excited every moment. He saluted the regiments and their colours as he passed them, and said something to each officer, warning the troops against committing such a foul act as that for which he was about to suffer. But, on coming to where the ——th were drawn up, he began with the Rifles, abusing them like pick-pockets in the most elegant terms which the Hindustanee language could command, evidently selected for the occasion; calling them cowards and old women, &c. &c. He bade farewell to the officers and saluted his colours.

On reaching the head of the column, his guard halted, awaiting the orders of the senior officer. While so halted and until they reached the place of execution, the unfortunate man ceased not to pour forth a volley of abuses and curses against the major who was riding at the head of his regiment, and even went so far as to spit at him! He completely lost himself by his conduct, and proved by his language, what he really was – a first-rate villain!

Military execution by hanging; the scene recorded here took place in Peshawar in 1850 when three sepoys were hanged for the murder of a comrade

Arrived at the gallows (which were formed of a *gin* for mounting and dismounting guns, or for raising great weights and other purposes), the brigade was formed into three sides of a hollow square – the light troops of corps holding the ground on the fourth to keep back the crowd; the prisoner was made to stand upon a platform cart, and the noose was adjusted round his neck. While this was being done, the poor fellow continued abusing the major and the Rifle company most *pathetically*, and catching a sight of W——t in the background he called out to him –

'W——t sahib! W——t sahib! I am going! Farewell! Take care of my poor father and young wife! Will you take care of them for my sake?'

'I will! I will!' replied W——t, with much emotion.

And the cart being driven from under him, the poor prisoner was consigned to his fate. He struggled most violently and was so long in dying that the men, who are always employed on these occasions (low caste shoe-makers, or *chucklers*, as they are called), were obliged one to climb up and pull the rope from above, while two caught hold of his legs below, to assist in breaking his neck!

In the evening, the body was cut down, and being rolled up in waxcloth, &c., was placed inside an iron cage made for that purpose; after which it was carried up the hill, and there suspended on a gibbet. I was present during this operation, and witnessed a most melancholy sight. The poor father and other relatives in great numbers had collected to take a last look at the deceased; the crying and lamentations which they made were truly affecting.

The natives of India of every caste have a peculiarly feeling way of mourning over their dead. On this occasion there was a long poetical recitation, mostly in Persian, composed evidently on purpose, making the dead one to be a perfect 'Nasherwan' and a second 'Roostum', (both heroes famous in Eastern romance), while the atrocious deed for which he had suffered was kept in the background, and looked upon most probably by some of them as one worthy of a Mussulman, a true son of the prophet! – that of putting an end to the existence of an infidel – a deed worthy of the reward of Paradise! His loss was deplored as of one cut off before his time; depriving his family of a member of whom they were so justly proud, and expressing pity for the wretched and bereaved parent of so excellent a son.

I left the ground shortly after hearing the guard receive strict injunctions not to allow anybody to go near the gibbet night or day, as there was a report that the relations would attempt to take away the body. The officer of the main-guard had to visit this spot during his *rounds*, and often did I go there in the dark and stilly night when nought was heard save the clank of the sentry's musket as he challenged; or the squeaking creak of the chain by which the cage was suspended, as it swung to and fro in the midnight breeze.

Some men there are in a regiment, who, to curry favour with their European officers, (who, I am sorry to say, always have their *pet-men* and favourites) are constantly to be seen at their quarters, tale-bearing, lying, and slandering, to a most shameful degree; shameful not only in the individual guilty of such mean conduct, but doubly so in the officer encouraging it. Such proceedings engender party-spirit and jealous feelings, and create all manner of double dealing, so as to destroy all discipline, and put a stop to that mutual confidence which ought to obtain amongst soldiers. Men quarrelling with each other, and the officers listening to one thing and disbelieving another, add fuel to the fire, which, though burning slowly at first, soon bursts out into a flame that causes an explosion in some act similar to that which I have just described.

I have known a case where a person has put an end to his comrade from envy, consequent on the former having been promoted before himself. Again, I know of one instance where a private shot his officer, who had tried to convert him to Christianity. Another man murdered a fellow soldier from pure jealousy in a love-affair; and there are various other causes for these misdeeds, but I think that the greater number of them can be traced to some mismanagement in discipline.

But the reader will probably ask what has all this to do with the affair of the murderer, Meer Emaum Ally? Simply this, that if ill-feeling and jealousy had not existed, and had there not been a kind of conspiracy against this brave but truly unfortunate man, and moreover, had such been crushed and suppressed in the outset, the miserable victim would not have been goaded on to the commission of an act, the very idea of which would in his calmer moments very likely have made him recoil with horror and disgust in the bare contemplation.

A strange fatality seems to have attended the military career of our lamented brigadier. I believe he had a narrow escape at the Vellore mutiny; for, being at the time the adjutant of his regiment (the identical one which did mutiny), he was supposed by the mutineers to be one of the principal causes of their grievances. When the rascals, headed by one of their ringleaders, entered his quarters with intent to murder him, and though they searched for him in every direction they did not succeed in securing him – the ringleader himself was all the time seated on a large wash-tub, making use of the most diabolical expressions, and abusing him in round terms.

The poor adjutant was in no very comfortable situation, for whilst the search was going on and the ringleader was giving vent to his feelings as above described, he was concealed under the identical tub in momentary expectation of having his throat cut. After this escape and even up to the day of his death, the poor man had a peculiar presentiment of a violent ending to his existence: and with such before his eyes what an unhappy life must his have been!

On the day of his death, he left his house on the top of the hill with a strong foreboding of evil. His son was with him at the time, a nice boy about seven or eight years of age, perhaps older. Before leaving the house, he called to his son and said, 'Goodbye to you, my boy; if anything happens to me you know where I keep my keys, and you know also where all my papers are to be found.'

The father parted from his son that evening for ever, for they never met again.

Emaum Ally's remains swung in the cage for some time after, until nothing was visible save a whitened skeleton, a severe and terrible warning to others. However, it was in the end handed over to his sorrowing old father, and found a resting-place in mother earth. The funeral was performed with great pomp as if for a hero, instead of for a murderer, and a great deal of fuss made on the occasion. A tomb about half a mile down on the plain towards St Thomas's Mount points out the spot where rest the relics of that extraordinary though ill-fated man, who had commenced his career most nobly, but had ended it in a manner not only disgraceful to the profession of a soldier, but doubly so to one who had in time of need proved himself a brave and gallant hero.

S HORTLY AFTER THE events detailed in the last chapter, an order came for the removal of the ——th to Madras. We marched down, and became stationed at that wretched receptacle for troops, called Vepery, a locality well known to my Madras readers, as teeming with every thing that is disagreeable, filthy, and disgusting.

Vepery is situated about two miles from Fort St George, and consists of a conglomeration of public buildings and private dwellings, well diversified with dirty hovels, mud-huts, and pig-styes. In those days, there were public quarters for the accommodation of the officers; such miserable tenements, that I declare without hesitation they were not fit for pigs to live in, far less for officers and gentlemen.

A whole posse of us scrambled into one of these wretched bungalows, appropriated to the dignified rank of ensigns of infantry; an abode, in truth, swarming with filth and vermin, occupied by the family of some discharged horse-keeper; the verandah tenanted by five or six goats, which were amusing themselves by rubbing their mangy hides against the pillars and walls; while the *godowns* (or outhouses) were occupied by another family composed of children, pigs and parriah dogs, all huddled together in dirty confusion; the two latter species of the creation forming the most prominent portion of the miserable multitude!

Walking-sticks and horsewhips having been effectually made use of, we got rid of these objectionables, bag and baggage, and, by the aid of half a dozen sweepers, contrived to make the place as decent and as clean as circumstances would admit, though we were covered with dust and vermin, and the smell of the place was insupportable. The walls of this mansion were bedaubed with various attempts at obscene representations, and the corners of the rooms bespattered with filth!

I remember our breakfast on the morning of our arrival at Vepery. Amongst the viands placed upon the table was a dishful of what *we* called '*shrimps*'. I was enjoying the treat (for so I thought them), and had consumed a considerable quantity, admiring their enormous size, and praising their flavour; so did the rest. Presently one of the older officers of the regiment came in to see how the 'griffs' were getting on, when I exclaimed:–

'Oh, capitally! Look here, what beautiful shrimps these are! We have but just bought them of a man who came with a basketfull! Do sit down and eat some; they are very fine, I assure you.'

Others repeated the invitation, but the oldster stared with apparent astonishment; and I observed that he eyed the dish with disgust. At last, he burst out into a laugh, and said –

'Do you know what those are?'

'No,' said I, 'except they are very large shrimps? Why, what are they but shrimps?'

'Oh, you griffin!' exclaimed he. 'You are a shrimp yourself! They are prawns! And where do you think they were caught?'

'Where?' inquired I, with astonishment.

'Why, in the Vepery tanks and river, to be sure,' said he; 'where all the dirt and filth of the whole town are thrown; and where these prawns breed in abundance! Have you never heard of Vepery prawns, before?'

'No! how could I?' replied I, turning pale in the face very suddenly. I jumped up from my chair, and made a desperate rush into a side-room. The sequel may be guessed – I was as sick as possible, as were also some of the rest; and I vouch for it not many of us ever after partook of those dainty delicacies, prawns (shrimps as we thought them), caught in the vicinity of Vepery.

Take my advice, young griffins, and never eat prawns; they are not only objectionable from the associations of their breeding, but unwholesome as food. Those caught and sold at Calcutta are generally fed and kept in the carcases of dead natives floating in the river. The fishermen secure the bodies by stakes to the bank, and sink them by means of tying stones to them. The prawns congregate in myriads, and feed upon the flesh. Those supposed to be caught in the skulls of the dead are looked upon as the richest and most delicate, from the circumstance of their having been nourished on the brains. The *Koi Hais* consider these prawns as dainties, and eat them in large quantities; a *jingee-curry* (prawn curry) being always a rich treat amongst them.

At Bombay they are a shade better, though there even bad enough. They are caught in the harbour, and feed upon all the dirt and filth from the ships, and the drainings of the town. So much for prawns, nasty things at all times and in all places, but at Madras, Bombay, or Calcutta particularly, they are horrible!

The arrival of so large a number of griffs attached to our regiment was a welcome addition to the roster of subalterns for guard duty, which, considering all things, was very severe, for there were two guards to furnish besides committees and courts-martial innumerable. However, notwithstanding many inconveniences, I liked the duty very well; it was a novelty to me, as we had to be on guard with European soldiers of HM ——th foot, then in the fort.

The main guard was a tolerably cool place, but the *Wallajah Gate* was quite dreadful. The officers' room was one of the bomb-proofs under the ramparts, as hot as an oven and swarming with mosquitoes of immense size, which sting like so many little devils. The gate guard was, however, done away with, in consequence of an officer dying there from the heat, which was at times insufferable.

The fort swarms with another abomination in the shape of soldiers' servants, who are the greatest thieves under the Indian sun. They rob from under the very noses of the sentries! I recollect a young officer, while on guard at the gate, getting up one morning and finding that his writing-desk, cloak and a blanket were all gone!

I do not think that being stationed at Madras tends to the good of either European or native troops. Both officers and men suffer not only in health, but in pocket, as it is a very expensive place for even the common necessaries of life.

As for amusements, there were many. Eating and drinking in abundance, with little of money to pay for indulging in either to any great extent. Our mess was kept up in first-rate style. There were plenty of parties, balls, and suppers; visiting and lounging about, billiards and rackets; then there were the evening rides on the beach, where all the beauty and fashion of the place resorted to *eat the air* and to talk scandal. The band performed twice a week, and enlivened us with good music.

We had also our rides in the country, which were certainly few, but such as they were I preferred them to going along the dirty roads of Madras itself. I generally passed my time at home; though my chum would often take me out to attend auctions and public sales, when I used to meet with and be introduced to many of the leading men of our army as well as civilians.

The only article I ever purchased was a tent, and that proved really serviceable. In selecting one, griffins usually go to the government stores, where such things are procurable, but I never saw a really good tent come from thence; no wonder, since they are constructed by contract and without much care and attention. Now, a tent from the stores is saleable at a fixed price without any abatement; the sum demanded must be paid; whereas, if you are bent upon having one, and are really obliged to have one, the best and cheapest way is to attend the sales. People dying or going away on leave dispose of their property to the highest bidders, and I myself purchased my tent at one of these sales for a quarter its original value; it was quite new, having been used but little, and one which had been made to order by an up-country man.

An ensign can set himself up with camp-equipage complete for between one hundred and fifty and two hundred rupees, whereas, by applying to the stores, he cannot do so under double that sum.

Griffins think that they must have every thing new, because they look well at first. I remember a young fellow, with a purse full of money, just let loose from his mamma's apron strings, calling upon me one hot day, looking very *knowing* at me, and rubbing his hands as if with delight at having done something worthy of applause.

'What do you think?' asked he, 'I have been purchasing – oh such useful things!'

'What?' inquired I.

'Something I would strongly advise you to buy, for they will be very useful to you when you march – no less than an extra pair of bullock-trunks, quite new. My *head-boy*, Appaoo, got them for me from a carpenter in Black-Town, and he tells me that they are dirt cheap, with locks, keys, and all complete.'

As he resided close by, I put on my cap and went to look at these rare articles. I saw at a glance that the poor boy had been taken in, and that Appaoo *was* a rascal, as I suspected. The trunks were old ones freshly planed over, with the brass clamps cleaned and polished. I do not think the pair were worth more than six or eight rupees. Appaoo knew me, and *was out* of course, though I contrived to catch a glimpse of the black scoundrel's face grinning at me, through the venetians, like a Cheshire cat.

The young man marched very soon after his purchase, and the said pair of bullock-trunks went to pieces before he had proceeded twenty miles. The honest, faithful, trunk-buying Appaoo made himself scarce a couple of days after with his master's silver spoons and gold watch. So much for new purchases and honest Appaoo; and I hope that my young friends will never allow their *head-boys* to make any bargains for them at all – depend on it, you will be cheated in the end. Those servants, yclept *head-boys*, self-styled butlers, are thieves of the highest order. Head-boy and thief are, in my opinion, synonymous terms. Ensigns have no business with them; if they employ such, they deserve to be cheated and robbed, as they most certainly will be.

The society of Madras is very stiff and formal, composed of the civil and military residents there, who hold the principal appointments. I mean not by this observation to say that there are not exceptions. But those individuals called 'big-wigs' are rare birds of their sort, and give themselves many airs, and fancy themselves very great people.

At home, we are all upon a par, as it were; but in India it is entirely a different order of things. Every person holds his place by rank and precedence. Birth, talent and refinement of character and mind, give way to situation and amount of salary, so that we frequently find the rich and ignorant *parvenu* jostling his poorer though better born neighbour; because the former holds superior rank, receives superior pay, and lives in a better house than the latter! Rank carries the palm everywhere, both amongst the military as well as the civilians.

If an unfortunate ensign, or lieutenant, dining at a friend's table, challenges the lady of a rich civilian to a glass of wine, or asks his daughter's hand to a quadrille, his doing so is put down as an act of bold effrontery; or, if the poor fellow should happen to offer his arm to a colonel's or a judge's lady to hand her down to the dinner-table, he is looked upon as an impudent young monkey; or, if he should address one of these ladies at table, hazard an opinion on the weather, or even steal a look at one of them! – *Ma foi!* if the husband did not call the poor offender out the next morning, he would look a sufficient number of daggers at him to kill him outright.

Then again there is a vast gulf between the high-in-office and their poorer neighbours in point of self-importance. The former consider themselves so far the superiors of the latter, that they turn up their noses at them as they pass, seldom or never condescending a bow or look of recognition, and fancy their dignity much hurt if they should happen to come 'between the wind and their nobility'. But a great deal of this *grandeeing* (if I may make such a word) originates principally from the vanity of the fairer portion of the community, the wives of these great folk. The airs they give themselves are perfectly disgusting. They think that the very ground they tread is not good enough for them; and, to talk to or notice the wife or daughter of those below them in *rank*, they look upon as something very condescending, something very patronizing. I have seen the wife of a gentleman, high in office, quit a quadrille at a ball, merely because she did not happen to *know* the lady standing opposite to her.

The nicest parties I ever went to were amongst the families of the regiments stationed at Madras. There I certainly experienced true hospitality and kindness, and enjoyed myself as I wished; but, as to the stiff *soirées* and formal dinners of the Madrassees, I declare I would ten times rather have gone on main guard twice a week to avoid one of them.

I do wish that the 'big-wigs' of Madras and everywhere else would but bear in mind what they once were; and then, probably, there would not be that space between them and their less fortunate fellow creatures as does exist at the present day.

It was in the month of March, of the year 1834, that the minds of military men became excited by warlike preparations being commenced against the Rajah of Coorg, an insolent fellow, who had for sometime past been causing the government much trouble by carrying on improper dealings, and being guilty of breaches of faith against us.

With a view to punish this refractory individual and bring him to his bearings, a large force was collected, and war declared against him. Being himself a bold and reckless character, he made every preparation for a determined resistance against a power which was supposed to be supreme in the East, but which he in his arrogance and boasted confidence presumed to despise. He raised troops, erected stockades, fortified the different passes and approaches to his country, and placed his capital, Muddekary, in a state of defence.

This war, or rather insurrection, was only a part and parcel of a well known general conspiracy, which would have taken place throughout the whole of Southern India, had the enemy been successful. Mysore, Kurnool, and other petty States, were all implicated in the rise, and the Nizam was suspected of having been tainted. A dreadful plot had been concocted and contrived amongst the native portion of the troops at Bangalore which, having been discovered in good time, was dealt with most summarily by the local government. The mutineers were seized, tried by court-martial and sentenced, some to be blown away from guns, others to be shot by musketry, and others to be discharged with ignominy.

Our troops were collected at different stations. The principal column was formed at Bangalore, while another was embodied at Bellury; a third, I think, at Cunnanore, and a fourth was prepared at Mangalore.

The Rifle company of the regiment to which I was attached, was amongst the troops ordered for this service. They were directed to proceed forthwith and join the column under General L——y, about starting from Bangalore. This company received the order for marching in the morning, and were off the following day. There happened to be two griffins doing duty with them, and, as they had been to the expense of procuring the Rifle uniform, and there were no other subalterns available, they were permitted to go, though I must say they were little fitted for field-duty, being both at the time on the *sick report*; they were not however to be deterred by that, so declared themselves ready to start.

The company was strong, in good order, and commanded by a very smart officer. He had with him one lieutenant, besides the two young ensigns. The whole marched beautifully, but the poor lieutenant was knocked up when they reached Arcot, having had a *coup-de-soleil*, which compelled him to return. The two ensigns travelled in sick *doolies* almost the whole distance.

The last march the company performed was one of forty-five miles upon a stretch without halting, being able thereby to join General L——y's column as it was on the move against the capital. The captain rode up to the general and reported his arrival, and begged permission to cover the advance of the force with his men.

'You must be all knocked up, Captain P——r,' replied the general; 'the company had better therefore fall to the rear.'

'We have marched a long way, sir, certainly,' said Captain P——r; 'but we have done so purposely to join the column under your command, in order that we may occupy the place we have always been accustomed to, the post of danger. You will find the men, sir, quite fresh for work, and I beg, sir, that they may be permitted to cover the advance of the column.'

'Be it so, Captain P——r,' said the general; 'let them relieve the skirmishers now in front!'

The general then gave orders for the light company of HM's ——th Foot to be called in. Meanwhile, Captain P——r took his men up to the front of the column, and relieved the light company above mentioned, the soldiers of the latter remarking upon the pluck of the little riflemen, as with rifles at the trail, their packs on and covered from head to foot with dust after their long and arduous march, they *doubled* past them in real soldier-like style, some of them shaking hands with the sepoys as they went by, giving them a hearty 'How are ye my boy Jack Sapay, how are you?' at the same time.

Two of the columns carried everything before them; that under the general commanding the whole, forced its way to the capital, which surrendered without firing a shot; and those from Bellury and Mangalore, both received serious checks, more particularly the former, under General W——, at Buck's Stockade (as it was called), where a most lamentable loss of life took place on our side, with every symptom of a defeat.

Buck's Stockade was, I believe, commanded by a discharged *havildar* of one of our Light Infantry Regiments, which happened to form one of the attacking force. I do not know why he had been discharged, but he recognised his old regiment when they advanced, and standing on the breast-work called out loudly for the colonel of the corps to come to the front and show himself, &c. &c.

He desired his men not to fire at the major of the regiment, as he was a good officer, but to shoot the colonel. It so happened that the colonel was on this occasion field-officer of the day in command of the rear-guard; he was consequently not present when this occurred. Seeing that the colonel was not forthcoming, the man commenced a long tirade of abuse, which, had there been anything hurtful in it, would have completely annihilated that gallant officer. The major escaped unharmed either by shot or *gallee* (abuse), and shortly after saw the rascally commandant of the stockade knocked on the head by one of his own men, whom he had called to by name, and whom he had commenced abusing in the same manner as he had done the colonel.

The European regiment employed at Buck's Stockade suffered severely. They lost their colonel who was killed, and several officers wounded. Three or four different times did the gallant soldiers of that regiment rush forward to secure the body of their colonel, and each time were those who made the attempt either killed or disabled. *The retreat* was sounded, and they were obliged to quit the ground. The enemy got possession of the colonel's body, and, cutting off the head, mutilated the remains most horribly.

During the retreat, the enemy came down upon the *doolies* carrying the sick and wounded; these had been put down by the bearers who had run away, leaving the poor fellows to their fate. The Coorgites dispatched every man, and they were found with their throats cut from ear to ear.

I recollect an anecdote told me of one of the wounded of this regiment. He had contrived to crawl away amongst some bushes, and had there concealed himself while the Coorgites with their long knives came out to put an end to the wounded, as was their custom. He remained unobserved for some time; by chance, however, one of the enemy caught sight of him, as he lay in a kind of hollow in the ground. The villain came up to him, and, finding him alive, drew his knife and aimed a blow at him, which he at once parried with his arm, receiving a severe wound in doing so. Such was the violence of the blow that the man actually tumbled upon his intended victim, and then the struggle took place for the mastery between the two; a mortal combat, a trial of strength for life or death, which was witnessed by no one, and which lasted for some time, terminating fortunately in favour of the brave son of Erin, who dispatched his swarthy foe with his trusty bayonet.

Disencumbering himself from the dead body of his foe, he made the best of his way towards camp, and arrived there in a wretched state of exhaustion from fatigue and starvation. I saw this man some months after, and had a long chat with him. He told me his story in that droll manner so peculiar to Irishmen, that he almost made me cry with laughing.

In the native corps an instance of bravery showed itself on the part of one of the men. He behaved beautifully before the enemy, and the European soldiers who witnessed his conduct, carried him before the general, and begged his promotion on the spot. This was granted, and he richly deserved it, too.

Muddekary fell without firing a shot. There were plenty of prize-money and plenty of *loot* (booty), all which were carefully collected and became the *spolia opima* of the conquerors. The Rajah himself was taken, and sent a prisoner to the strong fort of Vellore, where he was kept in durance vile for some time, after which he was removed to Benares, where I believe he now is, enjoying his handsome pension, the which I doubt not he prefers to being the king of such a set of cut-throat rascals.

All his property was disposed of by auction, and the proceeds of the sale added to the money already found; his stores of arms and ammunition; his elephants, camels, and horses; all shared the same fate. His country was taken possession of and is now a portion of our own territories, managed by a Superintendent, and yielding a tolerable revenue.

Thus ended the Coorg war.

The prize-money divided came to something very handsome. A subaltern's share being about three hundred pounds, and that of a private soldier three pounds ten shillings, one of the best dividends ever known in India. Many of the officers however despaired of ever receiving their prize-money; and, certain of them being then badly off for cash, sold their shares for what they could get, some for so little as sixty or seventy pounds.

There were several persons in the country who purchased up a great number of shares, so that when the prize-money was distributed, which it was very soon after, they reaped a plentiful harvest, and made an excellent business of the transaction. How disgusted must those officers have been who had sold their shares, when they found that they might have had such large sums of money, had they but exercised a little patience! Our troops were of course delighted at what they had got, and wished for another war, where they might obtain similar sums with similar ease.

Griffins are very foolish boys generally, and are guilty of innumerable acts for which they are often sorry in after life. None are more susceptible of the *tender passion* than griffins. They fancy themselves in love with every pretty face they see, and even go so far as to flatter themselves they are the admired of the fair sex: I make this remark because I have known several instances of such folly, and will cite one which recalls to my recollection an *affaire de coeur*, in which I very foolishly became entangled, and in consequence got myself into a sad hobble.

It so happened that a gallant officer of infantry arrived at Madras with his wife and family, together with sundry grown-up nieces, a whole host, enough to astonish anybody. They were all very fine girls indeed, one in particular, a lovely creature.

With these young
ladies came an officer
belonging to our
regiment who was
desperately in love with
this said pretty one, and
it was supposed that
something serious
would soon take place
between the two. He
took a fancy to me, and
introduced me to the
family above mentioned;
and particularly
commended me to the
notice of the fair Amanda, whose lovely countenance, bewitching eyes and
fascinating manners completely upset me head over heels into the sea of
love, and a very stormy sea it proved, too!

I also became desperately enamoured, and nothing could convince me
to the contrary, but I must needs fancy myself really and truly devotedly
attached to her! She was, indeed, a beauty! At least, so *I* thought; my being
smitten, therefore, was excusable; and, truth to say, I flattered myself that I
was not indifferent to the fair young lady.

Things went on very glibly; I visited the house every day, nobody
said me 'nay'; met her on *the course* of an evening; at balls at nights, when I
danced with, walked with, and chatted with her! In fact, I was regularly in
for it; my whole thoughts were concentrated in one focus. My friend had
proposed, and was refused! I did not attempt the same measure, because I
never thought or dreamed of such a thing; and I did not wish to run the
risk if I did, for fear of meeting with a similar fate.

This attraction drove all duty matters out of my head. My books fell
into arrears; my reports were never written; I made no inquiries as to how
matters were conducted in the company I commanded; I never went near
the men; and took an utter dislike to everything connected with my
profession, excepting my red coat, and that merely because I fancied I
looked well in it.

By degrees, matters became worse; the commanding officer had me
up, spoke kindly at first, then reprimanded me, and finally threatened to
remove me from the command of my company, if I did not reform. But
advice and threats I set at nought, and the climax was not long in coming.

It so occurred, that on one pay-day he had ordered a stoppage to be made from the men on account of the *dhobies* (washermen), who had to go some considerable distance to wash the clothes, which during the hot weather was hard work; so, to make it worth their while, he directed an increase to their monthly salary. The stoppage to be made displeased the men, more particularly as there were other deductions which told sadly against the sum total of their receipt.

I had on that day a particular engagement to go and see my fair flame, and consequently desired the *subadar* of the company to pay the men in the lines, making the deduction alluded to; the men were to be brought to my quarters the next morning for the purpose of signing the usual *acquittance roll*, which ought always to be done by each individual immediately on receiving his pay.

Away I went, nicely dressed, perfumed like a milliner, and my chin new reaped shone like stubble-land at harvest home; boots nicely polished, and everything as I thought quite killing! She was to sing '*Love not*' to me that day, too; a vain warning, indeed! But a man, or rather a boy, in love, is a great fool for his pains, and no mistake!

Away I went, never thinking of rupees, annas, or pice; never dreaming of the storm that was brewing for me, while I was sunshining with my beloved one like an egregious blockhead! I really do wonder I could have made such a downright ass of myself. *Mais allons*. My visit over, she, sweet creature, looking enchanting, I paid a fond adieu, and jumping into my *palankeen* returned home, where I found the *subadar* waiting and looking anything but what he used to do.

'What is the matter, *subadar*,' said I; 'is there anything gone wrong?'

'Yes, sir,' replied the old soldier.

'What is it?' I inquired, becoming much alarmed; 'tell me quickly!'

'The men, sir, objected to the stoppage on account of the *dhobies*, and would not take their pay! I talked them over and persauded them to do so; but they will not sign the roll; they wish to make a complaint to you, sir.'

I ordered the company to be brought to me immediately. They came, and, beginning with the non-commissioned officers, I made every man of them sign the acquittance roll, with only two or three who objected at first but obeyed in the end. The men were orderly and steady, however they objected to the deduction, upon the plea that living at Madras was very expensive, and that they could not afford any more stoppages. I mounted my pony and went to the commanding officer's. He received me most gloomily, and I reported to him all that had occurred. He was aware of it beforehand.

'Pay Day'; from Recollections of the East

'Who paid the company?' asked he. 'Did you pay the men, sir, or did you not?'

'No, sir,' replied I, 'I did not pay them; the *subadar* did so, in my absence.'

'That's enough,' said the major. Then, turning to the adjutant, who was present, he added:–

'Put Mr. Hervey's name in orders as having been removed from the command, and take that company yourself. Good morning to you; you may go!'

Go, I did; and I felt the degradation then most severely; and often have I called to mind those feelings with deep regret. The whole affair was a bitter lesson to me, and I hold it forth to others as one which may be of service to them, in case anybody should feel disposed to make a fool of himself as I did.

Thus, my young readers, did I reap the reward of my folly! Poor Amanda cried like a child when I told her what had occurred, and we agreed that it would be better for us both that the business should be at an end. It was soon over. She was to start in a few days for the up-country, with all her cousins, and I was glad when the time came for her departure. Our parting was indeed a sorrowful one. The bright sunshine in which I had been basking became covered with dark and murky clouds, which lowered upon me with foreboding aspect; however, there was now no help for it, and the sooner the cord of boyish love was sundered, and the spell which bound me broken, the better for me in every respect.

Now I think of it, I am surprised and astonished at the various tricks I then played. Often when on guard would I quit my post without leave, sally out of the fort gate, and go to the band, for the express purpose of seeing the object of my love! Often would I venture into the garden of the house where she resided, uninvited by the heads of the family, merely to exchange a few words with her. The former, a breach of discipline, by which I placed my commission at stake; the latter, one of etiquette, the thought of which makes me ashamed of myself. But I was a fool, and deserved what I got for my folly. The young lady proceeded up-country, and married in about a fortnight after her arrival at some station, and I got – what? A tin box with a slice of her wedding cake in it! And what did I lose? I lost my company!

I have entered into a detail of this foolish affair not without a blush of shame at the confession of the first false move I had made in my life; but I make the confession candidly, in order that my doing so may point out to my younger readers the danger I incurred in placing my commission in jeopardy, which it most certainly was, because I was guilty of neglect of duty, which might have caused a serious disturbance, if not a mutiny in the ranks of the regiment.

Never, my young friends, delegate to others a duty which you know you ought yourself to perform. It sets a bad example to those under you; for if you, as an officer, neglect your own duty, they will certainly neglect theirs.

All the recent disturbances in our native army, relating to *batta, pensions, foreign service allowances, &c.* are to be attributed, in my opinion, to the men not comprehending the substance of orders read to them on those points; and I think it will be acknowledged that such disturbances have been traced mainly to the neglect of officers, who have not performed their duties as they ought to have done.

It is folly and nonsense to neglect your duty, and still worse to *fall in love* before you know what love is, or to try to win the affections of a woman before knowing how to appreciate her. I very soon got over the love part of the business; but the consequences made an impression on my mind which damped my spirits for the time, and gave my character a stamp which has stuck to me ever since. I never neglected my duty again. I do not think it likely I ever shall.

THE INHABITANTS OF Vepery, and its environs, are composed generally of Eurasians, or Indo-Britons, (or to speak more plainly,
half-castes); some of them rolling in wealth, and aping all the airs
and following all the customs of consequential importance which that
wealth can command. They live in excellent houses, furnished in first-rate
style, keep up splendid establishments, and do all they possibly can to vie
with the European residents in the elegance of their abodes or the
brilliancy of their equipages.

These people have never been out of the country. They have been
born and brought up at Madras, and are consequently little calculated to
associate with the well-bred and educated families from England, who
compose the *élite* of the society. They try however all they can to induce
European gentle-folks to enter within the precincts of their houses, by
holding out to them all manner of allurements to gain their company, and
have their names down on their drawing-room tables. Time was when
officers of the Madras army used to mix promiscuously with them, but
such things never occur now-a-days.

In Calcutta they are numerous, and I have heard that the names of
many of them are down on the list of government-house visitors. They are
there admitted into society, and officers very frequently marry their
daughters. The *Koi-Hais* call them by the very queer term of *Chee-Chee*.
What that means I know not, but with us they go by the designation of
Vepery-Brahmins, and a very apt one too it is.

But to proceed. Many of the children of the Eurasian families (in fact
all) are brought up at schools kept by English people, who receive them as
pupils at moderate charges; and males as well as females are tolerably
educated in all the fine accomplishments requisite for ladies and gentlemen. They are taught English, also. But the way in which they talk, it is
quite a different thing. There is something so peculiarly *half-caste* in it, and
it carries with it such sounds and modes of expression, so different to what

the ear is accustomed in England, that the very hearing these people speak is offensive.

Their education finished, the females return to their parents, who do all they can to catch eligibles for their daughters; while the sons are generally provided for as clerks in the government or mercantile offices, or set up in business. They are thus enabled to gain an honest and respectable independence, without incumbering their relatives. In their own places and sphere the men are as they should be; but the slightest encouragement added to their wealth and self-importance renders them overbearing, and in every way objectionable.

Now, officers belonging to regiments stationed in Madras are frequently thrown amongst these dark-eyed bewitching syrens, and are very liable to become smitten with their charms. I must say the young women are very pretty, notwithstanding their colour. The consequences of associating with them are almost inevitable. Young, unthinking ensigns and lieutenants easily fall into the trap set for them; the bait is a sweet one; they propose, are accepted as a matter of course, and are obliged, *nolens volens*, to marry.

I have known several instances in which young care-for-nothing lads have been thus entrapped; men of excellent connexions at home yoking themselves with families far beneath them, and such as they would be

North View of Fort St George facing the Black Town; from a sketchbook of watercolours of Madras c. 1800

An officer of the Madras Native Infantry in undress uniform; from Costumes of the
Madras Army.

ashamed to introduce to their relatives. I remember there was a girls' school close to our mess-house at Vepery. Some of the pupils were very pretty, handsome young women, full of Oriental ardour, and anxious for husbands. In those days the school mistresses used to receive visitors, and many a young subaltern would go and take a *'look at the girls'*, as they would say, and rare were the goings-on at that establishment.

It so happened some years before we went there, that three young fellows, one day after mess, sallied out well primed with wine, vowing to each other that they would each propose to one of the fair demoiselles at this said school. There was a dance in the evening – that was the very thing; they went, handed in their cards, and were readily admitted. They entered the ball-room, made their bows to the lady hostess, who gladly welcomed them, and introduced them to the many belles who crowded the festive throng. A redcoat was as a bright diamond in one of their *assemblées*, so the rascals had it all their own way; they took their choice from among some two dozen of all sizes and colours, and danced and flirted to their heart's content.

Plenty of champagne was drunk on both sides, male and female, and our heroes were up to anything; the girls, equally excited, received their attentions and compliments most joyously. Pop went the questions, like the corks out of the champagne bottles, out flew the important affirmatives as quick as lightning – Yes! yes! yes!

They were all three accepted, and shortly after returned home to their quarters, as happy as 'wine and women' could make them. Next morning, when sobriety returned and whispered in their ears the occurrences of the past night, recollection flashed before them, and told them of what they had done; how it was to be undone they knew not. There was no retreat; regrets and explanations were vain. They were compelled to marry the girls, but how the matches turned out I never heard; *well*, it is to be hoped, though *badly* I very much fear. The man who marries a *Vepery-Brahmin* (except he be himself one of that fraternity) is a fool and is to be pitied. I would rather marry an Ourang-outang.

I do not think it does young officers any good to keep them at the Presidency, indeed, quite the contrary. Madras is at all times a very expensive place, and there are besides such temptations in the way, which induce men to purchase things they fancy they require, but which they can ill afford to buy. If they have not the money to pay for such things (as is often the case with almost nine out of ten) they run into debt, from which they are unable to extricate themselves, thus falling into difficulties which introduce them to the precincts of the jail, the ledger of the Agra bank, or of some money-lender (of whom there are many to be found at every station in India, more particularly at the presidencies), from the clutches of whom there is no escape.

The messes also are very expensive at Madras. There are constant parties given, and the charges are enormously high. Then young men *must* go out, and to do so they must be properly dressed, which entails an extra expense in uniforms, gloves, &c. &c. to say nothing of conveyance hire, if they do not keep such things themselves.

Then there is the famous club-house, one of the most splendid establishments in the Eastern world, to which they contrive to resort daily, and when there, they must have a 'tiffen', they must play at billiards or rackets, they must have their drink, they must have their ices, they cannot do without one thing or another; all this adds to their expenses, to say nothing of the dissipation. There are many other objections which I could bring forward, all tending to the same thing, and which will prove, that whatever others may think to the contrary, Madras is not the place for young boys to reside at.

I write strongly against young officers being kept at Madras; because I have myself experienced the dangers and disadvantages of the station. It is ruination to a lad's pockets, ruination to his principles, and ruination to his health; and I can only conclude the subject by saying that I think their being allowed to remain at the Presidency longer than is absolutely necessary, is a gross injustice to them. There is nothing like up-country and strict drill discipline, in my opinion.

A few months after our arrival at the presidency, the old general who commanded our division was taken ill and died. I shall never forget this officer's funeral. I must recount the occurrences of that day; fatal to many a poor brave soldier.

Being a general officer, the whole brigade at Madras was turned out to follow the remains to the grave. He was to be buried at St George's Cathedral, distant about three miles from the fort. The corps forming the funeral party were HM —— foot (recently arrived from New South Wales, and consequently not accustomed to the heat), and the ——, with which I was doing duty. The funeral was to take place at half past five o'clock in the evening, and the troops were ordered to be in position, forming a street to the burial ground, by five o'clock. Not being probably aware of the distance, and fearing lest they should be late, the colonel of the European corps paraded his men at about two o'clock, in the barrack-square, inside the fort, when the sun was most intense, and the ground burning like fire. Little did the gallant colonel know of the mischief that was being done.

We marched from our barracks, and came upon our ground in excellent time, but considerably after the other regiment. They had been at the cathedral some hours before us, and the effect which the march up had had upon the men was lamentable. They were all in full dress; the weight of those abominable chacos consequently added to their discomfort. A great many of the men were obliged to *fall out* on account of their inability to proceed; some tumbled down in fits, and when we came up we saw the roadside lined with these poor fellows lying in all directions.

I happened to be standing with my company close to where two or three of these poor soldiers were lying gasping. I therefore called my servant, and immediately mixing some brandy and water, gave each soldier a drink, as far as it would go. They thanked *my honour* most gratefully, and felt revived. These men, after drinking what I gave them, got up, brushed off the dust from their clothes and joined the ranks, while others were carried back to the fort, and I think I am not wrong in saying that several died from the effects of the exposure.

It was indeed a most distressing sight to behold men falling down and dying, when in the very act of burying the dead! All arose from mismanagement.

The funeral was a very grand and impressive one. The band with muffled drums playing the solemn *dead march*; the regular tramp of the troops as they moved in silent procession with arms reversed, the coffin with its military appendages, all combined to make a deep impression on the mind of the young officer, at least it did so on me; and I shall never forget the effect, the thrilling effect, which the roll of the three volleys of musketry had upon me; those three last tokens of military pomp and consequence, paid as a *requiem* to the departed one.

On an occasion of this description, *the soldier's farewell shot,* as it reverberates in the distance, tends more to fill the mind with serious feelings than any other part of the ceremony; but the business over, and when the troops return to their barracks to the spirit-stirring tune of some favourite quick march, those feelings become speedily dispelled, and the circumstance is soon forgotten, or treated as a matter of everyday occurrence. Such is the soldier's life, and such will it be, until wars shall cease and the profession of a soldier shall be as a thing that had no existence!

I remember a laughable occurrence which took place when our regiment was turned out for the Nabob of the Carnatic. 'Tis a high sounding title, no doubt. There might have been, in former days, some importance of power, wealth and grandeur attached to it, but it is not so now. The individual is but an insignificant individual, glorying in nought but an empty name, and keeping up no dignity whatever, with unsupported rank, and scarcely the semblance of consequence. He resides in a palace (as it is called), and spends his substance and time in dissipation and debauchery.

This said nabob pays annual visits to the tomb of his father (or grandfather, or uncle, I forget which), and on this occasion there is a grand procession, and one of our infantry regiments are sent to form a street and *present arms* to him. His highness rides on an elephant, dressed out in tinselled garments, chews *pawn*, and looks the picture of a young rake.

On one of these annual visits our regiment was in attendance, and we had to march down in the hot sun all the way to the dirty, filthy locality of the palace, called *Triplicane*. The crowd was dense, composed of all sorts of blackguards and ruffians from the surrounding buildings, most of them Mussulmans, coming to see the ceremony. There were guards of the Nabob's troops stationed at different parts, intended I suppose to keep the peace; I never recollect having seen such disreputable rascals before in all my life; thirty or forty ragamuffins, on bony horses, and about one hundred and fifty men on foot, armed with rusty muskets.

Arrived at our halting-ground, we formed the street, and stood a good half-hour waiting for this said Nabob, officers and men covered with dust and nothing to quench our thirst with except some filthy muddy water brought in leathern bags, the which I would not allow the men to drink – it would have given them the cholera to a moral certainty. At last, a cry of '*Nawaub ātā hai!*' (the Nabob is coming), put us on the alert; the corps *shouldered*, and all was ready. Presently some of the footmen (I will not call them sepoys, they do not deserve the name), came running by, and then two fellows on horseback, and then a *palankeen* with somebody in it lying at full length and chewing *pawn* most strenuously.

'This must be the Nabob,' thought the major. 'Regiment! pre – ee – sent ar – ms!' shouted he.

We presented arms, and the band struck up. Drums rolled and officers saluted, and all looked martial and proper. The man in the *palankeen* thus saluted was *not* the Nabob, but his barber. What a mistake!

Well, in about half an hour more, another cry startled us, and we stood to our arms again and shouldered. A similar procession passed, but there were more *palankeens* than one, and a couple of huge lumbering old-fashioned coaches, the blinds of which were down. The major was just on the point of shouting out again, when somebody standing by told him it was the *Lemrana*, and he stopped.

We were very tired of this farce, and felt in anything but a good humour, however at last the Nabob did make his appearance, riding on a large Elephant with *tom-toms* beating, 'colleroy-horns', and other instruments of Oriental music, making a noise fit to break the tympanum of one's ears. And then there was such a crowd, pushing and fighting, such shouting and such crying! Then the Elephants would begin trumpeting, which set all the horses rearing and kicking, while their riders held on like grim death by the pommels of their saddles. I never witnessed such a sight, nor do I ever wish to be on such a disagreeable duty again.

About the middle of the year 1834, some very extraordinary facts became disclosed, to the astonishment of the government and the public; reports upon which nobody could possibly have placed any credence, had there not been undoubted proofs to support them.

Captain D—— was a man well known throughout our Presidency; a general favourite in the circles of society; much given to hospitality; kind-hearted and benevolent; and looked upon by all the military authorities as a smart officer, and one well calculated to hold his responsible situation. He was in charge of the ordnance department at Bangalore, a large station in the Mysore country, where there was a considerable force kept up, consisting of artillery, cavalry and infantry. His appointment being a permanent one, he built himself a beautiful house, and was supposed to have expended much money in erecting and furnishing it. The grounds were nicely laid out, and the whole considered one of the handsomest and most tasteful at the station. So far so good.

In the course of time (which develops many a hidden secret) people began to wonder where all the money came from to enable the gallant captain to build, to embellish, to decorate, and how he could contrive to live in the way he did!

Various reports began to fly about, and suspicion was excited in the minds of those in office. Inquiries were then set on foot, and it was at last ascertained, upon proof indubitable, that the commissary had been guilty of embezzling government property, both in money and in stores! Public servants had been employed, and public property expended in building houses; and other irregularities discovered which were fully sufficient to warrant summary proceedings being instituted, for the purposes of investigation; and he was placed *in arrest*, pending the assembly of a court-martial for his trial.

In the instance before us, it would appear that Captain D—— was not in *close arrest*, for he was visited by several of his friends, amongst whom was a widow lady, with whom he was on terms of great friendship and intimacy. This lady was staunch and sincere in her regard for her unfortunate friend, and declared herself ready to do anything for him in the dilemma, from which he knew not how to extricate himself.

After serious deliberations held with his lady-friend, it was finally arranged betwixt the two that he was to fly to Pondicherry, and there embark on board of a French vessel then known to be loading for the Isle of France. The lady undertook to '*lay a dawk*' (which means to have relays of *palankeen*-bearers posted to carry on passengers without delay) from Bangalore to Pondicherry, as if for herself, and arranged that her friend was to quit the station in female attire! She arranged to come to his house with a dress of her own, and all the other et ceteras of a female's toilet. He was to have a suit of his clothes ready for her to put on, and they were to change places. He was to leave the house at the last moment, jump into the *palkee* and start at once, while she was to be walking in the garden as the prisoner! Capital!

On the evening appointed for the carrying into effect of this extraordinary arrangement, the lady came over to her friend's house with a bundle of her clothes in her hands. The change of attire was speedily accomplished, and, favoured by the darkness of the night, the gallant fugitive bade his fair coadjutor a fond and affectionate adieu, and, quitting the house, through the garden, hastened to that of the widow, where he found the *palankeen* all ready for him.

An Ordnance Officer from the Commissary of Ordnance, 1841; lithograph by H. Hunsley

He reached the French port in two or three days, where (having previously resumed the dress of his own sex on the road) he went to the house of an acquaintance, and shortly after embarked in the vessel which was destined to convey him far away on his flight from the land and scenes of his anticipated disgrace, thinking, poor fellow, that he had given his enemies the slip, and that now he was free from all chances of detection.

'Now I am safe,' thought he, no doubt, as the vessel, getting under weigh, sailed from the coast. But he was most woefully in error.

The authorities at Bangalore discovered the business very soon – sooner than either he or his widow-friend imagined, or expected.

The captain of a man-of-war lying at the time in the roads at Madras, was made acquainted with every particular, and he was dispatched forthwith in pursuit. With that smartness and celerity in movement so peculiar to our gallant navy, the man-of-war was off at once, and, cracking on sail night and day, contrived to enter Port Louis harbour a short time after the French merchantman with the fugitive on board had anchored.

Now comes the seizure of the runaway captain. Silly fellow! Little did he think when he saw a ship anchoring in the harbour, that she was a man-of-war sent from Madras after him.

The captain of the frigate, in the meantime, kept a strict eye upon the Frenchman. He ordered his boat to be lowered and the crew in her to be ready to start at a moment's warning. He presently saw the suspected vessel lower her boat, and observed a respectable military-looking personage, with a black hat on, go down the side into her, and seat himself in the stern sheets.

The captain went into his gig, and told the men to *give way*. Off she went in regular style; the coxswain kept his eye upon *the chase,* and watched her well. The two boats arrived at the landing place at the same time. Those in them got out. Mr D——s by himself, and the captain (in mufti or plain clothes, I believe,) by himself. A few man-of-war's men followed their officer a little behind by previous arrangement; they were to come up when required.

'All right,' thought poor D——s, 'I am now safe on shore, away from that abominable place Madras, and everything connected with it.'

'I have him now,' thought the captain, 'I'll go up to him at once.'

So he went up to D——s, and addressed him:–

'Ah D——s! How do you do? I have not seen you for an age!'

'Really,' replied D——s, 'I cannot call to mind where I could have had the pleasure of seeing you. What may your name be, sir?'

'The last time,' said the captain, 'that you had the pleasure to meet

me was I think at Madras; and that was some time ago; my name, sir, is
—— captain of his Majesty's ship ——, and I arrest you in the king's
name as a deserter; here is my warrant. Any attempt to escape is useless';
saying which he gave a sign to his men, who came up and seized him.

Thus was poor D—— taken and in due course of time brought back
in charge of a subaltern's party to Madras.

I was on main-guard one day, and happened to be seated in my room
writing, when I heard a tap at the door. It was the sentry, who informed
me that two officers in uniform were outside wishing to speak to me. They
proved to be the Town Major and Fort Adjutant. The former informed me
of the arrival in the roads of the deserter, Mr D——, (they did not call him
captain) and that he was to be confined in the guard.

The reinforcement to the guard was sent and located in one of the
rooms, while another was appropriated for the use of the prisoner, who
was shortly after landed and marched up under the escort which had
brought him from the Isle of France. What a degradation! What a fall!
When last in Madras, he was considered an officer and a gentleman; now,
he was a prisoner, marched up from the beach into the fort as a deserter.
My heart bled for him.

Arrived at the guard, the Town Major received the prisoner, and
handed him over to me. I showed him his room, and at the same time
placed two sentries, one at the front and the other at the back of his
apartment, with the necessary orders relative to their posts. I never saw a
man take things so coolly as he did. As soon as he entered his room, he
took off his clothes, and made himself comfortable in his sleeping drawers.
He lighted a cigar, and seemed to enjoy the comfort to his heart's content.

It so happened that the widow lady who had assisted him to escape in
the outset was down at the Presidency when D—— was brought back a
prisoner. The transaction had gained for her a celebrity at Madras, which
caused her to be looked upon as an object of interest and dread, as well as
of astonishment, to say nothing of the talk that there was throughout the
whole place of her conduct.

The officials at Madras determined that this lady should not again be
brought into contact with the prisoner; strict orders were therefore issued
not by any means to allow her to enter the guard, or to see him. I
remember meeting this lady one night at a party; she intimated to me a
wish to see D——, and even hinted at this being feasible the next time I
was on guard. I told her that the attempt would be useless with me, and
she had better therefore not make it. She acted up to my suggestion like a
wise woman.

A havildar of the 3rd MNI and a sepoy of the 43rd MNI; watercolour c. 1850

The prisoner was subsequently removed to Bangalore, there to take his trial. A court-martial being duly assembled, he was arraigned before it upon several charges, all which were clearly proved against him, and he was sentenced to be transported as a felon, I think it was for fourteen years, but am not quite sure. The sentence was confirmed, and in course of time he was placed on board of a ship with other felons as a convict, dressed and treated as such, and finally taken to the penal settlements in New South Wales.

In the course of the investigation at the court-martial, many a hidden secret was revealed, which put our sleepy officials on the alert; many an abuse was brought to light, which made people stare; many an act of rascality, embezzlement, swindling and thieving disclosed, which caused honest men's hair to stand an end! One or two *Jacks-in-Office* trembled, and were dreadfully alarmed. I remember one individual, high in position, was taken suddenly ill, and obliged to quit the country for the Cape on medical certificate. It was said that fright scared him away.

A general reform took place in all the offices. Men who had hitherto performed little or nothing, and had neglected their duty and left it to those under them, now worked hard and attended to what they were about. Staff-officers, who before did nought but scribble their names, write letters, eat sandwiches, and drink soda-water in their offices, now turned over a new leaf, and did their work properly. An occurrence of this description does much good. It corrects abuses, by making him who sleeps over his work watchful; by putting a stop to all manner of rascality; and by removing from responsible situations such men as are not deserving of their posts.

A grand fancy ball took place while I was at Madras, the first of the sort I had ever witnessed. The supper was an elegant one, the champagne in abundance; indeed there never is a lack of the good things of life at an Indian *fête*, and everything is of the best. The whole is done in style, and no expense spared. We had dancing to a late hour, and such flirtations! A fancy disguise is a capital cloak for such proceedings, which puts me in mind of one which occurred some few years previously to my arrival in India.

One of the party, a gay careless young fellow, appeared in the ball-room as a vender of sweet-cakes and macaroons, which he cried up and down, recommending them strongly to the fair ladies who lounged on the sofas and ottomans in every direction. He declared that he did not want money for his goods; all he required was a smile of approval from those who took them. The macaroons and cakes were partaken of by almost every individual in the room, from the governor and his lady, down to the *captain's wife* and the *subaltern's thing*.

Presently one lady complained of sickness, then another, and another, and another. At last, they were all sick, rushing desperately to the doors and windows, followed by the gentlemen equally affected.

The macaroon-seller had vanished. No one knew whither he had gone. He was not to be found anywhere. The cake &c. which he had imposed upon the guests had been highly medicated with *emetic*, and hence the cause of the sickness. He had retreated, changed his costume, and re-appeared in another, joining the unfortunate ones as if he were sick, also.

This untoward circumstance caused the ball to be broken up, and the festive scene was converted into one of groaning and disgust. People do not like taking physic when they do not require it; so dire vengeance was vowed upon the head of the offender, though how it ended I never heard.

I knew of another trick played off at one of these fancy-balls. A person came in dressed as a postman with a letter-bag, and amused himself by delivering sealed letters to certain ladies in the room, signed anonymously and written in objectionable language; suffice it to say it was not a very correct thing to do, and I heard that the individual was in a very awkward predicament in consequence, from which he with much difficulty extricated himself.

There *was* a time when some officers in India were given to much foppery and puppyism. But such time, I am glad to say, is gone by. We never now-a-days find gentlemen converting themselves into Bond Street hair-dressers, and such like characters. I remember hearing of people being so dreadfully eaten up with vanity and self-conceit, as to wear combs in their hair. Soldiers and officers, in red-coats and with swords by their sides, going about with combs in their hair!

There was one officer in particular who always wore combs. His hair was long and thin, without the semblance of a curl, so he took to combs and curl-papers to improve both the rat's-tails and his appearance. With such appendages (combs, I mean) attached to his head, he one evening attended a grand ball given by the commander-in-chief, and danced away seemingly enjoying himself to his own satisfaction, and little dreaming of the ridiculous figure he was cutting. In the course of the dance one of the combs fell, unobserved by him, to the ground, and was picked up by the gallant host.

After the dance was over and the couples were promenading the

A peon *or chit bearer in the Madras Club; sketch by Lt. Robert Thompson, c. 1851*

room, he placed himself in the middle, and, holding up the truant comb, that had so naughtily jumped from its affixed place, he cried out loud enough to attract the attention of every person present –

'Has anybody lost a comb? I have just found one.'

The owner of the article immediately put his hand to his head, and, finding one of *his* combs missing, took his glass, and, placing it to his eye, stalked up to where the crier was standing (calling for the owner of the said comb). He looked at it, and, with the greatest *nonchalance* possible, said:–

'Your excellency, the comb is mine.'

His excellency handed it to him, with an 'Oh! It is, is it? I hope it is not broken.'

The owner took the comb, and, with an air of the most consummate dandyism, replaced it in his hair, and walked away.

The consequence of this was a general order by his Excellency the Commander-in-chief, dated Head Quarters, Choultry Plain, &c. &c. prohibiting officers from wearing combs, or such like things in their hair.

A T LAST THE ORDER was out posting us to our respective regiments, and long enough had we had to wait for it, too. We had been doing duty with the ——th for a year and a half, and it appeared to us quite unaccountable how we could have been kept such a time without being sent to our proper corps, particularly when there were three or four vacancies in every one throughout the whole army.

A few days elapsed before we were finally disposed of, and I at length found my name down as third ensign to the 40th, then stationed at Mangalore, on the western coast of our Presidency, whither I determined upon going without delay, making up my mind to start at once by sea, so as to save all the trouble and extra expenses of a long and dreary march by myself, I being the only one bound for that coast.

Having drawn pay and garrison allowances beyond the regulated time allowed to ensigns on first marching to a field-establishment (or passage-money, if proceeding to join by sea), I was obliged to start on my own resources, which, considering I had been residing at Madras for a year, were, the reader may be sure, very scanty. What to do, therefore, I knew not, so I parted with my guns and horse 'to raise the wind', as the saying is, wherewithal to defray my passage-money, and set myself up with a regular kit for commencing life and keeping house.

My beautiful guns went for twenty pounds each, whereas they cost treble that amount; and I sold my horse at one of those abominable auctions for a trifle. There were others worse off than I was, and how they got on I know not. All this originated from a residence at Madras, and our consequent expensive mode of living. Oh, it is indeed a bad thing keeping griffins at the Presidency!

By the kind assistance of friends in a house of agency, I procured a reasonable passage in a country vessel going to Bombay, and with my servants and baggage embarked one fine evening on the 15th January 1835 quite delighted to get away from that detestable place, and earnestly hoping it might be many a year before I set foot there again.

The ship in which I had thus ventured my precious body and everything I possessed in this world, was a tolerably good one for a country craft. She had all those delights peculiar to vessels frequenting a tropical climate, such as cockroaches, scorpions and rats; and what surprised me most was to find out that she had as passengers a host of white ants, insects well known as destructive on shore, sufficiently so to render them objects of dread to everyone by whom they are visited; but what must they be on board of ship! Fortunately they did me no damage, though they might have sunk us. I always understood that white ants never touched teak-wood: this vessel was built of teak – an exception to the general rule, I suppose. But let us proceed.

The captain was an old friend, whom I had known many years ago as a boy; I was glad to meet with him, as he was very civil and attentive to me for old acquaintance sake. We had as passengers an old colonel and his lady going to Quilon to join a regiment stationed there. He a queer body, a good specimen of one of the ancient school of Madras officers, and she a delicate creature, evidently in bad health, never scarcely leaving her cabin.

Those who have sailed along the southernmost part of the western coast will agree with me that the scenery is very picturesque. At the time of the year when I passed that way everything was beautiful. The white sandy beach, with the tall graceful cocoa-nut trees crowding it in luxuriant verdure; the huts of the natives here and there, with sometimes houses in the European style in different places; the high hills and mountains in the background covered with thick forests; the light green colour of the water and boats out fishing; there was something extremely beautiful in all this, and I would sit on the poop of the ship all day pencil in hand amusing myself in taking sketches of those parts which I thought most suitable, though there was not much choice; for, where the scenery is all good, it is a difficult matter to make a selection.

Passing Cape Comorin with a fine breeze, we came upon Anjengo, where we anchored for the evening. The people of the place put off from the shore, bringing curiosities innumerable for sale; the most tempting were dolls or images, made of a composition very much like pitch, representing all the castes and trades of the natives of that coast, and so well executed, that the very articles of attire and ornament were minutely put on. The features and colour also were beautifully marked. They are well worth purchasing, and very cheap. I took a whole set for a mere song, and sent them to England, where they were much admired and prized. I think they are the best of the sort I ever saw.

The next place we touched at was Quilon, formerly a considerable military station, where a European regiment and other troops used to be located, but since reduced, in consequence of the climate not agreeing with the English soldiery. A skeleton of a native regiment now occupies the place, which is in a sad state of ruin and decay. Those beautiful barracks, which must have cost governments a mint of money, are now untenanted save by owls, bats and spiders, and the whole cantonment is fast going, following the many others all over the country which have been evacuated from similar causes.

From Quilon we came to Alleppie, a place belonging to the Rajah of Travancore. It is a tolerable town, containing several respectable English houses and a church. The inhabitants are Nairs and Mopley merchants, as well as natives from the interior. There is much business done here in pepper, sandal-wood and spices, the produce of the country, and which yield the Rajah a tolerable revenue.

The town is situated close to the beach, and is surrounded on all sides with thick groves of cocoa-nut trees, giving it a pretty appearance from the sea. Alleppie was the scene of some serious disturbances amongst the natives, and, if I am not mistaken, one of our civilians was most barbarously murdered by them. Those Mopleys are a troublesome set indeed.

We had a great deal of fun on shore at Alleppie that night. The captain took me to the house of the chief mate, a Portuguese, and there I saw a whole family of dark creatures, with whom I danced and flirted until it was late, and we did not get on board until long past midnight. The country-born Portuguese are a very respectable people, much more so than those *Vepery brahmins*, mentioned in a preceding chapter.

We quitted Alleppie the following morning; and, after a very delightful sail, anchored the next day at Cochin, formerly the principal Dutch settlement on that coast, though of little or no importance now-a-days. The town is a large one, composed of substantial houses, built in the old Dutch style, and laid out in regular streets and squares. There is, however, a general air of decay pervading the whole, and the place appears damp and unhealthy.

Some good fellows whom I had met at Quilon had been so kind and provident as to write to one of their own officers on out-post duty at Cochin, mentioning my coming, &c. &c., so when the ship anchored, this gentleman sent me a very warm and pressing invitation, requesting me to put up with him and to make his quarters my home during the time that the vessel might be detained there. This invitation I gladly accepted, and, packing up my portmanteau, I landed with the captain, whose wife and family resided in the town.

The scenery which opens to the view as you enter the river is extremely picturesque and pleasing. The great number of cocoa-nut trees growing close to the water's edge with their thick luxuriance of foliage, however, hide many drawbacks, and the eye very soon becomes reconciled to the ill-looking heavy buildings, which show themselves from among those trees, like so many hideous objects to interfere with the beauty of the lovely prospect.

I landed after a pleasant pull of about half an hour, and walked up to my friend's house. He received me with a most hearty welcome, such as travellers generally meet with in India. He had a nice room prepared for me, which I immediately took possession of, and enjoyed the delicious pleasures of a cold bath to my heart's content. Clean clothes and plenty of water, particularly in a warm climate, are indeed delights which none but those who have felt the comforts of both can possibly appreciate. I think that no luxury in the world can be equal to them. Oh how I long for an Indian life again!

Hospitality is a bright trait in the character of the English in India. I say not this by way of boasting. We are glad to see our fellow countrymen; delighted to receive any of them under our roof, be they our superiors, our equals, or our inferiors, from the general officer down to poor Paddy Malony, the private soldier, all the way from *ould Ireland*. A traveller always finds a door ready open to receive him at whatever station he arrives; and, if he is not comfortable and happy, it is his own fault.

There is nothing like Indian hospitality, and I defy anyone to deny the fact, that where they may meet with objectionable characters or cold behaviour, those are, as it were, thrown into the shadow by that predominating characteristic so peculiar to the English in India, viz. that they are verily *given to hospitality*, and, whatever may be their other faults or failings, hospitality, like charity, will cover a multitude of such sins.

I never recollect having spent such a pleasant time as I did at Cochin. I was twelve days there, during which period my host showed me all that was to be seen.

We visited the neighbouring country, and frequently went out snipe-shooting. The game was abundant, and we had capital sport; though I must own that I did not add much to the contents of the bag.

The old Dutch Government-house is a fine building, in a style of architecture peculiar to the times in which it had been erected, as heavy and massive as a Dutchman himself. It is however in a sad state of decay; the extensive grounds and gardens are quite neglected and overgrown with the rank vegetation of a damp climate.

We also went to Jew-Town, as it is called, a locality inhabited entirely by a colony of the scattered children of Israel. There they have resided for many years, and there they will reside I suppose until the times of restitution, when God's chosen race will be gathered together in the land of their forefathers, when Israel shall be again a people with the Lord for their God. These people at Cochin are a dirty squalid set, apparently suffering from a variety of diseases, the predominating ones being *ophthalmia* and *elephantiasis*.

The latter is a prevailing complaint at Cochin peculiar to the natives, known probably better under the denomination of '*Cochin-leg*'. People so affected are objects of pity. Their legs, from the knee downwards, become swollen to the size of those of elephants, the foot is covered over with an enormous quantity of extra flesh, and the toes have the appearance of large red *potatoes*: they are really disgusting to look at.

The military cantonment in Cochin; from a collection of watercolours by Lt. Robert Thompson entitled Sketches During Eight Years Military Honourable East India Company Service

Cochin has been and still is a famous place for ship-building. When I was there, I saw a large eight-hundred-ton veseel on the stocks, as also some smaller craft. The extensive teak-forests of Travancore, and the situation of the river, afford excellent facilities for that purpose. The Dutch used to build almost all their trading vessels as well as several ships of war at the place.

The bread-fruit flourishes here as well as along the coast. I saw one large tree in full bearing, and tasted once of the fruit; it very much resembled new bread, which reminds me of an anecdote I heard while at Cochin, which made me laugh very much indeed at the time. 'Twas a trick played off upon a greenhorn of an ensign, who happened to be passing through on his way to join his regiment stationed somewhere on the coast. He had heard of a bread-fruit tree in the compound of his friend with whom he put up, and expressed a wish to taste some of the produce.

'You will think it odd,' said his host, 'but the bread and butter which you will presently see on the tea-table are just as they come from the tree, except the outer rind which is cut off. We eat no real bread here; indeed there is not such a man as a baker in the place. All eat the fruit, which is considered much more wholesome, being free from yeast, or other ferment.'

'Really!' exclaimed the griff, 'I should like much to taste it.'

'So you shall; we will pluck a ripe one off the tree tomorrow morning for our breakfast, and I will have a few friends here to partake of it with you.'

The next morning early griff was up and moving, longing to see this famous tree which produced ready made bread and butter. But I must here inform the reader that, before retiring, his host had, with the aid of his chum and servants, contrived to cut up a quantity of loaves nice and thin, buttered them well, and had placed them together in slices so as to form two or three good-sized balls. These he had covered with the rind of the bread-fruit, sticking it over them by means of little pegs of pointed wood. He sent his servant up the tree, who fastened them in such a way that anyone below looking up would imagine that they really were the fruit growing on the tree. The trick was a capital one.

Everything prepared, a table was spread *sub tegmine* of *the* tree, and then the whole party assembled to meet Ensign ——, to whom the guests were severally introduced as they arrived.

'Now, my boy,' said the host, addressing his young friend, 'real bread-fruit you shall see, and you will also see that we eat nothing but this fruit in this place in lieu of bread.'

'What I tasted last night was very nice indeed,' observed the griffin, 'I should say that pulled fresh in the morning it will be delicious.'

In the meantime, the good host of the house sent his servant, who was a party to the trick, to climb the tree. He went up and picked two pointed out to him by his master; but, by some clumsiness or other, the fellow contrived to let one fall plump on the table. The fruit burst, and behold, the astonished griffin saw nothing but bread and butter ready for eating. The guests seized the rind and threw it away before there was time for the poor lad to think of examining it, and commenced devouring the remains as fast as they could, smacking their lips and pronouncing the fruit delightfully fresh.

The master gave his servant a pretended kicking, called him a clumsy rascal, and bade him run immediately, take off the rind from the other fruit, and bring it on table. This was done, and the bewildered greenhorn saw a whole round fruit of bread and butter fresh plucked in its natural shape. There was no doubt of it, none whatsoever; the fruit was culled and devoured so fast that he never once thought of looking for the pulp, or the seed. He ate and he believed, and went away the same evening so confident in his own mind that bread and butter grew on trees that he begged his friend to allow him to carry with him two or three, which he thought the ripest, as a supply for his journey in lieu of bread, which he had run short of previously to coming into Cochin. He was a regular griffin, was young ——, and there is no mistake about it.

We next touched at Calicut, where we took up a colonel and his lady proceding to Bombay, and from thence sailed on to Cannanore, the scenery all along being most beautiful, particularly that about Tellecherry. Cannanore is a large military station, being the headquarters of a division of the army, and a garrison composed of one of her Majesty's regiments of foot, two of native infantry, a detachment of artillery, &c. &c. I spent two days on shore, but did not go anywhere in particular, except to the commanding officer's for the purpose of paying my respects.

A few days after quitting, we made the Mangalore flag-staff. Here likewise is a river, or backwater, so that the pull to the landing-place is long and tedious. I had all my luggage put into two boats, and, jumping into the third, bade '*good bye*' to my friends in the ship, and pushed off.

In due time we landed, and I walked up to the cantonment, not very far off, and went straight to the house of one of my new brother officers, whom I had met at Madras some months before, little dreaming at the time that I was so soon to belong to his regiment. Here I found a home as a

temporary arrangement; and, as it was late in the afternoon when I arrived, I postponed my official visits until the next day.

Thus, kind reader, had I arrived at my journey's end in safety, having had a delightful trip of exactly a month from the date of my leaving Madras. I had derived much benefit from the sea air and salt water bathing, and was quite ready, after my holiday, to enter upon my duties in my own regiment, and to do everything in my power to gain the good opinion of my brother officers, who appeared to me to be a very gentlemanly set of men, and who received me most kindly as one of their own fraternity.

As a station for troops, Mangalore never was considered healthy, and that for more reasons than one. The backwater lies between the sea and cantonment, and between the former and the latter there are thick clustering plantations of cocoa-nut trees, the tops of which are almost on a level with the houses, situated upon a sort of high cliffy ground. The consequence is, that when the tide is out, and nothing but mud in the river, the sea breezes drive all the *miasma* right through those trees into the cantonment, rendering it really unhealthy.

In addition to this evil, the quantity of rain which pours incessantly during the monsoon renders the place very damp; this gives rise to noxious vapours, causing thereby fevers, rheumatisms, and a variety of other complaints, which play the deuce among the men as well as the officers. We lost several officers and many men here.

I remember one sad death which took place. It was that of one of our ensigns, a fine lad, a great favourite, and the quarter-master of the regiment. He died of *putrid fever*, a most dreadful, fatal complaint. When dead, the body was wound up in wax-cloth, to admit of its being lifted into the coffin. Decomposition had commenced before the vital spark had been extinct; and so infectious is the disorder considered, that his clothes and bedding were all burned, and the room, corpse and coffin, &c. &c. sprinkled with vinegar. Poor lad! He was a sad loss to his regiment.

The regiment to which I now belonged was composed of a fine body of soldiers, and I had every reason to hope that all would be well with me. Having commenced my military career afresh, as it were, with nobody to blame but myself if I went wrong, I resolved to put aside as much as I possibly could all boyish and griffinish tricks; to attend strictly to my work; to fag hard, and pass in the languages; to gain a knowledge of my duty; to become acquainted with my men; to do everything in my power to make them like me as their officer; to try all I could to please my commanding officer, and to make myself as agreeable as I possibly could to those with whom I had become associated probably for life.

I took a bungalow to myself, situated within a stone's throw of the mess-house, which, considering the heaviness of the monsoon rains, was very convenient.

It had been recently vacated by a captain of the corps and his family. I found it nice and clean. I bought up some of his furniture, and, taking possession of my new abode, made myself as comfortable as I could wish to be under ordinary circumstances.

I was as happy as an ensign could well be, and wanted nothing but my lieutenancy, and as that I hoped would come sooner or later, please God, I lived long enough to obtain it, I gave myself no trouble on the subject, resolving to draw my 181 rupees 5 annas a month, with philosophical patience, until I had a right to an increase to my salary.

Military duty is one of the *easiest* duties a man can undertake. Every single item of what he should do is laid down with such simplicity, and so well defined, 'that he who runs may read,' and, by a little attention on the part of the beginner, a knowledge of that duty is so easily attained, that it is surprising how anybody can mistake.

The adjutant of my regiment was a very proper sort of a fellow. He was extremely kind and attentive to the men, with whom he was a general favourite. He very often went out into the country, and brought home quantities of game, with which the neighbouring jungles abounded. Indeed almost all our officers were sportsmen, though none so devoted to it as the adjutant, whose bronzed countenance told of many-a-day's exposure to the sun in quest of the ferocious tiger, the cunning cheetah, the noble elk, or the bounding bison.

He had several live animals in his possession, quite a menagerie on a small scale. Let me see, there was a lovely male cheetah in a cage, full grown, but quite a kitten; another small one, a cub, and a full-sized bear. The former and the latter he had caught when quite young, amongst the wild forests of the Neilgherry Hills, where he had been stationed for some time.

The cheetah was not sufficiently tame to admit of his being at large, though I have often seen him charging after a sheep, seizing it with his teeth, and carrying it into his cage. The bear was a strange animal. He would stroll about very leisurely, either through the cantonment or amongst the men's lines, where he was well known and a general pet. He would come on to the parade-ground while the corps was under arms, and gambol about to the great amusement of every one. Poor bruin was also very fond of visiting the officers' houses, and purloining everything that was to be found. This he generally did at night, and, if he got nothing eatable, he would amuse himself by jumping upon the sofas, and tearing the linings of them all to pieces; he would pull out all the stuffing, and scatter it over the room. I remember catching him one night inside my house. He was on the point of mounting my couch, when I dealt him a blow across his snout (a tender part), which sent him rolling out in double quick time.

I was glad to find that our officers and men were great cricketers; a capital game among Europeans, but one which I had not the slightest conception would be played by natives; 'twas therefore quite a novelty to me. The adjutant was very fond of the game himself, and taught it to the men, who in a very short space of time became perfect adepts in the art of batting, bowling, and fielding.

We used to meet regularly every evening, and have capital fun, officers and men siding and playing matches. I do not remember ever having seen men enter into the spirit of this noble game as did our fellows: they have such quick eyes that their batting was capital, and, as for bowling, I venture to say that our best at it would astonish even *Lillywhite* himself.

At fagging they were untiring, and in catching particularly expert. They got into the regular way of play; made use of all the phrases and technicalities of the game; had their umpires and their scorers, and did the thing in a manner that quite surprised me.

I know some who objected to the officers and men playing together,

OUR CRICKET CLUB.
"Play."

upon the plea of its creating too great familiarity between the two grades. So far from such being the case, I never once saw an instance of even one man taking any liberties or approaching to any familiarity with the officers; on the contrary, they were ever respectful, and invariably kept themselves under proper restraint.

Any of the cricketers losing his temper, from any cause, would be immediately scouted by the rest, and not allowed to play. They were all led to understand that while playing they were supposed to be doing so to enjoy themselves; all squabbling was therefore forbidden; everybody was to be in perfect good humour; each was to do as he liked; there was no compulsion; but the rules of the game were to be strictly attended to.

Whenever there was a hunting or shooting expedition, or a picnic party, which was frequently the case, many of the sepoys, armed with their own private fowling-pieces, used to accompany us, and enjoyed the sport as much as we did. I remember an adventure which our gallant adjutant had one day with a cheetah, and which by the way might have ended seriously; the animal had been wounded by the aforesaid gentleman, and the enraged brute springing upon his foe had fastened his fangs into his cap (one of our English hunting-caps), which fortunately resisted the bite.

Had it not been providentially for one of the sepoys present, I cannot tell how the adventure would have terminated. The gallant fellow, seeing the danger of his officer, immediately rushed to the rescue, and with his hunting-knife dealt the cheetah such a dreadful blow on the skull, that it instantly killed him. This conduct on the part of the sepoy was not forgotten, and, being an individual of excellent character in other respects, he was at the request of all the officers of the regiment promoted, and otherwise rewarded. I have mentioned this and another case, and could cite a hundred more, proving the devotion and attachment of the native soldiery to their European officers.

Whenever there was anything going on in the way of amusements, our men were sure to join in the fun; no one forbade them; everybody who came was always welcome. There was a certain part of the backwater at Mangalore, near the entrance, or bar, where the water was beautifuly clear and deep, with a fine sandy bottom. Here we were wont to congregate almost every morning, officers and men, to enjoy the splendid exercise of bathing. This daily bathing in the salt-water not only kept the men from cutaneous disorders peculiar to the coast, (who has not heard of the *Malabar itch?*) but gave them plenty of healthful exercise. I was delighted to observe that in my new regiment officers and men went hand in hand together. There existed a kind of mutual confidence between the superior and inferior grades, which was indeed praiseworthy to all.

Let the day of trial come, and the despised sepoy will be despised no longer; it is only ignorance of their real merits which prevents many of our officers from knowing and liking them, and to know them is, in my humble opinion, to like them; we cannot do the one without the other. Let people say what they will to the contrary, we have all our failings, high and low, rich and poor; and, whatever our station in life may be, we should not judge harshly of others; and surely it is not *colour* that makes the man. Look at the native soldier with a generous eye, and all his faults will become concealed by his many virtues.

V ERY SOON AFTER MY joining, we had a new commanding officer posted to us, a lieutenant-colonel, well known throughout the army as a smart officer, kind and good-natured, but a bit of a martinet. He was an old and experienced officer, never having been out of the country from the day of his first landing. He had seen much service, but had been unfortunate in promotion. We liked him tolerably well.

He had many peculiarities, one of which was a strange habit of talking very angrily, and swearing a great deal when he meant nothing. He used to make use of very abusive language towards the men, notwithstanding that he liked them, and was very kind indeed to them. A kinder heart never beat under so rough an exterior as did his. Though much dreaded, he was, I think, liked by the men, despite his peculiarities and blustering manner, and he went by the name of the *angry colonel* amongst them.

I remember the first time I saw him. I thought I had seldom met with so handsome and so soldier-like a man. He was very tall and stout, with hair as white as snow, which gave him a very commanding appearance. He was an accomplished scholar; a tasteful musician for he played well on the flute; he was constantly reading; a capital chess-player, a game to which he was much addicted, so that, maugre his failings, he was an agreeable member of society.

He entered willingly into all our amusements; approved of cricket-playing and other games; used to come every evening to look on, encouraging the men whenever there was a good hit made, and abusing them like pickpockets if a ball were not caught, or stopped. He would sometimes take a bat himself at the spur of the moment, but being subject to gout he was not considered one of our *best* players. Poor Colonel F——! Alas! He is now no more! He was ever a kind friend to me, and sorry indeed was I when he was removed from amongst us.

There had been a shooting affair in this regiment, previously to my joining it. A private had shot a *subadar* on parade! This was another case of pride, jealousy, pique and spiteful revenge. Some misunderstanding had taken place betwixt the two, which the one took it upon himself on a fine morning to adjust, by putting a ball through his superior while the men were falling in, long before it was daylight. The trial had taken place, and the finding and sentence had gone to the Presidency for confirmation: in the mean time, the criminal was in close confinement in the guard.

A day or two after the colonel's arrival, the confirmed sentence was received and duly made known to the prisoner. He was to be hanged!

On the morning appointed, we fell in, and formed round the gallows erected for the purpose, and furnished by the civil authorities. We were drawn up in a hollow square, and the wretched murderer (a Hindoo) was brought out. He was dressed as if going to a wedding, covered from head to foot with wreaths of flowers; his clothes sprinkled with *huldee* (saffron); he was altogether quite a dandy!

On coming out, he expressed a wish to address the regiment. This he was not allowed to do. He mounted the ladder very steadily, and stood firm while the rope was being adjusted. When all was ready the signal was given, and the executioner pulled a rope to let fall the drop, but unfortunately the drop only fell half-way down, in consequence of something catching, so that the man was in a dreadful state, half hung as it were. At last, however, the obstruction was removed; he struggled and all was over!

After the usual time, the body was taken down and delivered over to his friends, who were assembled in great numbers, making a dreadful howling and lamentation, enough to distract any one. I was standing at the head of my company while this horrible scene was going on, and heard some of the men come out with exclamations of pity, such as that of 'Poor fellow!' 'What a death to die!' &c. &c. One of the elder sepoys said, 'Hold your tongues, my lads! It serves him right, the cowardly dog!' I must confess it made me feel quite sick.

It may seem that I was doomed to have something to do with the

Bandmaster and musicians of the Madras Army; coloured aquatint, 1845

subject of hanging, for we were seated one afternoon on the cricket-ground, when a man from the mess-guard came running to us and said –

'*Ao, āo, sāhib! Ghorā-wālā ăpué-tain phānsee dyā hai!*' (Come, come, sir! The horsekeeper has hanged himself.) Hearing this, we ran to the mess-stables close by, and there, sure enough, saw a sight which struck me with horror! Suspended from a beam over the doorway, the unfortunate man was hanging – quite dead! We forthwith cut him down, and tried to open a vein. However, it was all over with him.

Upon due inquiry, it was fully ascertained that the man had committed this act of self-destruction entirely because he had been thwarted in love. He had paid his addresses to a pretty *tŭnny-kerchee* (water-woman), who had at first looked favourably upon him. However, some more attractive swain made his advances likewise, and the frail fair one had taken to the latter, and jilted the former.

The man of gram-bags and currycombs could not stand this, so made up his mind to do away with himself, rather than bear the disgrace of belonging to what is called by us Indians the *juwaub club* (an institution composed principally of such unfortunate Lotharios, who have been disappointed in love, or refused in marriage, or jilted, even as was this poor man).

He went to work, it appeared, very determinedly and coolly, for (being a Roman Catholic) he had tied crucifixes to his hands and feet, and after that tied his arms in such a manner as to prevent himself from touching the fatal cord; he then stood upon the wall close by the beam, and took his last leap into the next world. His feet were within half an inch from the ground. This was in very truth a lover's leap.

The unfortunate cause of this desperate act, upon hearing the sad and dreadful end of one whom she had professed to love, threw herself into the river and was seen no more. A love-affair in India, amongst the natives, is looked upon in a different way to what it is in more civilized countries. I mean where there is a real feeling of affection betwixt the sexes.

Marriages are generally contracted among the Mussulmans without the parties seeing each other, with but few exceptions. I may say the same among the Hindoos and other castes; but the tender passion, when once it has inflamed the breast, is considered in a more serious light than people would imagine; and, when there is a rival in the case, none are more jealous than an Indian lover. If his love is likely to become thwarted, or his prospects of happiness endangered, the consequences are dreadful. The rival is either made away with by some desperate means, or, should he become successful, the disappointed lover falls a sacrifice to his own feelings, and generally contrives to put an end to his existence by the dagger, the cord, or the poison.

About a couple of months after my arrival at this station, from some cause or other, I found my health beginning to fail me, and I suddenly became quite an altered person. The climate was certainly against me. I did not at all like it. The days were hot and sultry, and the nights cold, damp, and otherwise uncomfortable; at least, so I fancied. I took plenty of exercise and lived moderately, too. Still all was not right with me, and I began to think an Indian climate not suited to my constitution.

The doctor took me in hand, and kept me very low indeed. There is nothing like living low in a country like India, when a man is at all indisposed. I was not often ill, but, whenever I felt so, I invariably took to broths and slops, though that regimen is deprecated by some of the faculty. People in general take no notice of a slight indisposition, but it is very wrong, for there is no knowing how such will end, and in tropical climates the most trivial complaint becomes, in a very short space of time, a very serious one, frequently ending in death.

'Tis the worst thing a man can do to neglect even a headache, or a cold; the causes of either may not be immediately known to the sufferer. I have heard some men say –

'Oh! 'tis nothing, merely a headache, it will soon be well.' The following day perhaps finds him stretched on a bed of sickness, or a corpse.

In India, disease works its way with rapid strides. Today, a man will rise up hale and hearty, with no anxiety whatsoever – that same evening he is in his grave. People may have a care-for-nothing feeling on these subjects, because they are strong and healthy; but in India, the strongest often go to the wall. Let my young readers then beware how they trifle with their health, that greatest of all blessings under heaven.

I found a confinement to indoor life very irksome indeed, and did not know what to do with myself. I would sometimes while away an hour or two in the unsportsman-like amusement of shooting dogs, of which a great number used to frequent my compound contiguous to the mess-house, from whence the brutes used to bring bones and offal, fighting and barking all day much to my annoyance. I was successful in slaughtering a few of them, but it was cruel work after all, and a pastime which was nearly attended with serious consequences.

I one day fired at a huge parriah dog, and somehow or other missed him; the ball flew through the open door of the mess-kitchen, and buried itself in the wall, whizzing close by the head of the cook, who was at the time pouring soup into a tureen. A narrow escape for both parties, and the loss of the soup, for the cook was so dreadfullly alarmed at the probability of his having been shot, that he upset what he had in his hands, and broke the tureen, for which, by the way, I had to pay; this was paying for one's fun, but it was better than being tried for manslaughter. I never fired at dogs again.

I have known many serious accidents from a too careless use of fire-arms. One officer I recollect of the Artillery was very fond of firing at marks with his pistols. He let fly at a bird in the hedge one day, and killed an unfortunate cow-keeper on the other side. Another officer shot a faithful old servant, mistaking him for a thief, in the dark. Another, carrying a gun at full cock, blew out the brains of his lascar, who happened to enter his tent at the moment. Another shot himself, and died of the wound. Another, from carelessly holding a pistol, crippled his left arm for life.

We had a very odd character at Mangalore in the shape of a *Moonshee*. He was a shrewd, intelligent old man, and a tolerable teacher. Although a Moslem, still he was very often in the habit of swerving from the strict regimen laid down regarding the indulging in wine and spirituous liquors. He used to take both *medicinally* – for the care of his body – to strengthen him in his old age! – to support the weakened energies of weary nature! He was particularly fond of cold claret; and a glass of that delicious beverage was a treat not to be despised by him. So, when old Ghouse used to come to me, to give me my lessons, and after they were ended I would say to him:–

'What say you, Ghouse, to going over to the billiard-room, and seeing that beautiful game played?'

'Very good, sir. I am your slave, and attend your pleasure. The game is indeed a scientific one.'

'And a little stuff to gladden your heart. Eh?'

'*La hillah!* (God is an only God.) Do not say a word about that, I pray, sir. I only take it as physic, and cannot drink it in any other way.'

And away we would go, old Ghouse nothing loth, to the mess-house, where several of our lads would be playing. Claret, deliciously cooled, was generally the drink, and as sure as it was opened old Ghouse used to have a goodly potation. He would look very sly – go to the doors and windows to see that nobody watched him; and, if he found all was right and the coast clear, he would take up the glass and empty its contents as quick as ligntning, smacking his lips and wiping his beard with the back of his hands, and exclaiming –

'*Ya allah!* This is indeed the nectar of Paradise!'

Brandy and gin old Ghouse did not relish so much as burgundy, champaign, or claret. The former he declared were fiery spirits, suitable only for English soldiers, parriahs, and cook-boys – while the latter were in very truth fit only for the true-believers. He was a drunken old rascal, was Ghouse; I have seen him toss off a dram of raw brandy with the greatest delight, notwithstanding his pretended aversion to it.

The Moslems and Hindoos in our part of India are not so foolishly punctilious regarding their religious prejudices as are those of Bengal and Bombay. This is the advantage that the Madras army has over those of the sister Presidencies. Our sepoys put aside those prejudices when the service is concerned, as an old *subadar* one day observed to me: –

'We put our religion into our knapsacks, sir, whenever our colours are unfurled, or where duty calls.'

Not being over particular, therefore, as regards the due observances of the tenets of their religion, nor overburdened with tender consciences, they indulge in the good things of life whenever it suits their convenience, much to the disgust of those high-caste bigots of the upper provinces, who look upon the natives of Southern India, and more particularly our sepoys, as a set of brute beasts not worthy to exist.

Our men in general care not what they eat, or drink. It is a well known fact, that our native troops are given to spirituous liquors. I have myself seen Hindoos and Moslems together, cheek-by-jowl, in the arrack shop, and I have also seen them rolling drunk in the ditch; their castes and their religion are matters of secondary consideration; these are *our* men; and again, I have met with men who have boasted of both, and declared their utter detestation of brandy or arrack, get so intoxicated from the effects of that pernicious drug, opium, that they have not been able to tell what they were about.

The evil effects of this propensity among the troops are more numerous than I can enter upon.

They are attended with most serious consequences; robberies, murder, mutiny, and insubordination, tending greatly to deteriorate from the good character of any regiment. But is it at all to be wondered at the common soldiery indulge in so baneful a practice, when they have so powerful an example set them by their own officers? Do not the orderlies on duty, coming to the officers' houses, see them drinking and smoking at all hours of the day? And do they not *sometimes* find them in such a condition as not to be able to do anything? Do not the men in the ranks see their officers sometimes even come on parade in a disgraceful state?

How is it that such doings are allowed to go on, unnoticed, unpunished; and yet, if a poor unfortunate private happens to be caught drunk, if he smells of liquor even, is he not instantly confined a prisoner and does he not undergo severe chastisement, while his superiors do the very same thing with impunity, and that too, some of them, every day?

We had been at Mangalore until May 1835 when a report came into the cantonment that there was a probability of our marching about the middle of that month. This put us all on the alert, and I for my own part was delighted at the prospect of quitting a place which I did not like, and which did not at all agree with me.

The reports relative to our marching were in a few days verified, as the order for our quitting Mangalore to be garrisoned at Vellore reached us, and all was bustle and preparation. We were to move by wings, that is, one half of the regiment, taking up the various outposts at first, and the other (or head-quarters) to follow.

When a regiment receives the order for marching, the first thing to be done or thought of is the disposal of one's property, to wit, household furniture and such other articles as are not absolutely necessary on the road. It is a very easy matter in setting up house to procure everything that is requisite, but the difficulty is the getting rid of the same on moving. I could not collect so much as one hundred rupees for the whole of the things disposed of. I think I got some seventy and odd rupees, and I had sofas, chairs, tables, pictures, glass and crockery, books and other things, all of the best description; and there was a rascally old Parsee at the place, who named his own prices, and gave me the option of taking what he offered or of carrying my things along with me. I had thus no alternative, and as money was the item most required, I was glad to pocket the one in preference to being burthened with the other.

We had great difficulty in procuring the necessary quantum of carriage for our baggage. There were scarcely any bullocks to be had, and several thousands were wanted. Our quarter-master had to go to the villages in the country, where, with the aid of the civil authorities, he was obliged to press into service as many as he could collect; such was the scarcity, indeed, that many were compelled to have their things carried by coolies instead.

I think I had six bullocks for my traps; two for my trunks, three for my tent, and one for sundries; in addition to which, I was obliged to hire six or eight men to carry my cot and other requisites. These last were engaged for the stage only, changing at each place, and receiving their hire at the end of each journey. Some of our officers were actually obliged to destroy part of their baggage, in consequence of the want of means of conveyance.

I must here inform the inexperienced reader, that a regiment marching in India is totally different to one in England, or anywhere else. To a thousand fighting men there are about four or five thousand camp-followers, and upwards; the families of officers and men, the servants of the former with their respective families, the bullock-drivers and bandy-men, the coolies, *palankeen*-bearers and others, form quite a host, to say nothing of the mixed multitude attached to the mess establishment.

I had two servants with me, and these, in addition to their relatives, as also my horsekeeper, grass-cutter, tent-lascar, bullock-drivers and coolies, made a total of about twenty-five souls to my single self; an ensign of foot, travelling with such a train, would appear almost incredible; 'tis however nothing but what is true. In the Bengal army, an ensign has, perhaps, double that number, but it is absolutely necessary; we cannot do without them, either in Madras or Bengal, whether we travel or are stationary; the number of servants to our establishment is quite ridiculous when we come to consider how very few are kept in a large family at home in Old England.

Each soldier has about three or four souls following him, according to whether he is married or not. The bachelor has his father or mother, or both, or perhaps grandfathers and grandmothers also, besides uncles and aunts, sisters and brothers, with probably some of their families. A married man, perhaps, has some of the above in addition to the members of his own immediate family; the old and decrepit, the weak and infirm, the sick and the lame, have all to be carried, and many is the poor sepoy, with nothing but his pay (or rather what remains of it, and that is little enough, God only knows), who has to procure carriage for the accommodation of these as well as for the conveyance of property; the number of living beings, therefore, and the difficulty of means of transport, may be conceived better than described.

As I before remarked, my health failed me at Mangalore; so that when we quitted that station, on our journey towards the Carnatic, I was in a very delicate weak state, and became fearful that I should not be able to proceed. The doctor told me, however, to try, and recommended my proceeding two stages by water, as far as a village called Buntwaul, distant by land, I think, about twenty miles from Mangalore. As our quarter-master (poor D—— C——) was going on in advance, it was arranged that I was to accompany him in his boat, sending on all my baggage and followers two days before me.

We had a delightful trip up the river; the scenery was very picturesque, the air cold and bracing, and the day beautifully fine. There were several of our sick men with us in the boat, together with baggage and other things; but, as our vessel was a large one, there was no lack of room for all.

About noon, we passed the regiment, encamped at a place about half-way between its starting-ground and its destination. While at this place I witnessed an animating and lively scene, the shore and rocks being occupied by many of our men and their families, washing, bathing,

In the field, the cook preparing his master's supper; from Lt. R. Thompson's album of watercolours

singing, and laughing, apparently quite rejoiced at getting away from such a vile place as Mangalore, and enjoying the delights of a holiday on the banks of a river.

We had a delightful run to Buntwaul, where we arrived in the evening, and, after landing, proceeded at once to the encamping-ground. I expected to find my tent ready pitched, but what was my disappointment, when, on my arrival, I was informed by my servants that my tent had not been erected, as I was not expected until the following morning. However, my kind friend, the quarter-master, invited me into his tent, in which I passed a comfortable night. As we had had no dinner, he asked one of our men to cook us up a dish of rice and curry, which made its appearance about half-an-hour after, smoking hot, and throwing out a most savoury enticing smell that made my mouth water.

We enjoyed our supper exceedingly, and finished the repast with a glass of hot brandy and water by way of a night-cap. A curry, made by a native in the way he himself eats it, is far preferable, in my opinion, to that which is concocted by our own cooks; there is something piquant and palatable in the one, while the other resembles a stew highly flavoured with spices and other condiments. Many are the times I have dined entirely off a dish cooked by one of my own sepoys, or bearers. Partaking of it in that way, I think it delicious and wholesome. Our men are always delighted whenever they are asked to cook for us, and on a line of march I invariably employed one of them for that purpose. Nothing pleases the poor fellows more than to be allowed to send their officers a dish of their own cooking. Natives are generally very clean in their culinary arrangements; I was therefore never apprehensive of anything dirty, or unwholesome, in the dishes they were in the habit of sending me.

I prefer eating from the sepoys' messes to the cookery of our own; and I have often stayed in my tent, and dined off a curry prepared by one of my company, rather than take my meals in the mess-tent. There is a particular knack, too, in boiling the rice, which the natives alone know; and the grain badly boiled, either done too much or not done enough, is always unwholesome.

This was my first night in a camp. I had never before slept under canvass. The novelty was strange to me, though we had everything as we desired it, and the interior of our habitation presented an air of comfort which rendered it quite snug, and made me feel as happy as if I were in a bedroom at home. Worn out and tired with the day's journey, I passed a very quiet night, and slept like a top until late the next morning, when the beating of drums and the sounds of martial music roused me from my slumbers. I jumped out of my bed, and, going to the door of the tent, beheld the regiment marching in; a very lively sight, and more particularly so to me, who had not witnessed such a one before.

Interior of a subaltern's tent during a shikar party; coloured lithograph by J.F. Fetheringham c. 1850

A LINE OF MARCH in India is a sight replete with interest and novelty. The enormous number of living souls in motion, the train of baggage, the quantity of cattle of all descriptions, the body of troops, small in comparison to that of the followers, the proportion being of three or four to each individual fighting man, this vast concourse of living beings moving together, and everything connected with them, renders the whole an exciting scene.

Troops in India move very early, according to the distance of the stage to be travelled, contriving so as to reach the camp as soon as possible after sunrise. As early as two and three o'clock in the morning, the families and baggage begin to be in motion, so as to get in advance of the regiment. Tents are struck and fires lighted, and the things placed upon the bandies; men, women and children talking, shouting, wrangling and crying. The order is that no one shall move before the beat of the drums, but this order (and a very foolish one, too) is never attended to; the families invariably try to start as early as they can, to avoid coming in contact with the main body.

At the time appointed 'the générale' rattles its startling sounds throughout the camp, when men and officers turn out; tents are struck as quick as possible; the baggage-bandies loaded and started off. It is quite dark, and preparations for moving are made by torch or candle-light. The whole camp, which was but a short while before sunk in silence and slumber, is now all bustle and stir. Officers and men, equally alive to their personal interests, are busy with their own concerns, attending to the dispatching of their families and baggage.

The servants are generally very smart: while the tents are being struck, one is attending to his master, the other is making tea or coffee (very necessary in marching, as it is always advisable to take something of the sort to warm the inner man against the morning air), the tent-lascar is busy in packing the tents, the horsekeeper in saddling his horse; and, if there is a lady in the case, the bearers are ready with their *palkee* to receive their precious burthen, who, wrapped in flannels and shawls, enters her conveyance, and starts on ahead.

Families marching have always two suits of tents; one is sent on in advance the evening before, with some of the servants, to prepare the breakfast, and the lady, with her young progeny (if there is any), moves on to make all ready for the reception of her lord and master, who follows with the troops.

The quarter-master of the regiment also starts the evening before, to select and mark out the ground for the next encampment, and the *jŭmmā-dānā*-guard (for collecting supplies) also accompanies him, to have all the necessaries of food and other articles ready. The mess-tent, and its concomitants, also leave the previous evening, so as to be ready with breakfast for the officers on the arrival of the regiment the next morning.

'*The générale*' sounded, the men begin to dress and accoutre themselves, and their tents are struck and carried away; all this should never take more than *half an hour*, when the next taps – 'the assembly' – are beat, and the troops fall in; the column is formed right or left in front; the advance and rear-guards are thrown out, and all move off at the sound of the 'quick march' from the orderly bugler; upon which the men generally give a shout and a huzzah, and away they go, leaving their old encampment, and looking forward with anxious expectations to reaching their next stage, and meeting with their families whom they have sent on in advance.

The guards and sentries are all withdrawn previously to starting, except the 'quarter guard', as it is called, which stands fast to protect the baggage and followers, and which does not quit the old ground until every soul is off it.

At first starting, the movement of the regiment is rather slow, owing not only to the darkness of the morning, but on account of the road being crowded with human beings, bullocks, bandies; obstacles which retard the progress of the redcoats, and render us anything but amiable, particularly as men are not much inclined to be in that mood on turning out sleepy and in the cold, to grope their way in the dark. However, we contrive to creep along, by means of torches and lanterns, until daylight, when the men jerk up their packs and start out boldly, calling out to those in advance to move on, and try to reach the encampment before the sun gets hot.

After clearing the old ground, the taps sound, 'unfix bayonets – and – march at ease,' when officers sheath their swords and mount, while the men march as they like, the pivots of sections, however, preserving their distances, and the whole push along as fast as they like, the men conversing with each other, the Joe Miller of each company telling his yarns, or cracking his jokes, some of the fellows singing, and others laughing. It very often happens that the officers are made subjects of mirth by the former, or of panegyric by the latter, as they are liked or disliked by the men.

Some light their pipes or cheroots, and smoke, as do also most of the officers. This latter is an excellent thing to do, because it drives away anything noxious in the morning air. I have known a whole regiment marching with pipes or cheroots a-light.

The band, drums and fifes, move at the head of the column; the men and boys composing them afford ample food for amusement, to say nothing of the censure attending their many tricks. I remember while passing through a village early one morning, there were a number of ducks waddling along to a piece of water hard by. Our drummers came right amongst them, several were snatched up unobserved, and crammed into the drums. At another time, we passed through a *toddy-tope*, where some of them contrived to get away and imbibe plentifully of the tempting beverage. They are strange rascals are our drummers, and up to all kinds of mischief.

In the rear of the column follow the recruits of the regiment (if there are any), and behind them again, the *recruit and pension boys*. These latter are lads kept up in our service by government, as a separate establishment in each corps. The lads are the sons of old and faithful men, brought up and instructed in all military duties, regularly mustered and paid. When arrived at a certain age, and if of the standard height, they are transferred to the ranks as privates, and generally turn out to be our best soldiers.

The 'recruit boys' are the elder lads, while the 'pension' are all the young ones; the former are made to do duty as orderlies, besides attending the regimental schools when not otherwise employed; while the latter are kept entirely at their lessons, coming out to be drilled regularly dressed in proper uniform; and it is quite laughable to see some of the smallest in their little military costume, with their caps on their heads, aping the soldier.

After the boys follows the adjutant, who rides, with the medico, in rear of the whole, and behind them again come the 'sick *doolies*', two-and-two, carried by bearers supplied by the commissariat or quarter-master general's departments. These *doolies* are comfortable conveyances, made up of strong framework well put together, and covered with blue or

Marching before dawn on route march to Bangalore; watercolour by Lt. R. Thompson of the 43rd MNI

white painted canvass: in them are placed the sick, who are accompanied by the medical subordinates belonging to the corps, together with the medicine chest, surgical instruments, &c.

On the reverse flanks of companies march the men driving bullocks, carrying large leather bags filled with water, a very useful arrangement for a line of march, particularly in hot weather. Then comes the rearguard, generally composed of one company thrown out in the usual way, and intended more for practice than anything else. Flanking parties are also in requisition, according to the whim of the commanding officer, who rides in stately grandeur at the head of his regiment, followed by his retinue of orderlies and horsekeeper, who watch him as closely as a cat does a mouse. A commanding officer of a regiment is a *very* great man on a line of march!

The column is usually halted half-way, to enable the men to rest awhile and eat something (if they have anything to eat), drink water, or take a puff at a pipe. On such occasions, they are moved off the road, arms are piled, and the men broken off; some lie down on the grass, others stroll about, while others sit on the road side and watch the baggage and followers marching along; some, again, more anxious, go down the road a little way to help on their families.

Officers dismount and sit chatting in groups, or, should there be any shooting-ground close at hand, or a *jheel* (lake, or large sheet of water) containing teal or duck, they generally take their guns and go and beat the one for partridges or hares, or try and have a shot at the wild fowl on the other. There is often much fun going on when thus halted, at the expense generally of some unlucky griffin.

My friend, who had but recently joined the corps, often gave us cause for laughter, and I may as well relate a trick played off on my young chum – by the old colonel, of course. While passing through a village, or rather the outskirts of it, the colonel spied some pigs grunting along the road side on their way to graze, driven by a little naked boy. He immediately called out to the youthful Nimrod,

'Come up! come up, as fast as you can, and bring your spear here! I see a beautiful boar, and a lot of others! Run, run, or they will all be off!'

'Where, where?' inquired he; and, snatching his spear from the hands of his horsekeeper, he charged to the front, and, not knowing a wild hog from a domestic one, laid his lance in rest, and bounded onwards. He rode over the poor black urchin, and flung his maiden spear against the sow, which scampered off, squeaking most lustily, the barb having grazed her skin. Poor B——! What a laugh did we have at him!

Married men while marching become great sportsmen; because the game they shoot supplies their tables, and consequently saves them the expenses of purchasing meat from the market. It was highly amusing to watch one (our doctor) in particular, who would rush after a miserable partridge which he might chance to hear calling in the jungle, or run up to his middle in water after a solitary duck, without bagging his bird. Poor doctor! his feeding must have been very second rate, if all he and his wife partook of were the produce of his gun; if he depended on that, they must undubitably have both been starved!

We had two married men with us in camp. One a captain, and the other the doctor above-named. The ladies must have had a very unpleasant time of it on first starting; for, independently of the inconveniences of early rising and travelling, they were exposed to the wet caused by the rains and the dampness of the tents in which they were obliged to reside.

The miseries of a march in the rains are indescribable, and are known only to those who have experienced them. Our clothes are damp; our tents throw out a disagreeable smell from being constantly soaked; the ground under us is wet and cold. Everybody in camp is grumbling and growling.

We have the rain pouring upon us on the line of march; upon coming to a halt, we have to wait for our baggage, which cannot proceed quickly on account of the state of the roads; and, when it reaches the encamping ground, the tents are pitched often on a swamp, and into them we have to go, miserable and discontented.

It is an odd and to me an unaccountable arrangement, that troops should be made to move at the seasons they do. They either march from one station to another in the rainy season, thereby rendering the journey one of discomfort, and engendering fevers and rheumatisms; or in the very middle of the hot weather, which causes cholera and other destructive diseases. Really, in these times, when disease and death are stalking with fierce strides throughout the country, carrying off thousands – scarcely a regiment marching without being attacked by cholera – it is a great pity that matters are not better managed than they are.

My own troubles on this march were not a few in number, incurred, no doubt, from inexperience, and a consequent want of good management. My bullocks annoyed me more than anything else, and my servants, who turned out all to be drunkards (how many ensign's servants are not?) were a constant source of vexation to me. My coolies annoyed me also, and my tent-lascar was a sore thorn in my side. On the march, it was a matter of everyday occurrence to hear of my bullocks having kicked off their loads, and scampered into the jungles; that the trunks, &c., were cast on the roadside without any prospect of their being brought on; and that their drivers had followed their bullocks in order to catch them.

My servant would be found lying by the trunks in a state of inebriety; my coolies would put down their loads also, and run back to the village from whence they came; and my tent-lascar would generally be found in a similar state to that in which my servant was – dead drunk – and fast asleep on the ground alongside of his comrade! Thus would I find matters almost every day.

I used to have all my domestics severely punished as soon as they reached camp; but really their drunkenness became so common, and their punishments having, to all appearances, little or no effect upon them, that I was constrained to let matters take their own course, consoling myself with the hopes, that, as their money could not last for ever, I should soon have them on their proper behaviour.

My lascar was a great rogue, for, independently of his profession as a pitcher of tents, he added the important knowledge of the mysteries of plate-washing and cleaning of knives, &c. These last attainments had full development in the mess-tent, whither he used daily to hie, for the purpose, as he called it, of assisting the mess servants, voluntarily of course.

This was a cunning arrangement on his part, inasmuch as that he thereby feasted upon the odds and ends which were brought to him, and imbibed all the wine and beer which he would chance to find in the glasses and tumblers left him to clean. The consequences were, that the fellow always got as drunk as possible, and I was thus deprived of his services for the greater part of the day, indeed I seldom could get even a glimpse of him, and as to his ever being sober, that would have been a wonder.

But I soon broke him of his tricks, for every time I found him tipsy I had him sent to the hospital-tent, where he was made to disgorge all he had taken, by means of a strong emetic, which was administered to him by the apothecary. Oh! the discomforts of a march with bad servants. The best servants are ruined on a line of march; mine could not be, for the villains were all bad enough before.

I remember on one occasion my servant came to me with a rueful countenance, saying that my cot-coolies had put down their load and had taken themselves off.

'Master, cot done, put em down, the coolies, sar, and run vay!' exclaimed the fellow, as he came up to me; 'no one got to make bring cot up to master tent.'

'Why did you allow them to run away, sir?' inquired I, quite angry with the man at thoughts of the probable fate of my bed, &c. &c. 'And where are they gone?'

A regiment of the line passing through a village; part of an extended panorama drawn by Lt. John Crealock in 1858

'What, I know, sar?' said the exasperated matey; 'I var foor man, sar. No rice this marnin, no nothing for me eat.'

'No nothing, say you, sir? You *have* been taking something as it is, and that's why the coolies ran away.'

'No, sar. I no take nothing. I foor man, sar; large fam'ly got. I *hanūsht* man. Neber drinkee nothing 'cept water. I Hindoo mans. Neber touch de 'rack, brandy, nothing, so help me Bob,' shouted the matey.

'Hold your tongue, you rogue!' said I, 'and don't make matters worse by telling lies.'

'I no tell lies, sar. I shtay with the thingis all time, and coolies get tired and put 'em down the cot; go drinkee vater, and then run ray, how I can help, sar? I neber drink, neber tell lies.'

'Of course,' said I, 'you took the coolies also, and they drank arrack with you, and then gave you the slip. Go this instant, and bring up my cot, and if it is not in this tent in an hour, I shall have you flogged at the bazaar flag-staff, you rascal!'

The colonel, who was walking by, heard the noise outside of my tent, and came up to where I was standing. He gave the unfortunate domestic one look. It was sufficient. He was off like lightning, and in less than an hour my cot reached the camp in safety, carried by the very coolies who had been supposed to have absconded. My domestic was sent, as usual, to the hospital-tent, and there under-went the usual discipline, which soon set him to rights; 'tis a capital plan, and one which natives dread exceedingly.

My Bucephalus was another grievance to me. Day after day there was sure to be something wrong, either real or imaginary. One day he would break loose and gallop all over the encampment, kicking and plunging in every direction, much to the annoyance of officers and men, old women

and children, who, doubtless, wished my old brute far enough! Another day the grass-cutter rogue could not procure a sufficient supply of grass, although the rest had abundance. The third day the beast would have a sore back, and a fourth day my man would discover and report that he had a loose shoe, and a fifth he would say that the animal refused his feed; every trivial thing was thus magnified into enormous disasters and misfortunes, so that I was in one constant state of ferment, and I had no peace night or day.

Mentioning horses, I may as well hint to all, as a general rule to be observed while marching, that it would be advisable for a man to look to his horses as much as possible himself, for the tricks that are played upon their owners are innumerable, and the loss of an animal, whatever its value, while travelling, particularly if possessed but of one, is a greater inconvenience than may be conceived. For instance, the horsekeeper, for want of better food, steals that intended for his beast, and feeds himself and family thereon.

In addition to these evils, the rascal horsekeeper is, during the cold nights, very fond of taking off his animal's clothing, and covering his own body therewith, to the detriment, of course, of his charge, which either gets an attack of rheumatism or a stroke of the land wind, which renders him weak in the loins, and consequently fit only to be shot.

I must observe, that in India our horses are generally fed upon green grass, for the procuring of which a man or woman, as the case may be, is employed upon a fixed salary of three rupees and a half per month, and this individual is obliged to fetch a fresh bundle of grass – a bundle of a certain size, too – every day for the horse; and really when we come to consider the daily labour and the distance (sometimes from ten to twenty miles) they have to go, before they can procure a sufficient supply, it would appear almost incredible that men or women can be got to do so much for so small a pittance; but so it is: and with this paltry sum the poor individual earning it is often times supporting a large family.

But let us get on with our march. Our route lay through a very woody country: the roads were execrable, and our movements consequently slow, not reaching the end of our stage sometimes till eleven o'clock! In course of time we came to the *Bessely Ghaut,* a pass that is very steep and rugged, covered on each side with enormous large trees and thick jungles. We were obliged to dismount and go down on foot, leading our horses, which, with shoes on their feet, was no easy matter. Many a fall did we see, and many a bullock, with its load, rolled down the declivity; any attempts to stop either, when once set going, were of no avail.

As a matter of course, my beasts of burthen were among the first to exhibit their clumsiness. Those carrying my trunks both came down by the run, and away went my unfortunate boxes, chasing each other down the steep in fine style, bounding and jumping over each other as if impatient to reach the bottom; one of the heaviest nearly killed an old woman, and another smashed an unfortunate dog to death, belonging to one of our men. 'Twas, indeed, a pretty sight to see those trunks *ricochet-ing* it down the pass; and gave cause of much amusement to watch the people getting out of their way: fortunately damage there was none.

At the foot of this *Ghaut* there is a rapid river, which is crossed by a ford, or causeway, very narrow and uneven, and made up entirely of large stones piled upon each other; the horses stumbled and sprawled about most unpleasantly; the stream was rapid, the water deep on each side, and swarming with alligators, which we saw in abundance.

As we halted on the one bank to allow the men and followers to cross over, we witnessed many an amusing sight; sometimes an old woman riding on a bullock, would flounder in the water, the unfortunate creature shrieking with fright; again some sedate *subadar*, riding on his tattoo, would come upon another, and the two animals would begin kicking and biting most furiously.

We amused ourselves by having shots at the alligators, one, an enormous fellow, *laying-to*, ready to pounce upon any body or thing which may chance to be carried off the ford by the force of the current; but no such luck attended him; all that he caught was a *tartar*, in the shape of a round bullet, which came with a sharp twang against his thick skull from one of our rifles. The huge monster gave a spring out of the water and then disappeared.

I had myself a narrow escape, being nearly carried into the jaws of one of these monsters. After the men had almost all crossed, I re-mounted my horse, and walked him into the water. My beast presently stopped to drink, and I, like a griffin, allowed him to do so, not knowing what was to follow. To my great surprise, I shortly found the horse settling down under me; and, had it not been for the promptitude of the horsekeeper, who was standing close by, he would certainly have taken a roll in the water, a trick which horses are very apt to play in a warm climate, not only with a view to cooling themselves but to get rid of the many flies which settle upon and sting them. I shall not, in a hurry, forget the narrow escape; my comrades, as usual, had their laugh at me, but I thought it no laughing matter, for an alligator's maw is no joke!

10

WHEN THE MORNING'S weary march is drawing to a close the men jerk up their knapsacks, and step out boldly; the fellows in the rear calling out to their comrades in front to push on – '*Chŭlloh! Chŭlloh bhāi!*' (Move on! move on, brother!) is the cry; and when the encampment, in its embryo state, appears in the distance, the *advance guard* shout out most joyously, '*Arrĕh dĕhrah! dekh dĕhrah! dĕhrah!*' (The tents! Look at the tents! The tents!) Gladsome tidings to all parties; for it not infrequently happens that, in consequence of the distance, or some other circumstance, the troops are not under canvass until past eleven o'clock, at which time the sun is *precious* hot.

When arrived at within a quarter of a mile from the camp that is to be, the '*Halt*' is sounded. Officers then dismount and fall in with their companies; the dressing and covering are taken up; trowsers that had been tucked up are let down; dust shaken off their hair and moustache; turbans (or chacos) and knapsacks cleaned, and everything put into apple-pie order previously to marching in.

When all is ready, the '*Quick march*' is given; the band strikes up a

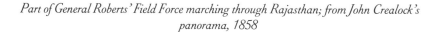

Part of General Roberts' Field Force marching through Rajasthan; from John Crealock's panorama, 1858

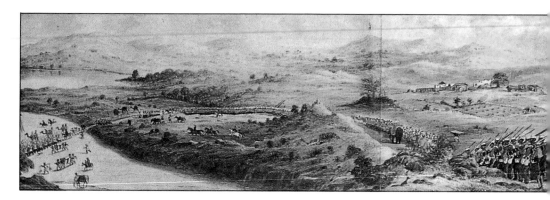

merry tune; the men step beautifully together to the exhilarating sounds; and the column winds up the road on to the alignment marked out, where it forms up into line, which is immediately dressed and corrected. The men for duty are marched to the front; arms are piled, and the regiment broken off; upon which the men generally give a shout of joy, unsling their packs, and commence taking off their accoutrements.

The Guards, being inspected, are marched off to their respective posts, sentries are thrown out over the arms, the colours are lodged in due form, and a guard placed over them. All the married men, as well as others who have relations and families, run down the road to help up their baggage and bullocks; while the care-for-nothing bachelors divest themselves of their uniforms, and put on the light, comfortable, and cool apparel of their country, and walk about, or assist in pitching their tents immediately in rear of their piles of muskets, which make a formidable show, regularly ranged as they are in one extensive line from right to left, with their angry bayonets glittering in the bright sunshine.

The European officers run off to the mess-tent, where, if the breakfast be not ready, a general shouting takes place for the eatables and drinkables. Hunger will brook of no delay, particularly if the means for appeasing the cravings of the appetite are procurable and not ready. Hungry men, just off a long march, are very impatient, and woe betide the unfortunate caterer or messman if they have to wait.

And, again, if each officer's servant is not ready, present in the tent, awaiting the arrival of their respective masters, with camp chair, hot-water plate, cup and saucer, knife and fork, silver spoons and muffineer, all prepared and arranged, miserable wretch! he is to be pitied indeed!

The uninitiated must be here informed that, in marching, the mess does not carry open any furniture, crockery, glassware, or cutlery; nor is the plate chest used. The officers therefore are obliged to provide them-

selves with necessaries for the table, and come to their meals in what is termed '*camp-fashion*', each individual making his servant carry a chair, three or four plates, a cup and saucer, knives, forks, spoons, and those invariable accompaniments to an Indian officer's plate chest, a pair of silver muffineers, one containing salt, and the other pepper.

A servant travelling thus laden presents a droll appearance. On his head is his master's chair; across his back is slung something resembling a bundle of clothes, but which, upon examination, will be found to contain a number of plates of a variety of patterns, and other articles of crockery, carefully wrapped up in the domestic's own pieces of drapery, some of them none of the cleanest. If any of the crockery is broken, others cannot be supplied, so the servant is obliged to be on the alert against any such untoward accident, or else he is sure to get a good *welting*. Then, in his '*cummer-bund*' (or waist-cloth) are concealed those precious articles, '*master's siliber tings*', one of each, with cutlery also.

This servant (yclept '*matey boy*') always starts on ahead, or follows in rear of his master's horse on the march, so as to be in time for him on his coming into the mess-tent. Arrived there, the domestic, with all dispatch, places the chair at the table, on which he arranges the plates, cup, saucer, &c., &c., having previously wiped each article with a towel, if he has one, and if not, with the corner of his jacket, or the end of his waist-cloth, taking care to impart to all a nice polish, in the same manner as the old apple-women at home do the fruit which they are vending.

These arrangements made, the faithful slave takes off his turban, from the folds of which he extracts his master's table napkin, neatly flattened and delightfully perfumed with cocoa-nut oil, which the natives use in great profusion for their hair. All this done, he awaits with impatience his master's coming; for, poor fellow, there is no provender for him until after breakfast, and then he feasts off the *débris* on his master's plate.

Breakfast after a march is a very delightful meal. We are hungry – and hunger is an undeniably exquisite sauce for all dishes; the viands are good, the tea and coffee excellent, and the whole very soon disappears. It is an amusing sight to watch the eaters, each man taking care of 'number one', and not minding his neighbour. For the first ten minutes or so, scarcely a word is spoken; some sit down as they enter, others more patient take off their uniforms, wash their hands, make themselves decent and comfortable in white jackets, and then come to the table.

Breakfast over and hunger appeased, conversation begins. The events of the morning are talked over, and the mode of spending the day is discussed; the laugh and joke go round, and all is merriment and fun.

Some light their hookahs and cigars, while others quit the tent to look after their own baggage, and to superintend the erecting of their temporary abodes.

Outside, a very busy animating scene presents itself; and the eye of the griffin sees many a sight to which he is unaccustomed. The whole ground is covered with living beings; cattle and baggage; men, women, and children; servants busily engaged in pitching tents, and wrangling with each other; horses and ponies neighing; officers and soldiers running to and fro; coolies coming in with their loads; *palankeens* and *doolies*; sick carts and bandies; stragglers arriving one after another; unruly bullocks kicking off their loads, and running helter-skelter; timid women and children screeching, and men hollowing; such a bustle and confusion, that, to the stranger the whole sight would appear as if there was great want of arrangement, and give him an idea of a sad state of discipline.

I remember well my utter astonishment the first time that I myself witnessed the scene I have so faintly described. I thought the people would never have done arriving, that the tents would never cease pitching, and that we should be in the same confused state the whole day. But how agreeably disappointed was I to find that in less than an hour's time the whole camp was as quiet and still as if we had been stationary for months! And this is indeed the case always.

Choosing a site for an encampment is no easy matter. At every town, or village, or halting-place, there is a piece of ground allotted for the use of troops, and the quarter-master of a regiment is always sent on with his establishment of camp-colour-men, for the express purpose of looking over the ground, pitching the flags, and arranging for the disposal of the followers, as well as of the fighting men.

The whole area or space is, as nearly as possible, a square, or, at all events, a parallelogram, inclosed within the camp colours, which indicate the bounds of the same. The front being decided upon, the first tent pitched is that intended to hold the advanced or *outlying piquet*, as it is called; this is usually placed some yards in front of the first line, which is composed of the men's tents, four to each company, and capable of containing each twenty-five men. In rear of this are the subalterns' tents, at a convenient distance; the next is the captains' line; but where there are so few officers present with a regiment as now-a-days, captains and subalterns generally pitch in one line.

The next in line is the commanding officer's, on each side of which stand the adjutant's and quarter-master's tents, his right- and left-hand men, his staff, the commanding officer's or head-quarters being distinguished by a large Union Jack flag floating on a tolerably-sized staff, or pole. On one flank of this last mentioned line is pitched the mess-tent, and on the other the hospital.

It still remains for me to touch on the other encampment for the families, out of which nobody is allowed, upon pain of severe penalty, to go. The families and other followers are permitted to erect their tents, or *pals*, or temporary huts, promiscuously, without any regard to regularity, as it would, indeed, be endless trouble to insist upon any observance of military regularity or precision, the which is more likely to give rise to grumbling and discontent, doing, thereby, more harm than good, by rendering the privacy of the women (of which the natives are peculiarly tenacious in all castes) liable to be intruded upon. This latter circumstance alone is apt to give dissatisfaction more than anything else; 'bully and tyrannize over us as much as you like, but do not meddle with our families,' is what is frequently said amongst them.

The appearance of this assemblage of tents, *pals* and hovels, of a variety of forms and sizes, presents a striking contrast to the regular encampment, consisting, as the latter does, of large comfortable coverings for men as well as for officers. 'Tis only the poverty-stricken married soldiery who are so miserably provided for, and it is they who suffer principally all the hardships and privations of a line of march, themselves

The 1st Division arriving in camp; from the panorama in watercolours drawn by John Crealock

having their respective duties to attend to, as well as the looking after and providing for their numerous families.

I have now only one item left in my description of an encampment, and that is one of the most important and most useful, as well as the most indispensably requisite. What I allude to is the *bazaar*, or sutlers' camp. Whenever any body of troops move from one station to another, it is the rule for the quartermaster-general's department to report to the civil authorities of the districts through which their route lays, informing them of the number of fighting men, and probable number of camp-followers accompanying.

This report enables the civil powers to make arrangements for the furnishing of supplies at the different halting-places, and this is done by the understrappers at the towns, villages and hamlets, directing the attendance in camp of a certain number of bazaar-men or shopkeepers, who are to bring with them supplies of all sorts for consumption.

A place is fixed upon by the quartermaster, where a large flag is hoisted on a long pole, and here the *bunnyahs*, or shopkeepers, are regularly ranged in line according to the articles they are vending; for instance, those selling rice, in one line; those selling grain, or vetch, or peas, in another; those with curry-stuff and other condiments, in another; then, again, the butcher has his stall apart; the poultry-man takes up his position here; the vendor of fish (if any) there; then the *pawn*-leaf man sits close to the flag-staff, and he of tobacco behind him; while the oil-seller

takes up his station on one flank, and the straw and torches are disposed of on the other.

Thus a plentiful supply of provisions is always in camp, and the articles are *supposed* to be of the best description. Nothing pay, nothing have, is the order; there is no *tick* allowed: the consequences are, that the dealings between the sutlers and the camp are all fair, or, at all events, they are presumed to be so; but it is to be feared that, as natives are great rascals in every situation where self-interest is concerned, there is much more knavery going on than people are probably aware of.

It is always customary, unless anything occurs to prevent it, for a regiment marching to have a halt, or resting-day, every third day; that is, there is no marching on the third. This enables both men and cattle to brush up and recruit from the fatigues of the journey, and also causes a break, as it were, which is in every respect pleasant to all parties. On such occasions, all damages to our travelling-appurtenances are repaired; horses are shod (that is, those that require it), broken tent ropes replaced, and rents mended; the men touch up their arms and accoutrements, while the old women and other idlers in camp wash their clothes.

The officers form themselves into parties, and go out shooting or hunting, followed by as many of the men as are fond of sport. The performance of all duties is strictly and regularly gone through; companies are inspected; arms and ammunition examined; the forms of guard-mounting are observed and everything is done to keep up that regimen of the military profession, so peculiar to the Madras army.

We invariably had a grand cricket-match on these days, if the ground admitted of it; the two sides playing for so many sheep, and having a good * zērāfut* (feast) afterwards. The officers always joined in the amusements, contributing all in their power towards that good feeling which should invariably exist in the ranks of every regiment.

There is always a grand dinner in the mess-tent on a halting-day, to which the ladies in camp are respectively invited, they coming as the rest do, 'camp fashion'.

A dinner of this description is a very merry one; we have plenty of fun, and eat and drink right joyfully. The old butler contrives to put on a capital dinner, and the wines are cooled with saltpetre, not only as a treat allowed on halting days, but because the ladies are dining with us.

The way we manage to cool our wine and beer on ordinary days is very simple. Take the bottle, and suspend it by the neck to the door of your tent, keeping the opposite one open to admit a through draft of air; cover the suspended culprit with a napkin or cloth, which must be kept well wet. The hot wind blowing upon this causes the water on the napkin to become cold; evaporation takes place, and imparts the coolness to the liquor, which renders it deliciously palatable.

Our water we cool in the same manner. The *goglets* (or earthenware bottles) in which we keep it are porous, and consequently the outer surface is always damp: the wind blowing upon them cools the contents sufficiently to obviate the necessity of using saltpetre. But water is an ingredient which is seldom used as a drink by itself; indeed, for my part, I do not think it wise to drink it plain, without mixing it with brandy, or wine; for there is no knowing where it comes from, and what poison may be in it.

But, to return to our dinner. The officers' servants don clean clothes, and get themselves shaved and otherwise brushed up; the plates and dishes, knives and forks, receive an extra superfine polish; the table looks nice and tidy, and the whole is capital.

While at dinner, the band is drawn up outside the tent, and we are enlivened with music, and in the evening, if the ground is even and grassy, we have a dance. Ladies are a great acquisition to a camp, in my opinion; although I know there are others who hold a different opinion. They have many inconveniences and privations to undergo, and some there are, poor creatures, who, with their young families, are exposed to many hardships, which it is a wonder their delicate constitutions can possibly undergo.

We arrived, without any extraordinary occurrence, at Bangalore, having been on the road for about a month, and, taking all things into consideration, after a very pleasant march thus far. True is it circumstances sometimes did happen to vex me, yet after all they were trivial, and then I was nothing more nor less than a downright greenhorn.

The cantonment of Bangalore is a very extensive one, widely scattered, but at the same time laid out in regular lines of houses, which are in general well built and compact, with enclosures, or compounds, according to the size of the dwellings. Many of the houses are large, and the rooms have fire-places, in consequence of the cold during certain months of the year. The appearance of the cantonment from the rising ground outside is certainly very pretty; the substantial buildings, the neatly trimmed hedges, the well made roads, and the church peeping out from among the trees, the soldiers' quarters and other barracks, and public stores, all form a striking picture to the eye of the stranger.

There is a large force maintained here, composed of horse-artillery, dragoons and native cavalry, foot artillery, European and native infantry, sappers and miners, and so on, intended chiefly to hold the Mysoreans in

The square and entrance to Tippoo Sultan's palace, Bangalore; coloured aquatint, 1804

check, for at this distant period there is still an ill feeling on the part of the Moslems, the old followers of the great Sultaun Tippoo, against the British government; and the *pettah* (or native suburbs) is swarming with the dissolute and discontented, as are also the neighbouring cities of Seringapatam and Mysore.

Our old European soldiers are very partial to Bangalore. They have been known to volunteer from one regiment to another three or four different times, to be able to remain in India in preference to going home. They live very comfortably, draw their pensions, which are ample for their own subsistence as well as for that of their families, and appear to be perfectly contented with their lot in life.

It is usually those attached to native women who remain in India; men with European wives generally return to England. I have known very few instances of the latter giving India the preference; there are connexions and associations which draw them to their own country, whereas the being united to females of colour with large families acts as a restraint, though many instances are known wherein European soldiers have deserted their wives and children, and gone away without them, never intending to return.

These pensioners are, however, considered very troublesome people, for they are much addicted to drinking, and are the means of corrupting the young soldiery, and making them intoxicated, after which the poor lads are turned out of their houses, and are invariably taken up by the patrols and punished the next morning.

The good folks at Bangalore, hearing of our character as cricketers, a challenge was sent us, and arrangements made for a match between the eleven of HM's ——th foot and ourselves; but this challenge was taking us at a disadvantage, for many of our best players were away with the *left-wing*: we were, therefore, badly off, though our lads were game to the backbone, and eager for the trial. Two of the best bats from among the officers volunteered, and were taken in for want of better to make up our eleven. Tents were pitched, the ground marked out, and the wickets placed by knowing hands, umpires selected, and scorers told off, all very proper.

Our men were nothing daunted, although they were much out of practice; they had never before played against Europeans, and their present antagonists, they were informed, were first-rate players. All the cantonment turned out to see such a novelty, viz., that of natives of India playing at that true English game; and it was a sight worth seeing, too; the whole ground was covered with European and native soldiery from the different corps in the place, besides ladies and gentlemen spectators, for whose accommodation tents were pitched and refreshments laid out by the mess of the gallant regiment to whom we were opposed.

The game was played very fairly and with great spirit, though it was evident to all present that the advantage was on the side of the Europeans. The first day's result was, however, in favour of our men, notwithstanding their want of practice. That of the second day was against us, which made the match in every way a drawn one, and both parties separated highly satisfied with each other, the Europeans in great glee, and our lads so excited that they declared, had the *left-wing* been present, there would have been no difficulty in giving the *soger logue* (the soldier-people) a thorough good drubbing. We were to have played the dragoons, but we left Bangalore before a match could be got up.

It was highly amusing to mark the behaviour of our gallant countrymen towards their darker comrades on this occasion. Not knowing the customs of the natives, the men had prepared a kind of collation with plenty of drink, to be partaken of by the sepoys as well as themselves. The soldiers came up to our men as soon as the game was over, and, slapping them on the back, one of them said:–

'Come along, boys, and take a bit of something to eat and a glass of beer!'

'No, sar! no can eat, no drink!' replied a *havildar* of ours.

'Arrah, honey!' exclaimed an Irish grenadier, 'we'll take no excuse; ye shall have a raal drop of the crater, too! come along!'

'No, sir! I Hindoo mans! I neber drink! I lose caste 'spose I take the rack!'

'Well, thin, lave the drink! Come in and take something to eat; do that now, there's a darlint, Jack Sapoy that ye are!'

'No, sar! *salam*, sar! *Main Mussulman hoon: makin ki sukta!*' (I am a Moslem: I cannot eat.)

'But ye are all a queer set of fishes, that ye are!' exclaimed the disappointed soldier. 'By the butt-end of my Brown-Bess, what is it that ye will do?'

'We go whome!' replied a Sepoy; 'go to camp. Roll-call *feade* got, we go, sar, *salam*, sar, *salam*!'

And away they went; thus ending the colloquy which I myself overheard. The sepoys were not accustomed to such instances of true English hospitality, and their caste prejudices prevented their eating and drinking with our gallant countrymen.

When I arrived at Bangalore, I was in a sad plight. The exposure to the sun had worked wonders with my smooth face and fair complexion. The whole was one mass of blister and *scarification*: the skin was peeling off in large flakes, and my poor nose was one great angry-looking thing, as if I had put it into the fire. I was quite horrified to look at myself in the glass, and dreaded the thoughts of visiting several lady acquaintances in the place.

On a line of march, when the young beginners are out in the heat day after day, without any shelter it is not at all to be wondered at that they suffer; there is no remedy for the evil, and the only way to manage is to let the skin come off by itself, and not pick and pull it as I did, thereby creating large sores, which are not only inconvenient and painful, but disfiguring.

I remember visiting a lady the day after our arrival. She stared in amazement at sight of me, and did not actually recognise me until some time after I had been in the room. Thinking that she would administer relief to my poor face, she hastily ran into her boudoir and brought out a bottle of 'Eau de Cologne', with which she wetted the corner of her *mouchoir de pôche*, and applied it to my nasal organ! The effect may be better imagined than described; I roared with the pain, and was glad to run away and plunge my head into a basin of cold water.

My rogue of a lascar was drunk every day while at Bangalore; the consequences were that my tent was never attended to, and I suffered accordingly. I threatened him with dismissal from my employment as a debauched drunkard, but he saved me that trouble, for he took himself off one fine day and I was thankful enough too, for a more determined arrack-drinker I never saw.

One dreadful storm I shall never forget. My pegs were not bushed as usual, and about ten o'clock it came on to rain and blow most furiously. I was on my cot fast asleep, when presently I was roused from my slumbers by hearing a loud noise resembling thunder, which made me fancy all sorts of things. This proved to be one corner of my tent, which had got loose, and was flapping about famously; presently, the whole fabrique came down with a crash! The pole fell straight across my cot, without however doing me any damage; and I should most probably have been smothered in the wet folds of the canvass, or had my back broken by the pole, had I not fortunately slipped off my cot, and taken shelter underneath it. As it was, I got wet through to the skin, and should have fared but badly, had I not taken refuge in my fellow griffin's tent for the rest of the night.

Servants in India of all classes, be they butlers, cooks, matey-boys, or tent-lascars, horsekeepers or grasscutters, or in fact anybody, must be dealt with in most rigid discipline, and then all will go right, but diverge from that, then farewell to peace and comfort. The master must keep himself in his own place; if so, the servants will know theirs; if they do not, they must be punished; but, if once there is a laxity in the discipline of the house, then, as I said before, farewell to every comfort, and farewell authority, and farewell to property also. There is nothing like good wholesome discipline even in one's own house.

AFTER RESTING FOR five days, we again broke ground and finally quitted Bangalore, in continuation of our journey towards our destination. I was beginning to be heartily tired of moving, and longed to reach the end of our march. The having to be in one constant state of bustle and excitement, was very tiresome, and the sameness of every-day occurrence was wearying to me. Our cattle, too, were beginning to evince signs of fatigue by losing flesh, from daily labour and bad feeding, and our men also were complaining of being badly off for the where-withal to prosecute their route. However, we had not much further to go. The 30th of June would find us at the end of our journey, and we hoped to remain quiet and stationary for three years at least.

The weather was very cold indeed at Bangalore, and continued so until we descended the Ghauts. When we turned out of a morning at three o'clock, the wind blew bitterly upon us, and both officers and men shivered and chattered as if they were half-frozen. I had no idea that it would be so chilly, and was always glad to wrap myself up in my cloak and stand by a fire until we moved, and then I used to march on foot almost the whole way, to keep myself from tumbling off my horse, for the cold used to make me as sleepy as possible. A hot cup of tea, or coffee, with a spoonful of good brandy in it, and a bit of dry toast, are capital preparations for a cold morning in India, after which, the warmth of a good Manilla cigar is really very comforting to the inner man.

The cold sharp air of the country through which we were passing was, however, very healthy and bracing, and was, doubtless, most beneficial to us all. We were in excellent health, having about six men on the sick report, and three were old ulcer cases, brought with us from Mangalore. The exercise of walking eight or ten miles every morning did me a vast deal of good. I enjoyed that part of the business considerably, and, when I arrived in camp, I had the appetite of a horse.

While thus walking, I would move between the sections of my own company, listening to the yarns spun, and conversing with and making remarks to the men as we trudged along. This the brave fellows liked very much, and they were always pleased when they saw me coming amongst them. I never once met with an instance of disrespect, nor did I ever feel myself lowered, in my own opinion, in the eyes of my men. Many a hearty laugh have I had while thus marching with my *sepahees*, and many a joke have I cracked with them, too. I recall these incidents often to my mind, and look back to those days with feelings of pleasure.

It is a long time now since I last marched with my men; when I became the company-officer, all familiarity was at an end and forgotten in the rigid discipline and demeanour of the well-trained soldier.

I firmly believe that if there were to be a better understanding between officers and men, there would not be half the disturbances, the mutinies, the desertions, the courts-martial, the everything that is objectionable amongst our native soldiery. No! The officers consider that they lower themselves by associating with their men. They think it *infra dignitatem* to be seen conversing with them, except at orderly hour, or on the parade-ground. Who, in the name of all that is military, should, if the officers do not? If they hold themselves aloof from their men, how can the one have any regard for the other?

In course of time, we came to the well known Nakennairy Pass, at which place we began to descend. The scenery at this part of our journey has something in it beautifully picturesque, and I may say grand. On our right, we beheld high hills in irregular forms, exhibiting a variety of rocky chasms, deep gullies and towering cliffs, covered with thick jungle and large trees. On the left the eye meets a series of deep valleys, prettily variegated here and there with sheets of water, thick clusters of trees, romantic glens and woody dingles.

In front, the eye rests upon the extensive plains of the Carnatic, interspersed here and there with small ranges of hills, dry beds of rivers, and watercourses, well cultivated paddy-fields, and broad patches of forest land, but the whole has an arid, parched-up appearance, nothing to be compared in general aspect of picturesque beauty to the country we had but recently traversed, and which was certainly far superior to that upon which we were now about to descend.

Mentioning the Nakennairy Pass reminds me of a strange story I once heard, but upon the truth of which I was rather inclined to be sceptical.

When the fortress of Seringapatam fell into the hands of British, after that ever-memorable siege which terminated in its capture and the over-throw of the Moslem dynasty in Southern India and the death of the Sultaun Tippoo, the quantity of treasure collected by the captors was not in any way adequate to what was expected or reported to exist in various parts of the city.

It was also a well-known fact that, when our gallant troops stormed the breach, there was a dreadful hand-to-hand fight inside, and that the enemy made a desperate resistance; and it is also well known that the Sultaun Tippoo, in attempting to escape in his *palankeen*, was attacked by an European soldier, who drove his bayonet at him and eventually dispatched him (not knowing, I believe, at the time who and what he was) and that he despoiled him of his rich belt and scimitar studded with precious jewels.

The Fall of Tippoo Sultaun; detail from an engraved aquatint, 1799. Unfortunately, Captain Hervey's romantic tale of Tippoo's death is not supported by eye-witness accounts

The story goes, that when this soldier rushed at the sultaun, the latter was so alarmed that he cried out for quarter, adding, that if he would spare his life he would tell him where a greater portion of his treasure was concealed, and that he should be made possessor of it all.

The soldier was moved for the moment from his bloody intent at hearing the important intelligence, and asked the terrified sultaun where it was. Upon which the latter, thinking doubtless that he had gained his point, whispered the secret into his ear. The soldier, exasperated at the improbability of a native confiding such a secret to him, a common man in the ranks, pushed the suppliant from him, and thrust his bayonet into his breast; he then moved on, leaving the slain on the ground where he had fallen.

The information which the British soldier had received made a deep impression upon him, and when he began to con the matter over in his mind in the cool of the night, he came to the conclusion that there might be some truth in what had been thus imparted to him, for the man he had dispatched had revealed the secret in the hopes that his doing so would be the means of sparing his life. He therefore resolved upon the first favourable opportunity to visit this spot, and to ascertain from personal inspection whether what he had thus heard was falsehood, or truth, keeping the matter meanwhile strictly locked up within the secret recesses of his own heart.

Having arranged his plans, he asked permission to proceed on sick-furlough, started with some details (men who had been disabled during the recent siege) then on the point of quitting Seringapatam for the Carnatic. In course of the march, the party arrived at the village of Nakennairy, where they halted for a couple of days, and, during this interval, the treasure-seeker managed to get away by himself, and went in quest of the place which had been told him by the sultaun, as already mentioned, and where the much-coveted gold and silver were said to be concealed.

He arrived at the mouth of the cavern indicated to him, and was on the point of entering it, when he was scared away by a roar. Looking up, he beheld to his great dismay, a huge tigress with two cubs standing close to him, and evidently meaning mischief. Treasure, riches, wealth, ambition, future happiness, grandeur, and everything else upon which he had been cogitating and dreaming for some time past, all vanished with the rapidity of thought. He quailed before his foe and slunk off as quickly as his terrified legs could convey him; coming back as he had gone, empty-handed, covered with mud and dirt, bruised and torn from the rapidity of his flight through the jungle, terrified and unmanned, broken and dispirited. His comrades thought him mad, and his superiors remarked that all was not right with him. He reached the Presidency in safety, but an altered man. The thoughts maddened him of somebody else knowing the secret, of the treasure being discovered, of others enjoying it, of others sharing it, when he might have had all, all!

Being a term-expired man, he had obtained his discharge from his regiment, and, free from the trammels of military discipline, he repaired to London, and laid a paper before the Court of Directors of the East India Company, stating that he had a most important matter to disclose to them, the which he would do, upon the proviso that the result should benefit him equally as well as themselves; that is to say, if there was any benefit derivable, he was to have half. The Court would not assent to his propositions, and offered him other terms, to which he would not agree; and the former, believing his information to be the workings of an unsettled brain, turned him out of the place, and told him he was mad. The man went away, and what became of him, no one knew.

The East India Company despatched secret instructions to the Madras authorities to the effect that trustworthy officers should be sent to search for treasure, which they had heard was buried in the neighbourhood of the Nakennairy Pass.

The government of the Fort St George selected two trustworthy men, the one in the civil service, and the other an officer in the army, and sent them with secret orders, in search of the hidden treasure, taking up their residence at the very same village from whence the poor soldier had started but a few months ago on the same errand as that on which they had come.

They sallied forth one day, well armed, in the direction of the hilly broken ground of the pass before mentioned; and there these two adventurers wandered about from morning till nightfall, continuing their search day after day, as if in quest of sport, without any success, bringing home with them, however, plenty of game, though *that* was not the sort of game which they were playing at.

One of the two, the military man, having separated from his comrade, came suddenly upon the entrance or mouth of what appeared to him to be a cave of considerable depth! He was presently joined by the absentee, and they both agreed that the cave, at the entrance of which they were standing, must be the one for which they had been directed to search, since they had been hunting up and down all over the neighbourhood, and had not seen anything resembling a cave anywhere else.

Proceeding cautiously, with guns ready cocked, in case of their approach being disputed, they had advanced somewhere about five or five paces, when they both detected a very strong smell, which there was no mistaking.

'I smell tiger!' said one.

'So do I!' said the other.

'Let us go a little further,' replied his companion, and they went a little further, when the leader suddenly came to a standstill.

'Oh, I see them!' whispered the military.

'See what?' asked his companion.

'Four huge glaring eye-balls!' slowly answered the other.

They made the best of their way back to their encampment, thinking themselves well out of the cave, and the jaws of the terrible animals they had seen in it. These were, I presume, part of the same family which had scared away the poor soldier!

The two treasure-hunters reported the finding of the cavern, awaiting the reply of government as to what further was to be done. Shortly after, a large party of sappers, miners, pioneers, and engineers, were sent up to the place; the unfortunate tigers were frightened out, the cavern was turned inside out, every nook and corner hunted, every inch of ground dug several feet down, but without success; nothing was discovered save whitened bones of deer and cattle, the *spolia opima* of the lords of the forest.

There was no treasure, that was evident; what then had become of it? People said it was all a hoax, and that government had been gulled; but I have heard say, that within a few years, there was a very old man residing in great affluence in some remote part of Scotland, who had been in former days nothing but a private in a Highland regiment, which had been some time in India.

I have heard that this self-same individual was no less a personage than the very soldier who had slain Tippoo Sultaun; who had also by much dint of perseverance, (how very persevering are the Scotch!) contrived to return to India; collected the money; and had carried the whole, amounting to several thousand pounds, up to his native village in the highlands of Scotland, where he had spent the rest of his days in quiet seclusion.

Besides being a beautiful musician and a first-rate flute player, our good old colonel was a capital hand at chess. So excited would he become on the issue, when so engaged, that I have known many refuse to play with him. He and our worthy quarter-master (a very talented young man) used to be constantly wrangling with each other on the subject; and even when employed on duty matters, the colonel would begin talking to him about the move of the red knight, or the checking of queen and castle; it was therefore a matter of difficulty with the quarter-master to get any business done.

In fact, we were quite worn out with hearing the old topic over and over again. The unfortunate official was the only person the colonel could get to play with him, and for want of others he would invariably give orders to the non-commissioned officer, going on in advance the previous evening, not to fail in securing for him the best chess-players in the village to which he was going; so that the poor man was obliged to hunt out and assemble all the chess-players, and select the best amongst them for the *Colonel Sahib*, on pain of his severe displeasure, in case he failed.

If the individual, whoever he was, pitted against the great man, beat him, he would give him a few rupees for his trouble, and bid him take himself off to the regions of *Jehahn-num*, a queer sort of a place, to which all true Moslems have a particular objection. If the man should have the good fortune to be beaten by the colonel, he would have for his reward nothing but a volley of abuse on his bad play, and being told that he ought to be ashamed of allowing himself to be beaten, that the little drummer-boy would play better, *et cetera*.

I remember, on one particular occasion, there had been a failure in procuring chess-players at one of the stages as usual. The colonel was talking to me at the moment when he was informed of the disappointment, and was very wroth. He declared that it was utterly impossible for a native village, with Moslem inhabitants, not to have a chess-player in it, and ended by asking me to go and fetch him a fellow, never mind who he was.

'Seize hold of the first you find!' said the colonel; 'the butcher or the barber will do; and if one or both cannot play at chess, I am much mistaken.'

I went accordingly into the village, and pretending to be in a violent passion, seized hold of the butcher, who, seated in his stall, was quietly vending his meat. I accused him of having cheated some of my men, and insisted on his coming instantly before the commanding officer. The poor fellow, quite alarmed at the earnestness of my manner, begged and supplicated, saying that he *was a poor man*, and had not sold a morsel of meat to any of the men of the regiment.

On my way back to camp with my prize in tow, I saw the *hŭjam* (barber) seated under a tree, shaving the cranium of one of our *subadars*. I called out to him to come immediately, as the *bŭrrah sahib* (the great gentleman) wanted to be shaved. The barber, delighed at the idea of having to perform on so exalted a personage as a colonel, besides receiving, perhaps, one rupee for his services, instead of one anna, instantly let go the half-shaved sconce of the *subadar*, and followed me to the big man's tent, where the colonel was seated in his *puijamahs* (long drawers), smoking his cheroot, with the chess-board all ready for action. He saw my two captives, and without saying a word pointed the chess-board to them, as much as to assert that they could play, and that it was useless denying it. The butcher said he could play but a little, and that he would not presume to compete with his 'Lordship, the defender of the poor!' The barber declared he knew nothing about the game.

The butcher was desired to sit down and do his best, while the barber was told to shave, and that when the butcher had tried his chance he should take his place. The action commenced, and in the course of two hours the butcher was the victor. The colonel threw his cap into the poor man's face and gave him five rupees into the bargain, telling him that if he would follow the regiment the next march he should not be a loser.

Meanwhile the barber took his seat with many salaams and excuses. The two played for nearly three hours, and the issue was in favour of the barber, who also received a good quota of abusive anathemas, together with five rupees. He, too, was engaged to follow the camp to the next stage, and the colonel's orderlies were strictly enjoined to keep an eye upon them, so that they should both be present to renew the contest the day after.

The butcher and barber thanked me heartily for taking them up in the way I did, adding that they would willingly accompany the regiment to Vellore, if there were a chance of their earning five rupees a day so easily.

'Wait,' said I, 'you'll see. Woe betide you, if you do not beat him tomorrow. If you win, well; but if you lose, you will be kicked out of camp, and have to return to your village without anything. However, try your luck; nothing venture, nothing have.'

They did venture, and got a sound drubbing both of them, in the short space of an hour each. They received a rupee for their trouble, and returned homewards much better off than I expected.

We were particularly fortunate during this march in regard to the health of our men and followers. The left wing, which had preceded us, had but one casualty, and that by cholera, and I am only surprised we escaped as we did. Our troops in India, and more particularly the native portion, have much to try them in marching. However strong, however brave, however patient, however willing, if they are tried above their

physical powers, they must fall; fall they will, and fall they do. Behold the man! The naked ploughboy, the artisan, the servant, or the well-clad wealthy native's son, whoever he may be, is transmogrified into a stiff, buckled-up-in-uniform soldier. His free and unfettered limbs are encased in tight scarlet cloth jacket and trowsers, in lieu of his light habiliments, whatever they might have been.

On his head he wears a heavy unwieldy *thing*, more like an inverted fire-bucket than a chaco, instead of his light *pugree*, or head cloth. In his left arm is placed a heavy musket, heavy enough for a roast-beef-fed Englishman to carry, but too much for the delicately-formed light body and slender limbs of the sepoy lad, who scarcely weighs one half of a European soldier!

On his back is slung a great knapsack, fastened to his body by means of leather-straps going round his shoulders and his chest, tight enough to cut him in two, in consequence of the weight of the pack. Across his breast he has two broad belts, held together by a brass plate passing on either side of him. To one of these is fastened his bayonet, and to the other his pouch or cartouch-box, large enough to contain some sixty rounds of ball ammunition, the whole sufficient to break a poor man's back. Round his waist passes another belt, intended to keep the others together, but tight enough to cut his very intestines out of him. On his feet he wears a pair of clumsy things called sandals (*chŭppŭls*, as the natives nominate them), such ungainly looking affairs that I really must be excused describing them, for I cannot.

Look at any of our sepoys in the ranks in *heavy marching order*. See him with his lumbering pack, weighing I know not how many pounds. This huge thing slung to a man's shoulders, with his great big firelock in his arm, his pouch full of ammunition, his body buckled up and hampered with tight fitting clothing and accoutrements, the accursed turban on his head – behold him! see how he stands!

The man literally totters under the weight! The perspiration pours from him in torrents; he is sick, and very often faints and falls. And yet the men are called unsteady under arms by reviewing generals, because, under such heavy burthens, they do not stand without moving.

Look at the sepoy again; see how he has to exert himself to throw musket up to his shoulder. He is obliged to bend down to lift it; and why? because it is too heavy for him. Look at the sepoy again, when firing ball. With what difficulty does he level his piece; and see – he pulls the trigger, and the discharge takes place. What a shock does the recoil give him! It frequently knocks him back. He has not the strength to wield such a weapon. Then, why give it to him? He would be ten per cent more efficient with a light *fuzil*. Surely 'tis not the size of the firelock, or that of the bullet, that makes the soldier; it is a mistake to think so.

Turn we now to a sepoy on the line of march. Before starting, a sepoy generally receives an advance of pay; perhaps he has it in full, or only half, according to the pleasure of the commanding officer. With this advance of pay he has to clear himself from the station (for probably he has incurred debts), besides paying an advance equal to one half, for the means of conveying his goods and chattels, as well as his numerous family, some of whom, particularly the young and aged, are unable to walk.

Exclusively of all this, he has to provide the means of sustenance for himself and dependants, and that with a total of perhaps two rupees in his pocket, for a journey of about two or three or four hundred miles! How can he do this? Impossible! He must starve and so must his family; at all events, they must from sheer necessity feed themselves upon the most economical plans that they can possibly devise.

Curry and rice are luxuries they dare not think of. Plain boiled rice is not so expensive, and of that they sometimes do manage to have a treat, about two mouthsful each. Bread or *chuppatees* (cakes made of rice flour), are quite out of the question. Butter-milk with a green chili after it, and now and then a bit of salt fish by way of a relish, is generally their sole food; and parched peas, or raw *chenna* (or grain), forms a kind of variety, which they chew, resembling the cud of bitter poverty in every sense of the word.

Upon this sort of diet have they to support nature, and be fit for the duties to which they are called in the camp and on the route. All this time he has to carry his pack, firelock, and accoutrements; his chaco, his pouch full of ball cartridges; the body emaciated and rendered feeble from want of proper sustenance; how is it possible for the wretched man to go through all this without breaking down?

I do not think that I have erred in what I have said. Indeed I feel confident I have not said one hundredth part of all these poor fellows have to undergo. The sepoy being thus badly fed (not fed at all in many instances!) and harassed in mind and body – the followers (thousands of them, too, to one regiment) being half-starved and miserably accommodated from want of covering against the inclemencies of the weather, badly clothed and helpless, can it be at all surprising that an epidemic should break out, and when it does make its appearance amongst them in the appalling form of cholera, that it rages with all its fury, and carries off the officers, soldiers, and the poor camp-followers by hundreds?

'What is to be done?' is the universal cry. Men at the head of affairs are at their wit's ends, and know not which way to turn. In very truth, it is 'the pestilence that walketh in darkness,' 'and the arrow that flieth by noon-day!' I must confess again, that it is my opinion, that if our troops were better fed, less worked, and more lightly armed and accoutred, the cholera, or any other epidemical complaint, would not show itself in our camps so often as it does.

Many a time and oft has the poor sepoy come to me begging to be let off carrying his knapsack, with distressing complaints somewhat to the following effect: –

'Pray sir, allow me to put my knapsack on my bandy; it will be well taken care of by my people. I am weak and unable to carry it as well as my firelock and ammunition. I cannot do it, sir, pray excuse me the knapsack.'

This is a common complaint; while another would come and say –

'Please sir, will you kindly lend me half a rupee? My family has not had anything to eat these two days, and I too am starving. I feel myself so weak that I cannot do my duty if I eat nothing. Pray be kind, sir, and lend me the half rupee. I will never ask again.'

A third would come and say –

'My bandy-man, sir, refuses to come on unless I give him some more money. What shall I do, sir? I have not got a *pice* in the world!'

These and many other similar distressing complaints and solicitations are constantly made, and in nine cases out of ten officers are unable to render any assistance. I will now take upon myself to mention the line of conduct I adopted, and what I used to do on the line of march, which I am now recording, and on similar subsequent occasions.

It so happened, that when we received orders to quit Mangalore, I disposed of all my kit of furniture, crockery, and everything else, for somewhere about seventy or eighty rupees. In addition to this sum, I received one month's pay in advance, besides some twenty rupees for a pair of old horse-pistols, which I sold as useless lumber; and I must here observe, that I made it a rule to appropriate my company allowance of thirty rupees a month entirely for the benefit of men whom I commanded. This I looked upon as a capital relief-fund, and so put it into the regimental cash-chest, as money belonging to the company, by way of security; keeping, however, some ten or twelve rupees in a bag for immediate use.

Every halting-day I treated my men to some sheep, and to those I knew to be hard up, I invariably dealt out so much rice, curry-stuff, or any thing else that they might require; or, if money was necessary, I made no objections to giving those that wanted a small sum, taking care to put down the names of all who benefited, for the purpose of avoiding, as much as possible, extending my bounty to the same person more than was absolutely requisite.

Whenever a man complained to me that he was unable to carry his knapsack, I always sent him to the doctor, and if he was reported weak, I invariably excused him the oppressive burden. If a man was lame or had blistered his feet, I would allow him to go on in advance with his family, or follow slowly in the rear.

In fact, gentle reader, I would busy my whole heart and soul in administering to the wants and comforts of my men; never a day passed without my assisting some of them.

I do not recollect having once detected any attempt to deceive me; indeed, the fellows knew me too well to try any thing of the sort. They were all perfectly aware that one case of deception would immediately bring condign punishment upon the offender. The consequences were, that I never had cause to repent of my kindness towards my men.

I cannot help saying, that so well behaved were the whole of my men during this march, that I only had occasion to resort to punishment once, and that was a case of drunkenness on the part of a recruit, the fellow having got into a *toddy-tope*, made a hole in the callibash with the point of his bayonet, and drank the liquor, which he managed to catch in his *lota*, or small canteen.

12

At length we came to the end of our journey, and entered the garrison of Vellore, after a march exactly of a month and a half, without having had a single casualty either of men, followers, or cattle. We were, indeed, singularly fortunate. I shall never forget the joy with which our men hailed the sight of the place as we neared it; nor shall I forget the delight I myself experienced at thoughts of once more becoming settled.

The meeting with our old companions in arms was one fraught with pleasure. Officers shook each other heartily by the hand, and men mingled

The 22nd regiment of Madras Native Infantry preparing to march from Vellore; watercolour by Capt. F.G. Bannerman Philips, 1855

in the ranks and embraced their comrades with delight. 'Tis indeed an exhilarating sight, and does a man's heart good to see such feelings existing amongst so large a mass of people; feelings which reflect credit upon and do honour to those in whose breasts they are engendered.

Chequered in truth is the life of a soldier, more so probably, than that of other professions, and still more particularly so in India. We are happy and joyous today; and tomorrow – where are we? Our friendships are formed and matured, but our friends are with us one day, and the next sees them in the narrow bed, the common lot of us all.

On our arrival, we were conducted to the barracks appropriated for our use, and as no lines were ready for the men, the encampment was formed and occupied until everything was ready for the reception of the families. The officers in the meantime rode about the cantonment in quest of accommodations for themselves; there were many houses vacant; many to pick and choose from, so that we had but one difficulty to contend with, and that was the rent, an important consideration, but which few take the trouble of making. The rents of houses in almost every military station are fixed and regulated by the authorities, according to size and respectability, so that no man is ever liable to be imposed upon, except by his own folly in entering a house with a rent too high for his purse.

The cantonment is composed of three long streets running parallel, with others intersecting, and the houses erected in compounds or gardens. The smaller and meaner buildings are situated at one end, while the larger and more respectable ones are located at the other. The quarters for the subalterns, that is to say, those of low rent (and they were high enough, too) were miserable hovels, some of them dirty, broken-down holes, which were quite disgraceful for so large a garrison.

The fort is situated about a quarter of a mile from cantonment. It is an old Maharatta fortification, built entirely of granite, with circular bastions, long curtains and narrow wet ditch; the water of which, being stagnant, threw out a stench sufficient to breed a plague! The houses inside the fort are substantial, but very old. The principal buildings are the palace, a very large pagoda or temple, converted into an arsenal, and the commandant's house, as also the barracks for European troops.

The interior of the Vellore fort was the scene of the famous mutiny. The barracks in which the European soldiery were so unmercifully massacred are still standing, and used as public offices. The visitor can to this day see the marks of the dreadful fire of musquetry which was poured in upon the poor fellows from the windows.

The dead bodies of the unfortunate European soldiers who fell were buried inside the fort and a mound marks the spot where their bones lay; those of the mutineers were taken out and thrown into a pit dug for that purpose, in a field shown to this day.

It must be borne in mind, that the country was then in a very unsettled state, and that the greater part of southern India had still a hankering after the late dynasty, particularly the Moslem population of the whole of Mysore and the Carnatic, where the late Sultaun Tippoo's power and name kept up the fire of revolt, which was still smouldering, ready to burst out into a blaze at the first favourable opportunity.

At Vellore, the native population was composed, for the greater part, of Moslems. The sultaun's whole harem were confined inside the fort, and it was a well-known fact that hundreds of his late adherents were residing in the *pettah*, or native town. These men were the means of undermining the fidelity of our troops from without, while the women from within were tampering with their allegiance to our government, promising all manner of bribes if they, like good believers, would rid the country of such *Khafirs* (infidels) as the English were!

These were the very people who excited, plotted and contrived the mutiny; while at the same time that they were acting thus basely, they (I mean those abominable old cats the women), were receiving handsome pensions from the hands of the very government whose power they were trying to subvert by their secret intrigues.

The *Mahal Sera* (or private palace), where the shrivelled remains of the great Tippoo's Harem reside, is an extensive building, surrounded by a lofty wall, high enough to prevent the entrance by escalade of any daring lover, had there been even encouragement for such an undertaking in the existence of any thing lovely or lovable deserving the attempt; but as there were neither youth nor beauty immured within the sacred walls, nothing but some dozen old women, the said high enclosure cannot be considered as being ornamental, or useful. Of the interior of this palace, I know nothing. No vulgar eye has ever pierced the mysteries of that seraglio. None were ever permitted to enter the precincts, excepting the brigadier commanding, under whose charge these state prisoners are kept; the fort adjutant, who goes with him, and the garrison surgeon, who feels the old ladies' pulses and prescribes something *nice* whenever they are indisposed.

The commanding-officer of the station had much cause of trouble and annoyance with the ladies. One day the water brought for consumption was bad; another day, the *pawn* leaves were objected to; a third, the meat was not eatable; a fourth, the sentries at night challenged too loudly, and disturbed their slumbers. And then there were frequent petitions against this person, or that; so that the situation of the brigadier in connexion with them, was anything but a *sinecure*.

The alligators are very dangerous creatures in the Vellore fort ditch. I have heard of several dreadful accidents happening at different times. I recollect one lamentable occurrence taking place shortly before our arrival.

It so happened that an unfortunate boy, while crossing the causeway, saw a large alligator close to him, and having some bread in his hands, stopped and sat down, with his feet dangling over the side, and amused himself by throwing in pieces of the bread, which the alligator snapped up. Little did the poor wretch know of what was coming!

Another large monster from behind crawled up the embankment, and seizing his victim by the hinder part plunged back with him in his jaws. There was no help; the boy could not have been saved; the sentry called out to the guard, but before anybody came the monster had disappeared with his prey, and all was still; the only thing visible of the catastrophe being the blood-stains in the grass and discoloured state of the water.

These monsters were first placed there in the days of Hyder Ally, as means of defence against an enemy, and with a view of preventing his prisoners from escaping. He had many confined in Vellore, and the neighbouring forts on the tops of the surrounding hills.

The authorities have oftentimes determined upon destroying these animals, but have been prevented doing so on account of the natives, who hold them in veneration in consequence of their having been placed there by so great a man as the tyrant Hyder.

These creatures are cowardly brutes, and nothing alarms them so much as the report of a gun. I was informed that the European soldiers in the fort were aware of this, and discovered that they always avoided that part of the ditch over which the morning and evening guns were fired; this latter circumstance they found out by throwing a dog into the water, the poor animal swam across and escaped untouched, whereas had it been thrown in at any other point it would have been snapped up immediately.

The soldiers would lower themselves from the ramparts into the waters just under the bastion, exactly as the gun fired at night, swim across the ditch without fear of the alligators, which they knew were not there, scramble up the ruinous counterscarps and steal into the *pettah*, where they would remain all night and return the following morning in time for the *reveillée* gun, swim back and get into their barracks undetected.

At Vellore, we had three regiments, including our own. The officers were all good fellows. The messes were always entertaining; and our commandant-brigadier was the very man to render himself liked and respected.

His lady was agreeable, and made herself much liked by her hospitable behaviour towards people passing through the station, whom she always invited to her house. Many have been the delightful parties I have gone to at that house, and many the nice comfortable dinners I have partaken of when on main guard.

The general society of Vellore was like that in most of our Indian stations, where we meet the same people, and see the same faces day after day, with little or no varying, to scare away the dull monotony of inactivity. The ride or drive in the heat of the sun, to visit the few ladies composing the female portion of our circle; the three o'clock dinner table; or the evening gallop up to the old race course, to breathe the hot air which comes down upon us from the neighbouring rocks; all this was stupid enough after all. Sometimes, an enterprising married man would hazard an evening party, to try and get up a little gaiety; the ladies found it too hot to dance, and the gentlemen would not attempt to dance at all, so between the two sexes that also was dull work.

People at Vellore in those days, had no spirit in them, excepting, by the way, at the messes, and there the jolly bachelors used to enjoy each other's society, and to live in first-rate style. But I took no delight in those noisy meetings. Smoking and drinking appeared to me to be but poor satisfaction, particularly with the concomitant evils of a sick head-ache the

Coffee after the parade; coloured lithograph showing officers in full dress uniform from the Horse Artillery, Cavalry, Irregular Cavalry and Infantry, c. 1850

next morning; such being the case, and for want of something better to do, I would wend my way home after my evening ride, have a cold bath, enjoy the delights of a nice cup of tea, and go to bed at times so early as eight o'clock. Vellore certainly was a very stupid place in the year 1835 – at least I thought so.

There was capital fox-hunting in the vicinity of Vellore. One of our officers kept some beautiful greyhounds, which he had bred himself, and with these he used to course the foxes. This may appear to the inexperienced a very unsportsmanlike thing, but a little explanation will, probably, serve to do away with such an impression. Many attempts have been made to introduce fox-hounds, harriers and beagles, into the country, but without success in any one way. Hundreds and thousands of these dogs have been sent out to India at enormous expense, and thousands of pounds have been spent in various ways in trying to keep up the necessary establishment for their care and management; but every attempt has been a complete failure.

The dogs cannot live in India. No sooner does a pack of them reach Madras, than they die by twos and threes a day. Few, if any, survive, and those that do, become mangy, and are of no use whatever.

The fox-hounds, harriers and beagles not being then equal either to the climate or the work they have to do, we are obliged to have recourse to greyhounds, which we breed sometimes entirely of English blood, but more frequently with a cross between an English and an Arab. The thorough-bred English dog is too heavy for this country, but the English blood in the Arab crossed, is a capital one for coursing.

There was also at Vellore a *bobbery pack*, as it is called. This strange denomination is applied to as strange a medley of the canine species. The pack is composed of dogs of all sorts and sizes; half-bred greyhounds, terriers, mongrel-curs, half-spaniels, poligars, parriahs, and half-bull, half-setters, and so forth. With such a combination, it is difficult for the inexperienced sportsman to conceive what can be its use.

But the *bobbery pack* afford good sport. They are fine at a run after jackall, or *dummall-gaudy*, alias hyaena; they will attack a village pig, or chase bagged hare. They are up to any fun, and really I have seen very good runs with them, far better than with Madras foxhounds. Almost every station has a *bobbery pack*, each member of the hunt contributing his share towards increasing the number of dogs.

The neighbouring hills, some five or six miles from Vellore, abounded with game of every description. We had snipe and wild-fowl in abundance, with partridge and hare as much as we wished. But game in the country of the Carnatic is particularly insipid, dry eating, and rather tough to boot; for nothing can be kept to get tender as in England; what is killed must be consumed at once, otherwise, it very soon becomes unfit to be eaten at all.

The best way to use game in some parts of India is, I think, to put it into *pickle*. Snipe, partridge, teal and duck, opened down the breast and put into salt for a few days, and after that dried in the sun, and then hung in the cook-room over the smoke of the wood-fire, make capital eating, and keep a considerable time; they are an excellent addition to the breakfast-table, particularly on a march, when good fresh provisions are not always procurable.

A roast hare is not eatable, from its being so very dry and tasteless; not even the accompaniment of jelly or tamarind sauce will make it palatable, nor is it nice in a stew; but potted hare, well concocted, is, I think, delicious, and can be used at any time for breakfast, tiffen or supper. It will, moreover, keep. I have seen hare potted in India ate in England, and it was just as good as when first done!

The reader may feel disposed to disbelieve me, but I can assure him that I have ate an excellent curry made from a young monkey! The meat was most tender, and exceedingly savoury. In some parts of Ceylon, the natives use the flesh of the monkey very often, particularly in broths and

curries for sick people. I have also ate a pie made of parrots and guanas, and an excellent dish it was, too.

In the month of May 1836, as I was desirous to pass an examination in Hindustanee I applied for leave, which to my great satisfaction was granted to me. I removed down to Madras, to the house of a worthy friend who was kind enough to give up the use of the bungalow in his compound entirely to me. And here I began in real earnest. I had two *moonshees* in my pay, and worked hard from ten in the morning until four in the afternoon. One *moonshee* kept me translating from Hindustanee into English, and the other *vice versa*.

These men used to do nothing but praise me up to the skies, and tell me to go up and apply for an examination committee, declaring that I should undoubtedly succeed with flying colours! The rascals told me that I was very clever indeed! Quite master of the language, and that I should pass a brilliant examination!

"There is not the slightest doubt of it, sir!" they would say.

Thinking them therefore sincere (and in doing so I acknowledge myself a great griffin), and that they were the best judges in such matters, I did apply for an examination, and on the day appointed underwent the ordeal; and, had it not been for the rascality of the *moonshee* who was present on the occasion (one of the very men whom I had been paying, and who had told me that there was not a doubt of my success) – had it not been for his rascality, the chances were that I should have passed.

Now, this self-same *moonshee*, be it known, solemnly promised me that he would make use of very easy language in conversing with me, and I told him that if I succeeded, I should divide the reward, viz., 180 rupees (a paltry reward indeed!) between the two teachers by way of remuneration. Instead of making my ordeal easy as he had promised, he did quite the contrary. Had I put fifty rupees into the hands of the *moonshee* just previously to my going up before the committee, in the shape of a *rishwŭt* (bribe), there is not a doubt but that he would have cleared the way for me.

And now, a word or two about these *moonshees*, or rather teachers. I look upon them generally as the veriest humbugs that can be met with among the natives. Habit and a wish to please make them adopt a line of conduct towards their employers quite at variance with honesty and sincerity. They assume a style of language and manners servile in the extreme. Everything they say has something in it of compliment to the person addressed; some silvery, flowery speech calculated to disgust far more than please; and their fawning, cringing ways of saluting, acquiescing, and smiling, are all very mean and deceitful.

The best and most efficient *moonshees* are those attached to regiments of the line. Interpreters of corps are the best calculated to judge as to the capabilities, characters and respectability of these men, and it is to one of these officers that I would recommend young beginners to apply for assistance and advice, on this important subject.

I was glad to be on my return to regimental headquarters. I detested the Presidency, and had hoped, when I last quitted it, never to go near the place again; but it appeared that I was doomed to do so, for no sooner was I away from it than I either found myself there, or on my way.

The manner in which I travelled on the occasion of my going back to Vellore was by posting, or *running dawk*, as it is termed; which means, travelling by relays of bearers, stationed at certain stages, where they change. When any one wishes to travel in this way, an application is made to the Post-office authorities for the relays of bearers being posted along the route he intends going; but, before this arrangement can be made, the traveller is obliged to pay a deposit of a certain sum, according to the distance.

The requisite sum being paid down, a day is fixed upon by the 'Jack-in-office' for the traveller's starting, a certain time being absolutely required for the posting of the bearers, which done, the bearers for the first stage are sent to his residence, and these men prepare the *palankeen* in their own manner, by lashing and binding, and a variety of other preliminaries, too numerous for me to detail.

A set of bearers consists of twelve men, including the *pŭdda-bhuee*, or head-bearer; besides these, there is a fellow for carrying the *massaul*, or torch, as also another for the *cavary baskets*, or *pettarahs*, which are a couple of baskets, or light tin boxes, generally painted green, slung on a bamboo, containing eating and drinking requisites for the journey. The whole set have a man of their own to convey their food and cooking utensils.

These poor fellows run for upwards of thirty miles, with scarcely any

rest, at the rate of four miles an hour, taking little or no sustenance all the time! When arrived at the end of their stage, they put down their load, and walk off, though some of them are apt to be troublesome, by begging a present, and it is generally customary to give them a rupee or so.

The new set are not long in making their appearance. They lift up the *palkee*, and trudge off without saying a work to the traveller; but they can never make a start without a great noise and wrangling among themselves, which it is almost useless to attempt to check; and in this manner they proceed, running along till they come to the end of their stage, quitting the *palankeen* like their predecessors.

Whilst I was at the Presidency a detachment of my regiment had been ordered off to Cuddalore, a station situated about one hundred and fifteen miles from Vellore; so that, when I returned, I was directed to proceed, without delay, to join that out-post, instead. I therefore packed up my traps again, borrowed a *palankeen*, and started two days after receiving orders to march.

I travelled this time by regular stages, and with only one set of bearers, halting at every ten or fifteen miles, at convenient places, where I would stop for the day, amusing myself either with shooting, or taking sketches of various ruins, with which the country abounded; the scenery, too, gave ample food for the pencil; I do not think I ever saw such picturesque views as presented themselves in every direction. I had capital sport, bagging partridge, hare, snipe, and teal in abundance. What a blessing it is that there are no game laws in India!

I met with few bungalows on the road for the accommodation of travellers; I was obliged, therefore, to put up in *choultries*, or under *topes* of trees, erected or planted by wealthy natives for the express purpose, for the use of their countrymen when travelling. These afford excellent shelter from the heat of the sun, and many is the time that I have pitched my tent under the covering of some huge *peepul*, whose wide stretching branches have waved over me, fanning the air into delicious coolness, and lulling me to sleep by the gentle murmuring of its sighs among the leaves.

Natives erect these *choultries*, dig the tanks, and plant the *topes*, at great expense, from charitable and religious motives. Some of these buildings are very extensive and well constructed, while others are mean and insignificant; but the will that prompts them to make the outlay and to raise the structures, amply compensates for their meanness, or want of accommodation; and when the benefits derivable for travellers are taken into consideration, the reader will at once say that their existence exhibits an excellent trait in the native character.

Whilst in Vellore my poor chum suffered more from white ants than any person I have ever met with. He kept all his uniforms, coats, jackets, pantaloons, epaulettes, sashes and belts, &c. in a very nice camphor-wood trunk (which, by the way, are supposed to be *anti-white ant*), safe, as he imagined, from all harm. This box he had raised from the floor, placing it upon four bricks. One day my friend went to the box to take his clothes out; he opened it, and, to his great horror and astonishment, discovered that scarcely any of his things were left! The greater part of his full-dress and other articles of uniform had been demolished by these dreadful visitors; the buttons and lace were found in the bottom of the box! Had he come somewhat later, there would have been nothing left to tell the tale!

I have myself witnessed some very extraordinary proofs of the mischief these creatures have done. When marching down from the Western coast in 1835, one of the men of my company had his firelock completely destroyed by the white ants! I recollect he was late for mustering, previously to marching off: the reason he gave was, that he could not make out what had come to his musket, which he had placed by his side during the night. He was found seated inside his tent trying to discover how it had become in that state, and, upon examination, we found that the insects had literally eaten away the stock; the lock fell out, and the butt-end was rendered quite unserviceable! All this was done in one night!

White ants are the most industrious creatures in the world. I have often watched them with a magnifying glass. They go to work with admirable ingenuity, carrying their earth and water in their bodies, and plastering as it were their winding passages for several yards with the greatest regularity, and in an incredibly short space of time; throwing out branching passages in different directions, by way of feelers. They will pierce through the cement or *chunam* on the floors, walls, or ceilings; and attack whatever is nearest to them. If they find nothing close at hand, they throw out their scouts to scour the country and report prey, and then do they set to work and sap and mine regularly up to the object of their destruction; and, when the business does commence in real earnest, it is not long in being accomplished.

Pictures on the walls of a room are destroyed in a most effective manner. The ants will work through a wall close up to a picture and take it in its rear, and no one knows what is going on until a large hole is discovered, and some valuable production of the pencil completely ruined. I remember a friend of mine who had two pictures, of his father and mother; they were placed close to each other. He came into his room one morning, and to his great disgust and sorrow discovered that the faces of both portraits had been entirely eaten away by the abominable wretches in the course of the night!

The best way to keep them from attacking clothes, books or papers, or indeed anything, is to get *paetrolium* (it is procurable almost everywhere in India), or tar, should the former not be within reach; and rub the legs of chairs and tables or the bottoms of boxes and trunks, and the backs of pictures, &c. &c. as well as to keep a bright look out against their incursions, having the carpets and mats frequently taken up, the floors well swept and sprinkled with wood ashes; all the incipient passages destroyed, and a little *paetrolium* poured into every opening. Your whole property must undergo constant watchfulness and examination, and there is a probability of your keeping them off; but if not, one night will be the ruin of you.

I REACHED CUDDALORE after a very pleasant though lonely journey of ten days, and took up my quarters with my old chum, who was glad again to have me with him.

I think Cuddalore a very pleasant station. It is situated close to the sea, with a back-water or river between it and the town, which is divided into two compartments, the old and the new town.

The largest building in Old Town is the jail. It is very extensive, and holds a great number of convicts, who are employed under the civil authorities on the roads or in the manufacture of a variety of articles, superintended by Europeans. Table-cloths, towels, and napkins, and also cloths of different textures are made here, and considered excellent materials, very durable and exceedingly cheap. I think these are the best of the kind I have seen in this part of India.

The church (apparently an old one) is also in the Old Town. In this place of worship, service is performed twice a day every Sunday, by a clergyman belonging to the station, and to which the European pensioners are regularly marched.

The pensioners' lines in the Old Town are extensive, and present a strange medley of neatness and cleanliness, together with filth and dirt commingled. The lines are laid out in streets; the houses or cottages are however irregular, some of them are large compared to others, which have more the appearance of pigsties than fit places for the veteran British soldier.

The pensioners consist of men of her Majesty's as well as of the Company's troops, who have attached themselves by marriage or other-wise to Eurasians and native women; few if any with European wives remain in the country longer than they are obliged, preferring rather to return home than live in the truly miserable manner which many of their countrymen with dark yoke-fellows are necessitated to do.

The British soldier, with his black or tawny wife, I can only compare to two things of a totally different nature, which never can agree. The man with the feelings and habits of his native home, and the female with those of her own country. He with one mode of thinking, she with another. He has nothing whatever to do; she has everything; he gets his pay and spends the greater portion of it in drink, reserving little for domestic purposes; while she has to supply the eatables without the wherewithal to pay for it. He lives upon drink, and his family starve!

I have myself witnessed many distressing scenes among the poor pensioners which I would not have believed on other testimony than that of my own eyes. Men and women lying drunk in the same house; children rolling about in filth and dirt crying with hunger; husband and wife fighting with each other under the influence of liquor; men lying in the ditches or on the road-side, or reeling home in a disgraceful state of intoxication! Many is the poor fellow or wretched woman I have been obliged to see locked up in the cells, raving from the effects of drink, knock-ing themselves against the walls and doors in frantic efforts to get out.

Many of them, for want of something better to do, go down to the water-side, and stand up to their middles for hours and hours together with hook, line, and rod fishing. At times, they are successful, and many is the basketful of beautiful fish I have bought from them fresh from the water, for the mere sum of one rupee, or even less.

I believe there is a circulating library for the soldiers, but few of them ever make use of it; the skittle-ground and arrack-shop are the places of general resort, and there they gamble, squabble and fight, smoke and drink all day long, and either come or are carried home in a state of brutal drunkenness.

Many is the anecdote of adventures by flood and field that I have heard, of bloody battles, of the perilous escalade, the deadly breach, and hand to hand conflict, which have made my blood thrill within me as I sat listening to the gallant fellows as they related them. These well-tried soldiers are worth knowing, for they are better calculated to give any young inexperienced officer an insight into the roughs of a military life, than he can possibly glean from the society of his own immediate comrades and associates. It is the poor man in the ranks who has experienced the real hardships and vicissitudes of a soldier's career. He it is who knows and has known how to bear the privations of the campaign, the toils of the march, the exposures of midnight bivouac. And he is the man that can tell the beardless boy what the realities of a soldier's profession are, and how he can best go through all that his duty calls upon him to perform.

Every one knows that Cuddalore was in days of yore the seat of the Madras government, or rather the seat of the government of that part of India. Fort St David is as famous in eastern history of former years as Fort St George; in fact much more so. Here it was that the immortal Clive first commenced his glorious career, and laid the foundation of the military character of our noble coast army. Here it was that our handful of English adventurers first held out in maintaining their footing in the East; where our gallant countrymen bravely contended against their European as well as their Eastern enemies.

But Fort St David is now no more; all that is to be seen of it are desolate ruins, dismantled walls, and dilapidated battlements.

Many a time and oft did I wander over those lonely ruins, a locality which was formerly the scene of military excitement, and the stage of glorious warfare. No gallant sentinel, with his trusty firelock and glittering bayonet, treads the pavement of the once bustling gateway; no watchman now, save the solitary screech-owl, seated on some dismantled bastion! No dashing officers, in the gay uniform of their noble profession, moving about in their various employments; not a soul, excepting, perhaps, the native shepherd-boy, as he basks in the glare, tending a few sheep or goats, which are nibbling the scanty herbage from among the scattered ruins!

The civilians stationed at Cuddalore all reside in New-Town (or as the natives call it, '*Mŭngēe-coopŭm*'). The whole of this cantonment is nicely laid out. The houses are large and commodious, with neat gardens and compounds attached to them; the roads and drives are good and the whole is a very agreeable locality for invalids.

I never, in all my life, saw snipe in such abundance as I did in the vicinity of Cuddalore. Snipe-shooting is, indeed, capital sport, and very exciting, for the game is, at times, so plentiful that a man must be a poor shot not to be able to bag as many couple as will serve to feed him and his friends for weeks to come. I have frequently brought down two brace of these birds with my two barrels, right and left.

As regards attire, I always wore a good thick flannel shooting-jacket (with skirts covering the hips), under which there was a woollen waistcoat. These are excellent coverings for the upper body, and sufficiently resist the hot winds, and prevent their penetrating to the skin, so as to check perspiration. Thick corderoy, or fustian trousers, fitting loosely to the body, and coming down to the ankles; worsted socks, and thick strong shoes, or laced-boots, completed the costume, with the exception, by-the-bye, of the hat, or cap. I always preferred the straw-hat, with a broad brim, and covered with white linen, of some sort, slightly padded with cotton. Inside I had some fresh plaintain or cabbage leaves, which offered a tolerable resistance to the heat of the sun, and kept the upper part of the head pretty cool.

My servant always carried a bottle of cold tea, covered with a wet towel, in case I was thirsty; and to avoid the chances of getting dry in the mouth, I always carried a *pebble* in it, or a bit of lead, which kept up the saliva, and prevented even the inclination to drink.

But, although the sport is excellent of its kind, I cannot help saying that it is a most dangerous pastime, attended with results serious, in more ways than one. In the first place, consider the exposure. The sportsman has to be out in the sun, from between nine and ten o'clock in the morning until three and four in the afternoon, with little or no rest; the hot, burning blaze above-head, and no screen from it, except a straw hat, with a plaintain leaf, or wet towel inside it.

In the second place the ground on which snipe lie, is invariably wet; so wet, generally, that the sportsman has to walk, for miles, up to his knees in mud; the feet must, of consequence, become wet, notwithstanding every means adopted to avoid it (no one can expect to kill snipe if he is afraid of wetting his feet); to say nothing of the probabilities of their being attacked by leeches, the bites of which frequently create ulcers, that take a considerable time to cure.

Snipe-shooting, therefore, though the sport is excellent, may, at all times, be looked upon as the most foolish and hair-brained amusement that can possibly be indulged in. I think so, decidedly, and I would not now go after such sport as I used so foolishly to do in former days, if I were paid thousands for it.

I have often seen men come home from snipe-shooting worn out with fatigue, the clothes wet from head to foot, the face burnt and red from the heat, and they have sat in their wet things for hours after, without even thinking of changing, but swallowing tumbler upon tumbler of cold sangaree, mulled claret, or beer, smoking cigars, and drinking again until they were perfectly overcome with the effects of their potations, and were carried to their beds in a state of insensibility. Yet people say there is no harm in it: wearied nature must be supported by the comforts and good things which she provides. A very foolish argument indeed; devoid of common sense, and showing nothing, in my opinion, but downright madness.

It so happened that the captain of our detachment and I, one day mounted our horses and went out in the direction of the Pondicherry district, with no other object in view than that of passing an hour or two before our dinner in shooting snipe, which we knew to be in abundance in that neighbourhood. We had frequently walked over many a mile of ground in the French territory, without any hindrance from the civil authorities of the villages, or from the natives themselves.

On the present occasion, we wandered about the fields, and shot away, uninterrupted by anybody; and accompanied each by our native servants, and our horsekeepers following the high road with our horses.

My comrade and I approached a field, in which two men were squatted, reaping; they were concealed from our view, and I think we must have been some ninety or a hundred yards from them. As we walked on, we were startled by some quail, which got up from under our feet; at these my friend fired, and killed two. The shot flew in the direction of the reapers; one of whom happened to get peppered pretty smartly, though not hurt seriously. I think about a dozen, or so, of the shot penetrated the outer skin, and drew a little blood. Upon being hit, the fellow jumped up, threw off his clothes (of which, certainly, he had not much), flung his reaping-knife on the ground, and yelled most vociferously.

We lost no time in running up to him, and examining his wounds, which we found were nothing at all; and that he had cried before he was really hurt. We told him not to be afraid; but the more we assured him, the more he capered about, and the more he howled.

The shrieking and yelling of this fellow attracted the attention of others in the neighbouring *khets* (or fields), and they came running up to where we stood, and crowded around us, to the number of upwards of a hundred and fifty men, armed with reaping-hooks, knives, and bamboos, with which they were one and all clamouring loudly to administer a little *addie* (as they call a beating) upon our sacred persons!

One man in particular (a huge fellow, standing six feet high, with a thundering big bludgeon in his hand, and a knife in his waist-cloth), kept shaking himself to and fro, and saying that we should be both well thrashed; that the man's having been hit was intentional, and that we were no officers, but a couple of runaway soldiers; concluding by declaring that they would take us up to the village authorities hard by, where we could make what explanation we liked. So there we stood, surrounded by these villains, when the head man of the village arrived. He was followed by three sepoys, in the French uniform; and a posse of others, who had evidently come out to see the fun. The former strutted up to us, and addressed us in French, bad enough, it was, too.

'*Vous avez blessé ce person ci,*' said the fellow; '*pourquoi avez-vous fait celà? Répondez vite!*'

My friend could not, for the life of him, recall the language sufficiently to enable him to answer; at last, he spoke; but whether the man really did not understand him, or pretended not, I am uncertain, though I suspect it was the latter.

'*Oui vraiment!*' answered my friend; '*mais – je vous assure que –* hang it – it was purely by accident – the deuce take the French.'

'*Que dites vous?*' said the man, pretending ignorance of the English, though he had it as easy as French. '*Il faut vous aller à Pondichère avec ces gens d'armes, donnez vous les armes!*'

Upon which one of the *gens d'armes* laid his hands on my friend's gun, and another seized hold of mine; to wrestle them out of their hands, and knock them both down, was the work of a moment. There were evident signs of a rush at us by the crowd, so I cocked my gun, and levelling it at the tall fellow above mentioned, I covered the rascal's heart; the crowd was closing on us, and the shouts became louder than ever; my finger was on the trigger, I was just on the point of pulling; a moment more, and the tall *ryot* would have slept with his fathers, when the muzzle was knocked up by my friend, who called out –

'For heaven's sake, do not fire! They are too strong for us. Give up your gun at once!'

I gave up my gun. 'Pity is it, indeed,' said I, 'that British officers should yield to such a set of rascals! How I should have liked to have knocked that tall fellow over, and sent him to the regions of darkness!'

'You were near enough doing so, you fiery young scamp,' replied my comrade, 'and glad am I you did not, for we should both have had our throats cut by them. You must prepare for a hot journey to Pondicherry; this villain of a *cutwaul* appears to be bent on our being taken there. But we will ride, I vote; where can our horses be?'

They were close at hand, so we dispatched one of our boys to call them. The prisoners (for such we were in every sense of the word) being then allowed to ride, we mounted our horses, and might easily have cleared ourselves of the crowd, and made off; but we were determined on revenge, so sate still until everything was ready for a start. We dismissed our two servants, and desired them to get to Cuddalore as fast as they could, to mention what had occurred to all our friends, and to send us a supply of clothes, uniforms, and other requisites.

The escort consisted of a corporal and three privates of the *gens d'armes*; they were natives, dressed in green uniforms, and black leather accoutrements, and queer looking caps, and armed with *empty bayonet scabbards!* They had not a firelock among them! They were fine looking fellows, and, I must confess, they were far better dressed than our men. The sun was terribly hot, and we were wet through from perspiration, besides being much fatigued; however, there was no help for it, and we thought that the best way was to put a good face on the matter, and enjoy our trip as much as we could.

It was highly amusing to see the people staring at us as they passed on the road, evidently wondering at the cause of our being so situated; and I must say, I could not help feeling an inward boiling of anger at being thus scrutinised, and, probably, taken for thieves, or murderers. I felt greatly disposed to knock some of our beggarly escort on the head, when I heard them answer inquiries made by the passengers.

'They are prisoners,' they would say, 'taken up for shooting a man!'

'They are a couple of European soldiers from Cuddalore,' another would say; 'they have been committing murder; they will be hanged!'

Before entering the suburbs, we halted, and my friend made the corporal and his guard fix their bayonets, and take their proper places; we only wanted a drummer to tap us into the town, to the '*rogue's march*', so as to give timely notice of our coming. We paraded right through the streets, my friend and I on horseback, our escort in front, flank, and rear, and, by way of retinue, followed by a motley crowd of upwards of two hundred natives, shouting and hallooing as we went along! What a sight! British officers, and gentlemen, brought in by a rabble crew, and that of the worst description of natives! And marching, as prisoners, into a French town!

We were halted at the door of the commandant's house, were marched in, and our arrival, together with their version of the circumstances connected with our arrest, duly reported. The commandant was at his dinner with his family: he jumped up immediately, ran out, and saw us standing in the verandah.

When he heard that we were officers from Cuddalore, that my friend commanded the detachment there, and that I was one of his subalterns, the commandant immediately put on his uniform, and quitted the house, desiring his wife and family to entertain us during his absence. I had, during this interval, contrived to win a smile or two from some of the owners of the bright eyes peeping through the venetians; and one by one the young ladies had ventured out, and by the time the commandant had left us, they were four of them as pretty girls as I would wish to see anywhere, standing behind my chair, making their remarks, and giving vent to their feelings by loud expressions of surprise and regret at the unpleasantness of our situation.

Wine, cakes, and fruit were brought and we amused ourselves exceedingly well until the return of the commandant with another military man in plain clothes, with the ribbon of the Legion of Honour in his button hole, who was introduced to us as the ADC of the governor.

This gentleman addressed us with much politeness, and assured us that the Marquis de Saint Simon, the governor, was much concerned at our detention, and desired to make us the most honourable amends; that we were at perfect liberty to return to Cuddalore at our own convenience, but that he trusted we should give him the pleasure of our company during our stay at Pondicherry.

This politeness in conveying a message in such very civil and apologetic terms, entirely did away with all angry feelings, and my friend bowed and bowed again, and a variety of complimentary language passed between the two.

The purport of my friend's reply was, that we should take advantage of the governor's permission to remain a few days at Pondicherry, and that we accepted with many thanks so polite an invitation to partake of the hospitality of so great a man as the Marquis de Saint Simon. He then inquired for an inn, and the ADC immediately offered to conduct us to one. Having made our acknowledgments to the commandant, we bowed to the whole party, and left the house, arm-in-arm with the ADC.

The day after the occurrences above related, we dressed ourselves in our uniforms and walked over to the Government House, which was not far from our hotel. On our arrival, we were ushered into the presence of the great man, who received us with that politeness of manner so peculiarly French; begged us to be seated, and forthwith apologized in plain language, on the part of the French Government, for the outrage that had been committed on our persons, by our being brought as we were to Pondicherry! Having accepted a most polite invitation to dinner, we were bowed out by his excellency very politely.

Pondicherry is, indeed, a very pretty place. It resembles very much, and reminds the traveller of, a French town on the Continent. The roads and streets of the suburbs are lined with avenues of trees; the roads themselves watered, so that there is little or no dust; giving the whole a cool, fresh appearance, instead of the hot, dry, parched-up aspect for which our cantonments are so remarkable. Nearly in the centre is a spacious square, laid out in walks, shaded by rows of magnificent trees, with the Government House on the northern face of it. This mansion is a beautiful building, surrounded by gardens and shrubberies, laid out in tasteful style, and the whole quite a fitting residence for the representative of the French Crown.

The villages and hamlets we saw, seemed to be clean and well-built; and the inhabitants in good condition, without that poverty-stricken look about them, which forms so remarkable a feature in the

Soldier of the Pondicherry Army; coloured lithograph c. 1850

peasantry of our own territories. It struck me that the whole of the French country was superior, in many respects, to ours; their roads are good, with trees on each side; their land seemed better cultivated, and better irrigated, by means of tanks and canals, constructed for that purpose.

The town's-people of Pondicherry are mixed. They are composed of Europeans, from the mother-country, or born and bred in India; half-castes; and the aborigines; the latter are generally Moslems of the Mopley or Lubby tribe, sea-faring men and merchants.

The Indo-French are, apparently, a superior set of people; better than the generality of half-castes and Eurasians to be met with in India. They have not that vanity and self-importance, so peculiar to those sort of people, in our parts of the country: besides that they talk French (a kind of patois), much better than our folks talk English, and have not that mode of expression so disgustingly – '*chee, chee.*'

Their women are superior certainly, in every way; there is a dash of the French in their manner and deportment, which elevates them considerably above our *fair* dames of Vepery celebrity; and their men are much better educated, and much more gentlemanly and civil than our Madrassees, who, with the exception of the clerks in the different public offices, are the most ignorant set of demons one would ever wish to meet with.

The greater part of the society of Pondicherry is composed of these tawny-visaged Frenchmen and their families. The Europeans, however, mix with them; intermarry, and connect themselves, without reference to birth, parentage, or education. It is no un-common sight to see a dark man with a fair wife, and *vice versa*.

Woman selling snipe; oil painting on mica by a local artist, 19th C.

We returned home to our hotel in time to make our toilet for the governor's dinner, after which we walked over to the big house, where the sentries presented arms to us, and we were ushered into the presence of the Marquis by his ADC. The Marquis received us with much politeness, discussed the state of the weather, the latest news from Europe, besides other topics, until the dinner was announced.

The Marquis seated my noble capitano on his right, and my little self on his left, and distributed the remainder of his guests on either side of us. These were severally introduced to us, and we sate down to our meal, which I must confess was the most *recherché* I had ever partaken of, served in the French style, and exquisitely cooked. The wines were delicious; there was no lack of champaign; the governor and his staff set us a good example, and the brilliancy of French vivacity had additional lustre imparted to it by the nectar which they imbibed, thereby giving zest and relish to our meal.

The marquis and my friend got on capitally together. His excellency had been attached to the emperor's staff in many of his campaigns, and was one of his most enthusiastic admirers. He was very eloquent in singing the great man's praises; and his gallant guest expatiated in such rapturous terms on Napoleon's great military genius, his splendid victories, his glorious career up to the very pinnacle of fame, and spoke so favourably of the whole French nation, that the marquis was delighted beyond measure, and embraced him with that excitement and ardour which are so peculiarly characteristic of the French.

The ADC had served in the grand army during the Russian campaign, and had been wounded on more than one occasion. He also had suffered severely from the horrors of the dreadful cold which had been fatal to so many thousands of his comrades, having lost all the toes of one of his feet. This officer was a fine soldierlike gentlemanly person, and chatted away with me for a long time.

And thus our Pondicherry adventure ended very agreeably.

I HAD BEEN NOT quite four years in the service when, in consequence of the adjutancy of my regiment falling vacant by the resignation of the then incumbent, I was agreeably surprised to find myself one fine day in the Gazette for the permanent situation, a circumstance of not very common occurrence in those days.

When I obtained the adjutancy I happened to be senior ensign of the regiment. The ensuing month found me a lieutenant, so that in this instance good fortune did not come singly, but smiled upon me most benignly.

I forthwith packed up my traps, bid farewell to all my friends at Cuddalore, and started by *palkee* for Vellore, in the same way and by the same route I had come, travelling in the morning, stopping for the whole day, and starting again in the afternoon after dinner. I amused myself as usual in shooting, sketching, and strolling about, though when we are alone the time is but dull and monotonous.

I was seated one day with my sketch-book in my hand, putting down, as fast as I could, a very pretty piece of landscape in a pass or road, between two hills, known as the Cunniambaddy Pass, half-way between Arnee and Vellore. The bearers had set down the *palankeen*, and I was thus amusing myself, puffing a cigar by way of companion to my occupation, while they were resting, squatted on the ground a short distance off, eating some cold rice. My attention was suddenly arrested by hearing a rustling among some bushes, and, to my astonishment, I presently saw a huge tiger slowly walking up towards me. I sate perfectly still, at the same time moving my right hand towards my pillows, and extracting therefrom a pair of pistols, which I carried loaded, in case of accidents. Mr Tiger walked up to within ten yards of me, and thinking probably that far enough, stood still, wagging his tail and making a noise, which with a cat would be termed *mewing*.

I saw by his open mouth that he had scarcely any teeth, and therefore looked upon him as not a very dangerous neighbour, though I dare say he would have given me a friendly pat with his paw, that would have done me irreparable injury. However, matters did not terminate so tragically. The brute was covered with mange from head to tail; there being little or no hair on him, and his *tout ensemble* proclaimed him to be rather ancient, but, at the same time, induced me to come to the conclusion that he had already tasted human flesh.

I had put down book and pencil immediately this visitor had made his appearance, and held one of my pistols ready cocked, to give him a salute, should he come too near; meanwhile, I picked up some stones with my left hand, and threw them at him with a view to driving him away.

In the meantime, the bearers sate eating their meal quite unconscious of the propinquity of so dreaded a foe. Presently, however, one of them came to the *palkee*, and seeing the animal, immediately shouted out, '*Bagh! bagh!*' (Tiger! tiger!) most lustily. This alarmed the rest, and all came running together, tumbling and sprawling over each other in most laughable manner, not knowing where the monster was; but when they saw him standing as I have described, their alarm became so great that it was with the greatest difficulty I could prevent their running away.

The noise and the hubbub caused by these men scared away the tiger, who slank off into the jungle, and the bearers begged me to fire at him as he moved, by way of farewell shot, for they all declared that he was the famous man-eater, so well known in that part of the country. This, however, I did not do, but got the fellows together, made them take up the *palkee*, and we reached the end of our journey that evening without further adventure.

An officer's menagerie; detail from a panorama painted by Lt. Charles Steeves showing the 'line of march of one of Her Majesty's Regiments in Guzerat', 1845

When I reached Vellore I took a nice house close to the barracks, and made myself comfortable. I found myself in a very responsible situation, and rather a peculiar one, too, the duties of which I had yet to learn, and a new commanding officer, to whom I was almost a stranger, my kind friend, the old colonel, having, during my absence, been removed to another regiment.

However, the old adjutant was a friend of mine, and gave me every assistance in his power, and, considering all things, I got on tolerably well. Everything was in my favour; I knew my drill and parade duties well enough, and had only those of the office to become *au fait* at; this I left to practice and time, hoping, in the end, to become more conversant with the work than I was at the commencement.

'There is nothing like experience,' is an oft repeated and well-known saying, and I found it to be too true in my own case, for I discovered, on entering upon the duties of my new appointment, that I had undertaken a task of no small magnitude.

My commanding officer, though a kind, good-hearted old man, was inclined to be a fidget, and, consequently, worried me out of my patience with constant and tiresome notes. He was ever on the tenterhooks of anxiety about one thing or the other, so that what with having to go regularly to his house, attending to the office-work, settling disputes, conducting courts-martial, and many other items, besides answering his innumerable notes, I had enough to do, and little time to spare.

A note-writing officer is, in very truth, a plague to his staff. I had been told, by my predecessor, that he was much addicted to scribbling long letters upon most trivial matters, thereby making mountains out of mole-hills, and giving much needless trouble to everybody. I had, consequently, made up my mind to receive, at most, about two or three notes per diem; but, when they came to me by sixes and eights almost every day, with little or no abatement, I was utterly astounded, and really became quite puzzled what to do, to stop such an inconvenience.

Every *chit* (note), however short, was written upon the same-sized piece of paper, regularly dated, and, coming in the number which I have stated, more or less each day, the collection soon made a tolerably sized bundle, about six or seven inches in thickness. 'And who knows, major,' I would say,' but we shall, one of these days, see your dispatches published to the military world? The great duke had his so published by one of his staff, and why should not I bring yours to light?'

A person given to note-writing, independently of being of a suspicious mistrusting character, is naturally a fidgetty one, and a fidget is generally considered, by all reasonable people, to be what is termed, in common parlance, an *old woman*; and he who has the name of one is unfit for his command, and only suited for the Invalids, or for comfortable lodgings in Bath, or Cheltenham, both places being famous for superannuated Indians from the three Presidencies; far better for them, I think, than at the heads of regiments, in which situations all they do is to worry those under them in such a way as to render their duties irksome in the extreme.

At the present rate, many of us can never expect to be majors under thirty-five years service, and then, what shall we be fit for? Nothing but the invalid or pension establishment! If our commanding officers of regiments were more effective, the army would be so also; but at present the class of men in general at the heads of divisions, brigades, and regiments are old and worn out, while the young and the effective are becoming non-effective, from this slowness of promotion. As we now stand there is little or no hope whatever except by purchasing out our seniors from our own resources. There is scarcely a regiment but what is made to suffer very heavy stoppages in liquidation of loans from houses of agency, or the famous Agra bank, of enormous sums borrowed to buy out some worn-out major or disgusted captain; and yet there is no alternative but to purchase out those above us. We require reform, and there is no mistake on the subject.

Very soon after my having become re-established in my quarters at Vellore, the European regiment which was stationed in the neighbourhood, at Arnee, received orders to move, *en route*, to Bellary, a large garrison in the Ceded Districts. They passed through Vellore on their journey, and, as that was the first time I had ever witnessed a King's regiment on a line of march, I had a good opportunity of observing how matters were conducted.

This corps had been a long time in India; they were, consequently, more orientalized, as it were, and more accustomed to the mode of proceeding on such occasions; but with them, even, there was much to animadvert upon, and, consequently, much that was irregular. On the morning of their coming into the station, I rode out for several miles, on purpose to meet, and have a good look at them. As far as the main body was concerned, everything was as it should be; the column, *en route*, was correct to the letter, and presented a very soldier-like appearance in every sense; there was the advanced guard, the band, drums, and fifes, and then the sections of the column; the men looked very well as they trudged along with that regularity of step so peculiar to the British soldier.

I could find no fault with the column of march, none whatever; but what astonished me was, when the main body had passed me a considerable distance, to see the great number of stragglers. The whole road, for several miles, was lined with them; and what the cause could be I was at a loss to conceive; I could not, however, help thinking it strange, that so great a number of men should have been allowed to fall to the rear, nor could I help remarking how many of them there were not over and above steady in their gait. I do not think I am wrong in saying that I observed a sprinkling of certain individuals with one, two, and three stripes on their arms, amongst the lower classes of the inebriated.

When the regiment, or rather the skeleton of it, marched into Vellore, th sight was certainly not a very pleasing one, owing to the number of men in the rear, or who had been left behind to follow; the baggage and camp-followers were enormous; I had no idea that an European regiment could have had so many.

I do not think I am far out in my reckoning, when I say that stragglers, by twos and threes, were passing through Vellore for upwards of a week; and the manner in which these unfortunate people did travel was truly pitiable. The soldiers themselves, mostly on foot, followed by their children, many of them barefooted and bareheaded, their women also walking, or riding inside their bandies, or on bullocks, and from the objects they all presented, many of them must have been destitute of food, to procure which they were carrying their necessaries in their hands, and selling them to the sepoys, who purchased the things for little or nothing.

I remember several of the soldiers coming to me with their *ammunition boots* for sale, to scrape a little money together, some to get the wherewithal to eat, and others, of whom I fear the number dominated, to purchase a dram or two. One poor man came to me in a truly miserable plight, with a pair of these boots in his hands.

'Is it a pair of stout boots, y'er honour will be wanting this fine sunshiny morning?' said he, 'I have a pair here, sur, that'll just fit ye; ye may have em, sur, for half a rupee, which will enable a poor soldier and his family to get a bit of somewhat to eat for our breakfasts, y'er honour.'

Upon my word, I could not help feeling for this poor man. The idea that he was actually going begging, as were many more of his comrades, was truly distressing.

'I do not want your boots, my poor fellow,' said I, 'or, if I did, I would not encourage you to break through the strict rules of the service, which prohibit a soldier disposing of his kit, or any part of it. Why sell them at all? Have you not received your advance of pay?'

Watercolour of a havildar of the 3rd MNI with sepoys, c. 1850

'Pay, sur? Not a bit of pay have I seen!' replied the man. 'Isn't it my pay that has gone to pay that black nigger of a bandy-man, to carry my wife and the childer, and the thraps in? Not a farden have I, y'er honour, to feed them, or get a drop of drink either. I must sell the boots, y'er honour, or starve! I have no other means of getting a breakfast!'

'Well,' said I, 'you shall not starve if I can help it; but nevertheless, I will not be the purchaser of your boots. Keep them yourself, and when you muster them at your next kit inspection, think of me, and scratch your back, and thank your stars that it is not scratched by the cat instead!'

'Thank y'er honour,' returned the Hibernian, 'I will do that same: I'll think of you at every kit inspection, if it will please you.'

'It will please me indeed,' said I, 'if your doing so will save you from the disgrace of being publickly flogged! Where is your family at this present moment?'

'I have left them, y'er honour, under a tree about half a mile out of this place.'

'Go and fetch them all here, bag and baggage, and you shall have a good breakfast, every one of you; but mind, leave those boots here.'

'God Almighty bless y'er honour!' exclaimed the delighted soldier, and, leaving his boots, he quitted my house to go fetch his family.

This, gentle reader, was one, out of many of the wretched soldiery who continued passing through Vellore for the number of days I have mentioned. Many a poor wretch did I see rolling along the road in a state of intoxication, exposed to the heat of the sun (for they marched at all times of the day), without any covering except that of their heavy chacos, or their small foraging caps; covered with dirt and perspiration from head to foot, unshaven beards of three or four days' growth, probably destitute of food, the only thing which they may have taken being some horrible buttermilk, or what is as bad, if not worse, a draught or two of toddy accompanied by sundry drams of arrack.

As before observed, I invariably experienced much delight and satisfaction in showing hospitality and kindness to all classes of my countrymen, whether officers or private soldiers. I therefore never hesitated for a moment in calling in a poor way-worn soldier, and giving him a day's rest and a hearty meal, an act of charity which costs one nothing, and which I do wish I could see exercised by others a little more than it is.

In about half an hour's time or more, my friend Terence O'Brien arrived, bringing his family. Let me see; there was his wife; she was a respectable looking woman, with an Irish brogue that rendered her language perfectly unintelligible to me; then there were four children, besides a baby in arms, and one on the stocks, if appearances spoke the truth; strange that poor people always have most children; and last came Terence himself.

I looked upon this circumstance as a capital opportunity of showing our sepoys a specimen of the lower classes of our countrymen, and giving them an idea of their mode of proceeding in private life; so, as there were many of our fellows at my house on business at the time, I mentioned to them what was going on, and what I was going to do. They consequently loitered about, peeping through the doors and windows, to have a look at a novelty which, perhaps, few of them had before witnessed.

Terence brought the whole of his party up into the back verandah, and, I must confess, a more pitiable sight I never saw; misery and starvation were the predominating features, and they really looked as if the sun had exerted his utmost in endeavouring to roast them; the poor woman and the children were burned most dreadfully, and this, added to the filth and dirt of some three or four days, rendered their appearance anything but pleasing to the eye; however, with the aid of plenty of clean water and soap, we contrived to make them somewhat respectable, and the exertions of the barber, on Terence's chin, worked wonders on his visage, which had not been touched by a razor for a week.

When their breakfast was over, I desired the poor soldier and his family to remain in the house until the evening, when he could start afresh on his journey, after having had some dinner, which I would order for them at four o'clock, so that they should not be put to any extra expense. To this, of course, he readily assented, and a room having been cleared out for that purpose, their bedding, &c. was brought inside, and the whole of them turned in, to take a sleep, which I suppose they had not enjoyed for many days.

At four o'clock, I had a dinner for them, consisting of a good piece of roast beef, vegetables, and plum pudding; the débris of this meal were also put away in the basket, with sundry loaves of bread, and the remains of an old cheese, which I happened to have in the house. I gave them some beer to drink, and before they started, my servant put up some tea, sugar, coffee, and rice, &c., in small quantities, and handed them over to the poor woman, who did nothing, all the time, but give vent to tears of gratitude; coming out with strange Irish expressions, which I never recollected to have heard before. In the evening, they prepared for a start, and, when all was ready, the Irish soldier came up to me, and while the tear-drop glistened in his eye, he thanked me for all I had done for him.

'Thank ye, y'er honour!' said he. 'You have saved me from ruin!

Your act of kindness this day to me and mine has opened my eyes, and I shall never forget the advice you have given me, or the warning either. May God bless you! and if poor Terence O'Brien can serve you, remember, his heart's blood is your's!'

'Remember the boots, Terence;' said I, 'don't forget them; and, as you are but a young man, I hope that they may yet be the means of your becoming a serjeant. In the garrison, in the camp, on sentry, or on your cot; in the battle-field, or on the breach, don't forget the boots!'

I then shook hands with him, as also with the good woman, during which latter ceremony, I placed a small packet in her grasp, containing ten rupees, for her own private use.

'Do not open this,' said I, 'until you reach your next stage. I place it in your hands; let not your husband know of it, but keep it yourself, for your road expenses; and, whenever he feels inclined to drink, or do anything wrong, remind him of this day, and his boots!'

'That I will, sur; and God bless you a thousand times!'

And the bandy left the compound, followed by a whole posse of my men, who, I afterwards learned, had gone out, stopped the soldier, and insisted upon his accepting a small sum of money, amounting to some five rupees, which they had collected at the moment. Noble, generous fellows! Has not the poor, despised sepoy a feeling heart? Who ever says he has not, does him an injustice, as great as it is undeserved.

I am of opinion, that no regiment should ever break ground in the way this one did, and as many others do; not a soul should move until all is ready, and then let the whole start off together. Discipline would thus be maintained, and not suffer; the men, and followers and baggage, would be kept in a collected state, and be under the control and surveillance of the proper authorities. But, disorganize a regiment in the manner this one was, and it will not be matter of wonder if good order flies to the four quarters of the globe. When once broken into small parties, discipline is at an end; it becomes a case of every man for himself; and soldiers, once led astray, are worse than little children, without any control, without the power of acting for themselves or the inclination to do what is correct.

A very romantic affair occurred at the palace inside the fort, shortly after my return to Vellore, showing what women will do when they are determined. There happened to be a young Mussulmanee girl attached to the household of Tippoo's wives. She was termed a *loundee* (slave girl), and had belonged to the palace establishment from childhood. She had grown up to be a very fine creature, of about sixteen or seventeen years of age, and it was said that she had experienced severe treatment from the old ladies to whose authority she was subservient, to such a degree indeed that the poor girl's life was a perfect burden to her. She was plagued to death by the old catamarans, and her situation was anything but an enviable one. She therefore determined upon an escape from the prison within the miserable precincts of which she had been so long immured.

What was this poor girl to do, then? How was she to escape! The walls of the palace were high, and, if she did contrive to get herself on the top of them, how was she to descend on the other side? The fall would be a very dangerous one, but she cared not for that. Liberty was her guiding star, and liberty she would have, come what would. She resolved trying at all events, and not even the fear of pain or of a dreadful death could divert her from her fixed purpose.

She fixed upon a storm-threatening-night, when the stars hid them-selves behind the sombre curtains of murky clouds, when the thunder crashed above, and the forked lightning played around her; the rain poured down in torrents and drenched her to the skin, but she feared not, and undertook her enterprise with daring courage.

The slave girl contrived to get herself to a window, latticed with a kind of iron net-work, so that those inside could not be visible to, or observed by, others outside; this obstruction, old and rusted, the heroic girl managed to break through, thereby making an aperture sufficiently large to admit of her getting out. This she succeeded in doing, and hanging on by the frame-work of the window sill, she trusted herself to the protection of her *Allah*, and dropped to the ground, a height I should say of upwards of twenty feet!

It was about three o'clock in the morning when this took place; a patrole was going the rounds at the time, and happening to pass by just at that particular moment, the men composing it beheld an object falling from the window to the ground. A wild shriek rent the air as the girl was descending, and then a heavy sound reached the ears of the spectators, as the body fell on the green sward below; there was a cry of pain and agony, and all was still save the howling of the wind among the trees and adjoining buildings.

The *naigue* (corporal) who commanded the patrole, went up with his men to the spot where lay the apparently lifeless body of a female. She was not dead, as they shortly after ascertained by her groanings; and, as the place was not very far from the hospital, one of the party was sent to call for assistance, while the *naigue* stood by and ascertained from her who and what she was, which he was able to do as she gave signs of returning reason.

In the meantime, people came from the hospital, and the poor girl was lifted up, quite insensible from the pain she suffered, and conveyed to the female ward, where it was ascertained that she had fractured her left leg midway between the knee and the hip. Early that morning several medical men examined the limb and pronounced the injury of such a nature as would admit of setting, and eventually of healing, provided she remained quiet and allowed them to do what was necessary.

In the meantime, there was no small hubbub inside the palace, when the report and fact of Fatima Bee's escape and accident became known to the old ladies. They were perfectly furious, and vowed vengeance upon the head of the culprit. They became so excited and worked themselves to such a pitch of rage, that I verily believe the circumstance took a good year from the total of some of their lives. They sent messages innumerable to the brigadier, desiring this, that, and everything else, declaring that the girl had disgraced them by exposing herself to the gaze of a man, and making matters worse by allowing a parcel of English doctors to handle her about and set her leg, which she ought rather to have allowed to drop off; ending their tirade by requesting that the vile wretch might never be allowed to darken the doors of the palace, but be turned out of the place as not worthy of its protection.

The unfortunate Fatima Bee, after a lengthened sojourn in the garrison-hospital, during which period she had been seen and admired by many (for as I before said she was beautiful), at last recovered the use of her leg, and became what she had so long wished for, a free-woman; and, finally, the lawful wife by *shadee* (marriage) of the aforesaid handsome Mussulman *naigue*, who, in the occasion of his first seeing her fall, happened to catch a glimpse of her features, and became enamoured at first sight of the lovely fugitive.

Women when once seen by men are considered, by Moslems, as polluted; and this poor creature had become so in every respect, if the circumstance of her having been seen (and the *naigue* saw her himself) could possibly contaminate anyone; the gallant soldier should not, according to his creed and the customs of his sect, have connected himself with one who had so disgraced the rules of decorum. But she was a beauty and no mistake; he thought her so, and cared not for caste prejudices.

To become the lawful wife of a dashing soldier, after having been buffeted and beaten as the slave of a set of old hags, was a bargain too good to be despised, so the suitor was accepted by the lovely girl herself, who had also seen and become smitten with the handsome manly countenance of her gallant lover. The arrangements were made, and the marriage-ceremony performed in great state, and the young bride was made happy, and exulted in the issue of her undertaking. She was heard to say, that she recommended all females similarly situated to cast off the trammels of bondage and to be free at all hazards, as she herself had done.

During the dry, hot, sultry weather, when everything exposed to the influence of the sun is parched and withered up, and the ground itself gives strong and convincing indications of opening by cracks and fissures in all directions, sighing, as it were, for the cooling moisture of the absent and lingering monsoon, and when all nature assumes that arid aspect so peculiar to the season, the greatest care is necessary in the use of fires or lights inside houses. The least spark alighting on any substance is almost certain of bursting out into a destructive flame, reducing every house to ashes in an incredibly short space of time.

During our stay at Vellore, and at the time of the year I have mentioned, we had many such conflagrations, not only in our own lines, but in those of other corps, as also among the native huts, in every direction; and it always happened, somehow or other, that the bugles would sound, and the drums beat, just as we were about commencing our dinner in the evening, a most inconvenient time of the day the reader will allow. How our hungry young subs would grumble and growl at being

obliged to relinquish their comfortable meal and well-cooled wines; to exchange the clean white jacket for the buckled-up uniforms, and to be going into the midst of burning huts, to get covered with dirt and black from head to foot in helping to extinguish the flames, pulling down houses, throwing water over the fiery ruins, and bawling themselves hoarse in giving orders to do this, that and the other.

When I inform the reader that I have witnessed so many as three or four fires in the men's lines on one day, the troops having to turn out each time, he will be able to form some conception of what we have to undergo in endeavouring to put out the flames, and prevent the whole of the huts being swept away by their force. This turning out at all hours was really a great nuisance; but what was more annoying than anything else, was the circumstance of our knowing that the trouble we were put to was the consequence of premeditated mischief on the part of a set of rogues, in nine cases out of ten, who went about for the purpose.

There is a certain class of natives in every place, who earn their livelihood by erecting and constructing the lines of the troops. While some are engaged in raising the walls, others procure the materials for the roofs, such as bamboos, and palmira or cocoanut-tree leaves, which they dry and manufacture into a sort of matting, for the outer covering of the buildings.

These individuals, in order to ensure a sale for their wares, employ secret agents from among their own sect, who go about the villages and lines, and slily insert pieces of slow-match, or burning tinder, under the thatches of the houses, or huts. The dry rotten leaves, or straw, afford an easy prey to the fire, which, being fanned by the violent gusts of wind, very soon raises a conflagration, laying all in heaps of ruins before the least thing can be done.

Our people contrived, one evening, to catch one of these rascally *Swings*, red-handed, in the very act of stuffing a piece of burning rag into the thatch of one of our men's huts. No sooner was he detected, than the men surrounded him, vociferating loudly, 'Hang him up! Hang him up at once!' And one of the fellows had actually put a rope round his neck, when the officer of the day, who happened to be in the lines at the time, came to the spot, and prevented anything further taking place, otherwise the offender would have had a swing for the trouble he had taken in attempting to burn down the huts.

Our sepoys lost much property by these frequent calamities, exclusively of their huts, the re-building and re-thatching of which came heavily upon their scanty purses. Everything that can be got out, on such an occasion, is thrown promiscuously on the ground, and the many spectators (light-fingered ones also) find no difficulty in helping themselves, and carrying off whatever they can lay their hands on. The noise and confusion caused by the fire, the crowds of people, and the darkness, materially assist these rogues in making off with their booty.

The only way to stop such mischief, that I could think of, was, to have a certain number of men (out of uniform) always on the look-out; two or three of each company, in their respective lines. These being obliged to stay in their lines all day, their comrades were made to do their duty for them at barracks, &c. By this plan not a single stranger could possibly be seen about without being questioned by these men, and if in any way suspicious, they were immediately taken up and duly examined.

The way we contrived, whenever a fire broke out, was to have a working party always ready, told off at the evening roll-call parade. These men, under the command of non-commissioned officers, were divided into three parties. Some of one party were appointed to mount the tops of the houses nearest to the fire, and pull down their roofs, whilst the remainder threw water upon those furthest from the fire, so as to prevent their catching, from the innumerable sparks falling on them. Another party was employed in fetching water from the nearest wells; and the third threw water on the flames.

I frequently obliged our fatigue-parties to practise as if at drill, to make them expert, though there was not much necessity for that, there being so many conflagrations at one place or another, at which our men were invariably employed, that they became first-rate firemen, and proved themselves most useful on every occasion.

IN THE MONTH OF September 1837, we received orders to march down to
be stationed at the Presidency, a piece of intelligence we were anything
but glad to have conveyed to us, as we all knew from experience what a
disagreeable station we were going to in every respect. However, it was of
no use grumbling about it – for '*The king commands, and we must obey*'; so
we set to work with our usual dispatch, packed up our traps, and were very
soon on the road for our new destination.

I was sorry myself to quit Vellore again, because I had become so
comfortably housed in very nice quarters, and had made up my mind to
have a rest of at least a year before I marched again. I had had enough of
knocking about ever since I first joined my regiment; but so it is in India. A
poor man no sooner gets himself settled, and begins to *feel* himself a little
as it were after the shock upon his purse, which is never very full, when he
is moved off again, and he becomes as badly off as ever.

Our friends at home fancy that we Indians are as rich as Croesus, and
can command as much money as we like whenever we choose to shake the
famous *pagoda tree*, but those days are long gone by. All the money that
was to be made is now in the coffers of the English at home, while those
abroad are really and truly as poor as poverty can render them, and that is
poor enough. The constant marching and counter-marching to which the
poor regimental officers are subjected, prevents them from saving money,
so that they are obliged, *nolens volens*, to stick to the service, and the higher
grades of lieutenant-colonel are only made to quit it by their being
knocked about from one station to another, so that body and mind grow
weary of journeying to and fro, and the pocket becomes so exhausted by
the expenses that they are compelled to retire either by taking some bonus,
or, if such does not offer, by taking their pensions to which from length of
service they are entitled.

We started our march towards the Presidency without any particular occurrence worth noticing. We passed through a very flat uninteresting country; uninteresting in regard to appearance, but every inch of it rendered famous in the history of the wars of Hyder and Tippoo, and which had witnessed the march of thousands and thousands of the Moslem host, and the handful of our own gallant troops who so boldly contended against their numerous enemies.

On our march, we passed through the town of Conjeveram, a place famous for its enormous pagoda, or Hindoo temple, which has the celebrity of being of very ancient construction; and to visit which, natives from all parts of India perform many a weary pilgrimage, to pay their devotions at the shrine, and to fulfil certain vows which they undertake from various causes.

Conjeveram pagoda swarms with a peculiar species of the monkey tribe, which are held sacred by the natives to the famous deity, Hunnamun, and the circumstance of any of them being wantonly injured is sure to be visited by condign punishment upon the heads of the offenders. Some years ago, a party of ignorant griffins, travelling through the place, contrived, unwittingly (but, at the same time, cruelly), to fire at and kill one of these creatures. They were instantly surrounded, and mobbed; and had it not been for the timely presence of a detachment of soldiery then passing through, the probabilities were, that mischief would have been done, even to bloodshed. As it was, one or two got well drubbed, and the fowling-piece of the offender was broken to atoms, and thrown into the fire.

Young men first travelling in the East should be very particular how they play such tricks, by interfering with, or encroaching upon, the religious prejudices of the natives. There is nothing that they will not do for Europeans; but, at the same time, there is nothing they will resent so much as an insult offered to their families, customs, or religion. Many think it very fine and praiseworthy to deride the heathen, injure their temples or idols, and do everything in their power to aggravate the poor natives; but it is very bad taste, and worse policy.

Were a set of heathens to enter one of our churches, and desecrate it, who would more readily resent the insult than ourselves? Besides, our doing such things is not the best way to show them our superiority, either in point of civilization, or as regards religion; decidedly not: to insult and maltreat is not the best way to win the heathen from the worship of 'graven images, the work of men's hands, wood and stone'.

This requires a very different line of conduct, diametrically opposite to that generally adopted; rather should we show ourselves to be

Christians; and, unless we contrive a surer way of proving that we are so, we can never expect that the name of Christ, or his worship, can take the place of idolatry, which, alas, still exists to such a fearful extent in our Eastern possessions.

On arriving at the last stage but one from Madras, our commanding officer determined upon halting a couple of days previously to marching in, so that he might put everything into apple-pie order, to cut a fine figure on his entering the Presidency. The place where we halted was, I think, at the village of Cunnatoor, and the encamping ground low and likely to be swampy in the event of rain. The major was all anxiety and bustle. The men's arms and accoutrements were burnished up, and a goodly quantum of pipe-clay administered to the belts; knapsacks were repacked, pouches polished to the brightness of looking-glasses; turbans or chacos underwent a similar process; and all the *dhobies* in camp set to work to wash and iron all the men's haversacks; second-best coats were ordered to be worn; and the men actually told that they were to carry their *sandals* in their hands instead of on their feet which were not to be encumbered with them until marching into Madras, for fear of their getting soiled, or dirtied!

I was myself worried beyond my patience during the whole of this memorable day, a day big with the fate of the major and his corps! If I went to his tent *once*, on that day, I must have done so full twenty times; and as for those abominable notes, I am not far wrong when I say, that I received two or three every hour; and my mind was not at ease that night at ten o'clock, until the orderly came to my tent and imparted the important and comforting assurance in a whisper, that the 'Major Sahib' was asleep!

Joyful intelligence, indeed, and on the reception of which I fancied

that I should have a little rest. But, alas! I was mistaken! For, worn out and fatigued, I had slumbered sweetly for about a couple of hours, when I was roused by an orderly bearing another dreadful note! The reception of such a thing at so late an hour of the night would induce any one to imagine that the contents of it were of consequence, but it was not the case; for the major *merely* wrote to know how many files there would be on the ground in the morning, and also the names of the two officers warned to carry the colours! Perfectly preposterous I declare.

But to proceed. I told the major during the evening that I feared all his arrangements and the trouble he had taken would be of no avail; for I thought it would rain before morning, and so it did, for shortly after midnight we had such a downpour that the tents were soon saturated, and the whole camp in a swamp. Many of the tents were blown down either from the force of the wind, or fell from the weight of the canvass.

The water was flowing through my tent upwards of a foot deep; my trunks and boxes I had taken the precaution of placing on the top of a table covered with a tarpaulin, so that nothing was spoilt, and by remaining on my cot I escaped getting wet. As for any communication outside, that could only take place by wading knee-deep through the water.

The poor men suffered severely; almost all their tents came down; their muskets and nicely whitened accoutrements covered with mud and dirt; their knapsacks thoroughly drenched, and rendered three times as heavy in consequence; their pouches were all soaking, and the cartridges in them greatly damaged; in fact, all the preparations we had been making were knocked on the head. The anger and vexation of the major had no bounds, and he gave vent to his irate humour in volleys of curses and oaths quite sufficient to send all the elements out of their elements, were such a thing possible.

When our column of march came to be looked at by daylight, it presented a most distressing, ungainly sight. What the neat and gold-laced staff officer, who came to show us the way, thought of us I cannot say, but our appearance was anything but what we wished, and our poor major was so much put out, and so irate, that I thought it would have broken his heart. The dirty, filthy, muddy, drenching state, in which all of us marched, was indeed anything but favourable to our good name, and I longed for the time when we should all get under cover, so as to conceal the besmirched condition of our array from the eyes of those who invariably make it a point to criticise and find fault.

Our route into Madras was anything but a good one. In some parts, the men had actually to wade above their knees in water, and the whole of the way it was ankle-deep in mud. The state in which we were, when we arrived at the outskirts, and the red dust with which we became covered, in moving through the streets, adding to our sorry plight, made matters worse than before, and, I must confess, that I never recollected having seen troops in such a condition in all my life, and I hope I never shall again. When arrived at the barracks, we found that the regiment which we had come to relieve had not vacated their lines, and that the usual committee for the valuation of the huts had not even assembled; that in fact nothing was ready for our reception.

Such a state of things was most annoying, to the men particularly, who were, in consequence, obliged to locate themselves, and their host of families, on the small confined space near at hand, which happened to be in a dirty swampy condition, not fit for the Vepery pigs to wallow in, far less for troops to encamp upon. This piece of ground was about 150 yards long, and 50 broad. There were no tents for the men, that is, not for them all, so that many with their families were huddled together in those miserable little *pals* already described, while many took shelter in the verandahs of the several buildings close by.

Under these very trying circumstances, it was not at all to be wondered at that the cholera very soon made its appearance, and carried off the followers by scores, creating quite a panic throughout the regiment. We had many cases among the men, of whom we lost altogether about twenty, as well as I can remember. In addition, we lost one of the finest young officers in the regiment, our grenadier subaltern. His death was matter of regret to us all, for he was much liked. He was taken ill at about twelve o'clock at noon, and was in his grave before the sun was set the following day. I was surprised that more of us were not attacked, our quarters being close to the scene of death, and the continual noise of native music and beating of tom-toms, together with the howling of women and screeching of children, added not a little to the probabilities of our being affected.

The medical men were indefatigable in their exertions, and many cases taken in time were successfully treated. The officers had no easy task to perform, their men were continually coming to them for brandy, and calling to them to help them and their perishing families. Cholera in a regiment is in truth a dreadful calamity. No one can conceive the pitiable state to which it reduces the men, who, from being brave soldiers, are reduced to the verge of despair, and demean themselves like little children; men who would shrink from nothing in the performance of their duty, become unnerved, panic-stricken, and quite unmanageable.

After the cholera had subsided, as a matter of course our first thoughts were how to render our men's lines as free from filth and dirt as we could. They were in a shameful state when we took possession, and we had a difficult task in clearing them and making them habitable. The disease left us about a week or ten days after it first made its appearance, and those who had been attacked and escaped, recovered very soon and returned to their duty; but we were fearful, from the dirty conditions of the lines, that we should again be visited by that dreadful scourge.

The men underwent much personal expense in rebuilding and re-thatching their huts, and this alone involved them in a way which they could ill afford. Anybody visiting Vepery, and looking at the wretched assemblage of huts and hovels, the dirty burying-ground in a swampy state, the receptacle not only of the dead but of filth of every description, the several stagnant ponds, or rather ditches, teeming with slime and dead dogs and cats, the swarms of pigs and the heaps of rubbish in all directions; and above all, the stench sufficient to breed a plague, would, I am sure, coincide with me in the opinion, that there could not be a worse place for troops.

Why should not poor Jack Sepoy's health be consulted as well as that of the European soldiers? Why should his comforts be made of secondary consideration? And why should he be looked upon with indifference? And why should not government lay out a few thousand rupees in erecting proper places for the native troops to reside in with their families, instead of making them dwell in such wretched abodes, really not fit for pigs?

Our commander-in-chief, Sir P. M——, was a great stickler for all the minutiae of dress and the little observances, which were a source of much annoyance to the officers at the Presidency. Several long orders were issued respecting what officers should put on before eight o'clock in the morning, what after that hour, and what during their evening rides, or drives. Swords and belts were in great vogue; a man could not stir out of his house without having both fastened to his side, the general himself sitting down to his meals with a huge sabre hugged between his knees. If a button was open, a poor man was sure to be found fault with; and, if the chin strap of the cap was not down, buckled under his chin, he was equally culpable.

Officers' whiskers were made to be clipped in a certain way, from the tip of the ear to the corner of the mouth in a straight line with hedge-like precision, not one hair above nor one below; the incongruity in appearance was thus worse than before; some had a good show, while others sported only a small tuft, and others, again, only a half dozen hairs on either side.

The hair, too, was ordered to be kept close cut, and I do believe, if it could have been possible, the teeth would have been put under military restrictions of some kind or another.

This selfsame gallant chief was particularly fond of exercising the troops in large bodies at sham fights; a capital thing, too, the very best that he could do; so that, notwithstanding the folly of all his other peculiar hobbies, this one of his was decidedly the best. The first time I have reason to recollect very well, as it was attended with some ludicrous occurrences.

A day or two previously to our going out to this famous sham-fight, the commander-in-chief directed that officers commanding regiments, with their flank-company captains and adjutants, should meet him at a certain rendezvous, at a certain hour, on a certain morning.

The meeting accordingly took place, and his excellency (a fine, active old fellow) galloped over a great deal of ground, followed by about twenty or thirty officers, all mounted. He went at a smart pace, and that caused much emulation among the train that followed, to keep up with their leader – horses jumped about, reared and plunged, and their riders held on famously, as if a staff-appointment depended on their keeping their seats.

To this mode of proceeding, and the speed at which the whole cavalcade dashed along, neither our worthy commander nor his charger had been accustomed. The latter, never having been out of a walk for a considerable period, thought, doubtless, that it was capital fun, and nearly ran away; and the former was in such a state of mental agony, and lost so much leather, that, when he reached home, he was in a sad plight, and kept his room for the whole day; but this did not end on that day, for there was a repetition that same evening, and twice the following day.

The exertions which he had undergone, added to those of the fight, quite upset our commandant. He was confined to bed for a whole week, with physic and *simple dressing*, and did nothing but give way to bitter invectives against new-fangled commanders-in-chief, who introduced a system to which he had never been subjected before, and declaring that it was time enough to fight when there was real necessity for it, and, as for galloping through the streets like a madman, it was preposterous, and the whole party ought to have been stopped by the police, instead of their being permitted to frighten all the foot passengers who crowded the place.

The scene of action was situated in one of the principal parts of Madras. There was a river, a bridge or two to cross, high roads, hedges, ditches, houses and huts; but not one yard of ground to enable troops to manoeuvre upon. The whole force consisted of about 4,000 men of all arms, divided into two portions, opposed to each other. Cavalry rushed

upon infantry squares; then infantry charged through rivers and took the
cavalry in flank, when they thought it time to be off, so off they went in a
great hurry. Then the banks of the river were lined with skirmishers
opposed to each other; and there was such a fire kept up on both sides, that

Gunner sepoys of the Madras Artillery; watercolour by Capt. T.J. Ryves, 1st Madras Fusiliers, 1837

had there been bullets, the whole would have been annihilated in no time. There were such popping of musquetry, roaring of cannon, such drumming and bugling, such dust and such heat, such bawling and squalling, that it appears to me the whole was a scene of confusion worse confounded, and I thought that if there was so much of bungling and such a host of mistakes in a *sham* fight, what a precious business must a *real* one be! The commander-in-chief gave one order, and his staff gave another; and commandants of regiments gave a third, so that there was really no knowing what to do.

The only drawback (the heat not included – and that is always one in India to everything) to our doings on these occasions, was the enormous number of spectators who congregated to see the spectacle. They quite clogged up the way, and there was no moving on account of them. Nothing could be done with steadiness, or precision; the noise and yelling they made rendered it an impossibility to hear the different words of command, and when they are not understood, troops cannot act correctly. The galloping about of mounted officers, the puffing away of buglers, the rubb-dubb-dubbing of the drummers, go for nothing; and all the troops would have been much better in their quarters, with their arms and accoutrements resting clean in their racks, instead of undergoing wear and tear, and being dirtied to no purpose.

In consequence of the exposed state of the roadstead, the monsoon, or rather the effect of it, is felt much more at Madras than anywhere along the coast, thereby rendering it very dangerous for shipping lying at anchor. It is considered to be so hazardous, that the flag-staff is struck during its prevalence, as a signal for all vessels to leave the anchorage, giving timely warning that it is not safe to remain there longer than is absolutely necessary. All the smaller country craft invariably quit, and nothing is to be seen in the roads at such a period, save the larger vessels, and of these only a very few.

The communication from shore with ships in the roads is very hazardous, owing to the surf which rolls upon the beach with terrific violence, causing its roar to be heard for several miles inland. It not unfrequently occurs that ships and other vessels are cast away, and many lives lost.

I myself witnessed a truly distressing circumstance of the above description, during the monsoon, when a very beautiful ship was completely lost, and the fortunes of the commander blighted for ever. She had come into Madras, laden with teak-timber from the Tenasserim provinces. The day after her arrival, it blew a dreadful gale, so much so that all the different vessels, large and small, slipped or cut their cables and stood out to sea, but the *Th*—— held her ground beautifully, and weathered the gale, which blew with unabated fury for the whole of that night.

The day following there was a lull, and the captain determined on shifting his berth and bringing her close in shore, so as to be able to float out and land his timber in safety. He was advised by many seafaring men at Madras to remain where he was, as her anchor had good holding-ground, and there was no necessity for his landing his timber in such a hurry.

However, he shifted his ship's berth and coming close in shore, commenced landing his timber. So secure did he consider his vessel to be, that he actually slept on shore that night, leaving the ship in charge of his chief officer. It blew a perfect hurricane during that awful night, and the sea rose tremendously high, and beat right into the buildings on the beach.

Towards morning, the hapless ship was discovered to be dragging her anchor, and drifting fast in shore. The mate saw the danger in which his ship was placed. He therefore let down another anchor, in the hopes of bringing her up, but such was the violence of the sea, and the consequent strain upon the cables, that in a very short time the chain of the last snapped like whip-cord, and the vessel came rapidly and struck the shore. I never can forget this truly appalling sight. A huge vessel, as she was, carried by the force of the mighty waves, as easily as a piece of cork, and dashed on to the beach, within twenty yards of the high road.

The agony of mind which the unfortunate captain suffered must have been intense. I saw him standing on the beach, no doubt reproaching himself for his obstinacy in not having taken the advice of his friends for the safety of his ship. Shortly after she grounded, ropes and hawsers were passed on shore, and the whole crew, including officers, were landed in safety. The surf made a clean breach over her, from stem to stern, dashing the spray into the very houses, and drenching the thousands, who congregated to see the spectacle, to the skin. She was so strongly, and so well put together, that she lay on the shore for several months after, and was eventually taken to pieces by degrees.

The captain was from that time a broken-hearted man. He quitted Madras soon after, and went to Rangoon, where he died, without relations or friends to cheer his last moments.

We of the 40th are certainly very much attached to the navy, and I trust we shall always be so too. The men used to take up the same feeling, and frequently went on board the *lŭrraee jha*ʒ (fighting-ships), to see the sights, and talk with the *sailor logue*, as the sepoys call our gallant tars, and it was highly amusing to see the latter with the former, cracking their jokes and trying to make them drink grog and taste a bit of salt junk; and, when the ship's crew were at quarters, and went through their evolutions, working their guns, handing their sails, and doing everything with that peculiar smartness for which the British Navy is so famous, our lads would stand on the poop in silent admiration and wonder. Can there be a more beautiful heart-stirring sight than that of a man-of-war's crew, either at the daily routine of exercise, or in real action?

We were frequently guests on board the *W*——, which was for a considerable period the only ship of war in the roads. They had other visitors on board, of course, as well as ourselves, and that every day. Under such circumstances, it was as well to avoid putting their hospitality too often to the test; but some people never think of the expense which they put others to, as long as they themselves have not to pay the piper. This was exemplified in one individual, whom I remember seeing every time I visited the *W*——. He was decidedly a standing-dish either at the

Madras Beach from the south, showing the newly-built ice-house for storing ice from North America; watercolour by Lt. R. Thompson

ward-room or at the gun-room mess-table; and almost lived on board.

This personage was a great connoisseur in beer, which he would drink to such an extent, that I am really afraid to say how many bottles he would swallow at one sitting. It was quite a wonderful and a curious sight to watch the manner in which this poor man drank his beer. No sooner was the glass to his lips than the contents disappeared in a trice! I tried to do the same one day, by way of experiment, and only succeeded in half choking myself.

The officers of the *W——* very soon became weary of this every-day occurrence. Had the man been an agreeable companion, or in any way amusing, they might probably have been induced to overlook this propensity; but he had not one redeeming quality in him, so that he soon became a perfect nuisance. But this daily intruder on board the seventy-four did not continue his visits for any length of time. One day, the admiral happening to be on the quarter-deck when he tumbled up the ladder, he was seen, and got a hint to quit the ship, such as he could not well help taking, much to the delight of all the officers.

At Madras, I had purchased a very fine young Arab horse for a charger. He was a beautiful dashing creature, and one day while I was riding him on the evening promenade, the beer-drinker caught sight of him, and admired him much. He said that he thought the animal would make him a capital parade-horse (he was in the cavalry) and offered to become a purchaser if I wished to part with him.

He offered me a couple of hundred rupees in addition to what I had given for him, and I agreed, provided that he liked him after a fair trial. I jumped off the horse, and he mounted with considerable difficulty, nearly tumbling over the other side. He set spurs into the horse's flanks, and although his rider was a very heavy man, (being fat and bloated from good living and beer-drinking), the animal made no difficulty in galloping off with him as hard as he could go. I saw at once that it was a regular runaway, the rider had no power over the horse, and in turning a corner over a bridge was thrown with violence against the parapet, and conveyed home in a state of insensibility. I do not exactly know what became of him but I think he went into the Invalids, and died shortly after of apoplexy or *delirium tremens*, one or other, the dreadful effects of drink.

The blue-coats and red should, and always do, move hand in hand wherever they go. There cannot possibly be two nobler professions. Hurrah for the wooden walls of old England, and the gallant hearts of oak which guard them; and hurrah for the red-coats, too, who fight shoulder to shoulder with them by sea as well as by land!

ARLY IN THE YEAR 1838, the government deeming it prudent that the number of troops employed in the Tenasserim Provinces of Burmah should be increased, in consequence of an expected rupture with the Burmese, a brigade of two regiments, consisting of HM ——rd foot, then stationed at Arnee, and my own corps, were ordered to prepare for foreign service as an augmentation, sufficient in strength it was supposed for the holding in check the warlike spirit and hostile intentions so evidently gaining ground at the court of Ava. We accordingly received the *hooken* (order) to make all necessary arrangements preparatory to embarkation.

I must explain here that a regiment of native infantry going on foreign service (which signifies quitting the continent of India for China for instance, or for the Straits' Settlements, the Tenasserim Provinces, or Aden, or Egypt) are obliged to leave their families behind, they not being allowed to accompany the corps. In fact, it could not be done. The government are liberal in the extreme on these occasions, and readily make every arrangement in their power for the comfort and maintenance of the numerous host, which is always attached to a native regiment.

Each soldier previously to his following his colours on such an occasion is obliged to register his nominated heir in a book in the adjutant's office kept for that purpose. This record is corrected every quarter by a committee, giving the soldier an opportunity to make what alterations he may please, according to the current circumstances of life.

This book is one of the greatest consequence to the interests of the soldiery, and consequently requires the greatest care and minutest supervision in being always kept complete and ready for reference. As casualties occur among the men, the nominated heirs benefit, accordingly; those for pension obtain the salary allowed by the regulations for their life-time only, it not being transferable from one to another, and ceasing immediately on the decease of the individual holding the certificate.

The soldier himself receives an increase to his monthly salary, and his family is taken every care of during his absence; and, if anything happens to him one member of that family, at least, obtains a stipend for life of half the amount of the pay received by the soldier while alive. Can there be anything more handsome, or more liberal? In addition to this, he is enabled to transfer a moiety of his monthly pay, amounting to one half of the whole, to his family for their support, for the period of his being sundered from them in the performance of his duty.

I think it of the utmost importance that the officers of a regiment, from the senior down to the youngest ensign, should give their whole energies and attention to the necessary arrangements of preparing for foreign service. Personal supervision in composing the requisite documents, of which a great number have to be written, is a matter of most urgent attention.

The disadvantages of neglecting such important matters are greater than the careless or the ignorant can conceive. Witness some of the disturbances in certain corps, in which the men have positively refused to go on board, openly avowing their determination not to do so until they were made aware of what they were to expect, declaring that they would not quit the shore, except every doubt and misunderstanding were cleared up.

Our arms and accoutrements were taken into the arsenal in the fort, and there carefully packed up in large chests and boxes. Our people were very loth to part with their firelocks, but they would have been in the way, and probably injured on the voyage. But the principal cause of their being put away is in compliance with a line of policy adopted by the government for being on the safe side, in case of any discontentment and consequent outbreak, while on board, among the native soldiery, which would render them a powerful enemy to deal with, possessed, as they would be, of their own weapons.

Provisions and water were shipped in large quantities; and in this government were not in any way stinting, every article for culinary purposes having been abundantly supplied for daily consumption during the passage. The water-casks were filled by high-caste Rajhpoots of another regiment, detached for that express duty; and in this, too, they are obliged to be exceedingly particular, because neither Hindoo nor Moslem will touch anything that has been defiled by other people; whereas, Rajhpoots and Brahmins, being considered by both sects as high-caste men, are deemed quite unobjectionable, though a Moslem employed for the purpose will render the water as tainted, and, consequently, unfit for

use of the Hindoo, while the sons of the Prophet have no such feelings of
punctiliousness with regard to their brethren.

The men were all strongly recommended to start their families off as
soon as they possibly could to get them out of the way, and a day was fixed
upon for every living camp-follower to leave the lines upon pain of severe
censure. But this was of no avail; for, although they did obey orders and
quitted the lines, still they lingered behind to have a last parting with their
relatives, thereby making matters worse than they were. Do what we
would, there was no getting rid of the old women. They stuck to the men
like leeches; and what was to be done we knew not.

I shall never forget our march down to the beach that morning. The
men were at intervals shouting, as if on purpose to keep down, or drive
away, their own sorrows, and the lamentations of the thousands who
followed them on either side of the road. The morning was a fine one,
though the night had been stormy. The surf was, therefore, very high
indeed, and it was at first feared that we should not be able to embark.

The band played away some spirit-stirring tunes which added to the
excitement of the moment, and I felt as happy as possible at the thoughts
of a trip to sea after our disagreeable sojourn at Vepery; added to which,
we had the prospects of seeing some service, which contributed not a little
to our delight. We reached the beach at about six o'clock, and there found
HM ——rd Foot, the regiment which was to accompany us, already on the
point of embarking.

The two corps cheered each other loudly as we came up, and the
soldiers and sepoys shook hands as merrily as possible. The line having
been formed and other arrangements made, we proceeded to apportion the
men to the *massulah* boats, which were all drawn up on the beach with their
crews ready for work.

The noise and hubbub caused by the presence of women and children,
old and young, big and little, all howling forth their lamentations, and
imploring blessings from their deities upon the heads of their departing
relations, were truly distressing and the heart-rending shrieks and piercing
cries of some of them, as their husbands, trying to smother their own
feelings, leaped into the boats, and pushed off from the beach, were
piteous in the extreme, and sufficient to unman the stoutest there present.
Many a gallant fellow did I see almost choking with emotion, trying all
they could to conceal their feelings, and dashing the tear-drop as it forced
its way, despite of their efforts to conceal it. Many, alas! parted from their
dear ones never to meet again!

But the parting once over, and the men in the boats rowing off to the shrill music of the merry fife and the rattle of the drum, they took off their caps and shouted their war-cry of *'Dheen! dheen!'* until they made the neighbouring buildings ring again!

Husband and wife; painting by an Indian artist showing a Madras sepoy and his wife, c. 1810

Our old commanding officer was himself so excited that he stood on the beach waving his cap, and bawling most lustily, little heeding my adjutant-like efforts to keep him from being overtaken by the surf. There he stood, calling out most frantically, and moved not until a huge wave broke and covered him from head to foot, very nearly carrying him into the sea by the receding of the water. As it was, we had a difficulty in pulling him back. He got a thorough ducking for his obstinacy, and stood dripping with the briny element. But the best of the joke was that he laid the whole blame upon my poor shoulders, and declared that I might have saved him from the wetting if I had liked.

The last batch that left were the commanding officer, his staff, with the colours and guard.

As we pushed off from the shore in the boat, we were greeted by a long and piercing shriek, or rather yell, from the numerous people assembled; the families of the men paying a last farewell to the big man who had the interests and welfare of their relations in his hands; the shouting became more and more faint as the boat distanced the shore,

Embarcation on Madras Beach; aquatint by T.B. East, c. 1856

many of them lingering behind to take a last look at us as we neared the ship.

We arrived at the beach I think at six o'clock, and, if I recollect rightly, the ship's bell struck *six* when the accommodation boat came alongside.

When the commanding officer's boat came alongside, we found the men already on board, in a miserable plight, from the effects of sea-sickness. The whole of both upper and lower decks was covered with men lying promiscuously in all directions, vomiting, and groaning, and moaning in the most distressing manner possible. 'Twas, indeed, a most piteous sight; but we thought the best way was not to interfere with them for a while, and allow them to remain where they were until somewhat recovered from the nausea.

In the meantime, our active and intelligent quartermaster, with that *best* of quartermaster-sergeants, old M—— C——, bustled about, and made the necessary arrangements for berthing the men below, knowing that the sooner they were got out of the way, and comfortably stowed, the sooner would they recover, and find their own places, and look about them. The men were, therefore, called down by sections, commencing with our grenadiers, and their respective places assigned to them for the rest of the voyage.

I forget now how many there were of our party altogether, but the ship was full from stem to stern, with little or no spare room for anybody.

The European officers were accommodated in the poop-cabins, while the whole of the gun-deck was allotted to the troops. There were large gun-ports on either side, which, being opened in fine weather, gave a free circulation of wholesome air, and made the place nice and cool for the men.

The height between decks was sufficient to enable our tallest grenadier to walk about without knocking his head against the beams. There were large wide hatches with wind-sails rigged down each, so that as far as comfort was concerned, the men and officers had every reason to be satisfied with their berths. The men slept on the deck by ranks, foot to foot, on each side, being ranged by companies, subdivisions and sections, with non-commissioned officers between each, and the native officers at the heads of companies. The width of beam was sufficient to admit of a tolerable space between the men's feet to pass backwards and forwards when necessary. I never would wish to sail in a better transport than was the *N*——. Her only fault was her age; may good luck attend her and her worthy skipper, wherever they go!

I shall not forget the first night we had on board, when I wandered out of my roost, in quest of water, without a light, and, when groping about in the dark, my putting my hand into the gaping mouth of some slumbering son of the sea, and being duly rewarded for the insertion by a bite, which made me roar with pain! Nor shall I forget the ghost-like apparition of our night-capped commandant, who, roused out of his sleep, thrust his head out of his cabin, and, in a towering passion, inquired who it was making such a noise; and, on being informed of the fact, that it was no less a personage than his adjutant, exclaimed, 'Why, what a row you're making, man, I thought the old ship was on fire!'

There are always a certain number of *cabooses*, or cooking-places, supplied according to the size of the ship, or the number of troops on board. We had, I think, six of these appendages, three for the Hindoos on the larboard side, and three for the Moslems on the starboard; the Christians, Parriahs, and other low-caste men, were cooked for by the Moslems. In addition to these *cabooses*, there were huge cauldrons, with ladles, &c. for boiling rice, as also small utensils for making curries, as well as stones, with pestles for grinding the curry stuff, &c. and making chutney, and so forth.

These culinary utensils, &c. are served out to the cooks, who are held responsible for their safe keeping, as well as for the cleanliness and preservation of the *cabooses*. Sentries are posted over them to guard against fires (which are invariably put out at *retreat-beating*) as well as to prevent those who have no business there to come near, or to touch them. This latter arrangement is on account of the prejudices of caste, the natives having a particular objection to anything connected with their eating or drinking being defiled by unworthy persons.

In serving out the food, after its having been cooked, each man comes and receives his own by rank; that is to say, the commissioned officers first, and then the non-commissioned, and so forth. Those of the lower *castes* come last of all; and the remains are kept until evening, when the whole is warmed up for a kind of supper; what is then left is preserved till the morning when those who like can warm up the cold rice, or make themselves *chuppaties*, or flat cakes, which, with the aid of a small curry, make the men a capital breakfast. There is no lack. The men can be eating all day, and yet there would be plenty, and to spare.

Our sepoys do not mess together. Their eating and drinking are left to themselves. Some of them, however, do club together, and make what arrangements they please. I do not approve of messes amongst natives, though I have heard people say that such could easily be established.

The water is given out every morning under the superintendence of the European officer of the day. The duty is an unpleasant one, inasmuch as that the place where the water is kept being in the ship's hold, the heat is insufferable, and that added to the filthy state of such localities, renders a visit to those regions of darkness by no means delightful.

The Rajhpoots and Brahmins had water given them separately from the rest of their comrades. A *scuttle-butt* was handed over to them for their own special use, and this was hoisted up from the hold and lashed in a convenient place on deck. The precious butt was an object of the deepest interest and care among those concerned. A sentry, one of their own *caste*, was posted over it in order to guard against defilement. When emptied, the butt was replenished, but in strict conformity with rules as regarded quantity per diem.

This arrangement effectually prevented clashing or disputes among the men, though many were the amusing scenes we witnessed when any of the crew in the performance of their duty would unthinkingly place his unhallowed feet upon the sacred receptacle for water. What shouting there would be! What angry looks! And how coolly would the ignorant sailor take the matter, hitch up his trousers, turn his quid, and tell the sepoys to go to a certain warm place which I will not mention.

But the ship's crew and our men pulled capitally together, as I can vouch for. Our sepoys were ever ready to assist them in the duties of the ship, and they invariably did all they could to please their dark-visaged passengers. It is to me a delightful thing to see the European and the Indian together – when the former looks upon the latter with friendly feeling – when we see the blinded prejudices of ignorance overcome by the more generous and nobler feelings of the heart.

In consequence of the scarcity of the good things of life at the place whither we were bound, we took with us stores of wines, and beer, and other requisites; and all these put together occupied a considerable space in the hold, and were stowed away in what we considered a safe place. We discovered when too late that we had been labouring under a delusion.

Our worthy friends of the midshipmen's mess were always mightily civil to us, and frequently asked us to take a glass of grog in their den of a berth. At the early part of the voyage, our friends treated us with some abominable trash in the shape of English brandy, and gin, more resembling turpentine than real Hollands: but after we had been to sea, we were agreeably surprised at having much better of both descriptions of spirits than hitherto, but what was more, we discovered a most palpable similarity in our drink to our own brandy and gin!

The midshipmites, on being asked where such excellent spirits had been procured, very coolly replied that their mess-supplies had been got from our mess-agents (and so they were certainly), and that their best had been reserved for their friends on their becoming better acquainted! What will the readers say when I tell them that on our unpacking and examining our stores after landing, we discovered sundry dozens of brandy, gin, and beer, sherry, madeira, and port; champaign, hock and claret; jams, jellies, and other preserves; hermetically sealed provisions, and many sundries, *minus*, and wanting?

So the murder was out; the middies had helped themselves to their heart's content, and we had ourselves helped them too in demolishing our own goods, little dreaming at the time we were doing so of the trick thus played off upon us, and that the *Jacks* had got the blind side of us *sodgers*.

Thus our trip passed happily away. We passed the Andaman Islands on our starboard bow, sailing pretty close to the principal one, and at last arrived in safety off Amherst, the entrance to the river leading up to our destined port.

Towards the evening, a pilot boarded us, saying that he had come to take the ship up to Moulmein, at the turn of the tide. He was a fat over-fed European, a first-rate vulgarian, and evidently possessed of a no small fund of what is termed a good opinion of himself, to say nothing of impudence. He swaggered into the cuddy, where we all were at our wine; talked loudly, murdering King's English most distressingly, and addressed some of us in a tone of familiarity, as if he had known us for years.

This man was with us a couple of days altogether, that is, the whole of that afternoon and the next day, when we arrived at Moulmein. At meals, he proved himself a capital trencher-man. This I can vouch for, as he sate next to me at table, and I saw him demolish a whole baked sheep's head with the *garniture* in an incredible short space of time. We will make no allusions to the oceans of beer, wine, and brandy pawney, which passed down his capacious throat.

I must here observe, that the Salween river is a particularly winding one, and full of shoals and sand-banks, which are constantly shifting; the navigation, therefore, is one of no easy accomplishment, requiring the greatest care and attention, particularly with vessels of much draft of water, such as our own.

The sagacious and accomplished individual alluded to, however, affected to think little or nothing of the duty upon which he was employed, walking about the ship with a long cheroot in his mouth, which he was constantly lighting, calling out to his servant (for he had brought one with him) to fetch this and that, and swilling brandy and water to an extent which perfectly astonished me! How the man kept sober I cannot imagine; as it was, I looked upon him to be in a state completely unfitted to do his duty, and how he got the ship up in safety was a mystery to me.

We anchored at Moulmein sometime between two and three in the afternoon, and immediately began disembarking.

On landing at the wharf, we were saluted by a tremendous shower of rain, by way of welcome to the Tenasserim Provinces. After we had got thoroughly wet, the men were marched off by companies, to a place about two and a half miles away, where tents had been ready pitched for their accommodation, while the officers were left to find shelter for themselves wherever they best could. The way up to our new cantonments led through a long street, composed entirely of Burmese houses, so very different in construction and material to those of India, that we were taken

British troops march into Rangoon during the First Burma War, 1824; Coloured aquatint from Moore's Burma Empire

by surprise; the appearance and dress of the natives, men and women, also attracted attention, and we could not help observing the fine make and looks of the former, and the handsome tasteful character of the latter.

The natives of Moulmein, and indeed those of the whole country, are a stout muscular race of men, of fair complexion, and, in many instances, of handsome countenances. The women are generally good looking, clean and well dressed in silks and muslins, the manufacture of the country; but I will not trouble the reader at present, on these points.

Our situation on landing was anything but agreeable or pleasant – I mean that of the men, and a few of the officers. Let the reader picture to himself a whole regiment of infantry, with all its stores, and other appurtenances to boot, encamped on a piece of ground barely clear of brushwood and jungle, the rain pouring down in heavy torrents, and no covering overhead save that of the tents.

Our gallant men were not, however, left for any considerable time in this truly miserable condition. In about a week's time the main building, or 'place of arms', was sufficiently completed to admit the greater part of the corps under its shelter; the mess-house, and one large bungalow were also completed; in the course of a few days more, a considerable piece of ground was nicely cleared away, and regular lines marked out and commenced upon for the hutting of our men.

There were then ten huts to each company in each line, exclusively of those belonging to the native officers, who were allowed quarters for themselves and those whom they chose to reside with them. We had a first-rate hospital for our sick, which in due course of time increased beyond our expectations; the building was, however, very capacious, so that there was plenty of room.

Then we cleared and levelled an open piece of ground for our parade, and upon this we forthwith commenced operations as soon as our arms and accoutrements had been served out to us, and began in earnest to brush the rust off after our sea voyage. I think I may safely add, that by the time we had been six weeks at the place everything was as correct and regular as if we had been there a whole year. Nothing could exceed the cheerfulness of our sepoys; their behaviour was indeed worthy of the regiment to which they belonged.

The monsoon at Moulmein is, in my opinion, second to none. In troth, it is a monsoon in every sense of the word, what John Chinaman would call 'first-chop'. I never before nor since saw such rain. It seemed to fall in real earnest; no nonsensical little drizzling showers, but good fat downpours, with such thundering and lightning, and such a noise as it

British infantrymen at rifle practice in barracks near the Great Pagoda, Rangoon, 1857; watercolour by Lt. R. Thompson

rushed down, that it appeared to me always as if the flood-gates of heaven had been opened, and that we should all be afloat.

But although the rain falls in such torrents and for a considerable time, without any abatement, still there were always parts of the day when it would clear up and be as bright and sunshiny as a summer's day in old England; with the air so cool and delightfully pleasant, that we would wander about in perfect safety without the fear of the sun doing us any harm. I have frequently rambled over the country without even a hat on.

The roofs of our habitations being composed entirely of thatch, made of cocoa-nut leaves, the fall of the rain, as it pattered on them, caused such a din and noise, that, until accustomed to it, we could scarcely hear each other speak, unless we bawled out at the top of our voices. But, with all its drawbacks of rain, thunder and lightning, dampness, spoilt things, mildewed clothes, and other inconveniences, we did not dislike the monsoon.

We became located at Moulmein about the middle of May 1838, and I do not think that a finer brigade than that at Moulmein, at the time I allude to, could be assembled anywhere. The two European regiments were the most efficient I had ever seen, and the detachment of artillery, composed of as fine a body of men as ever formed in battery. The force was commanded by an old and experienced officer, who gave us little or no trouble, but kept everything in fighting trim; and we jogged on in the same peaceful hum-drum routine of daily duty, without any variety, or the slightest prospects of a brush with the Burmese, as our reinforcement had led us to expect.

The climate was very salubrious during the three years we were quartered there, notwithstanding its dampness; at least, it suited the European constitution, but the native soldiery suffered much. We lost upwards of a hundred men, principally from dysentery, and a disease termed *berri-berri*, but the complaints from which they died were brought on chiefly by intemperance. The soldiers of the European regiments were very healthy indeed. I think they lost not more than three men to our ten!

But I must, at this portion of my narrative, beg the kind reader's permission to curtail a lengthened period of three years, and all that took place during that time, in which I may have been concerned. I have my reasons for doing so; the principal of which is that, in the event of this, my present humble production, being dealt with in such a manner as to induce me to come before the public again, I hope to be able to bring out another effort of my pen and produce an account of a residence of those said years in the provinces of Tenasserim, which will, I trust, serve not only to amuse, but give an insight into that interesting part of our eastern possessions.

As before observed, we went through our three years' service in Tenasserim, at the expiration of which time we were relieved by another regiment of Native Infantry from Madras, which took up our lines, the officers purchasing our houses for little or nothing. The order for our embarkation having therefore come, we found ourselves in due course of time comfortably berthed on board the good ship *B—— M——*, a seven-hundred-ton ship, a detachment of the regiment preceding in a smaller vessel.

Our sepoys, having been to sea previously, got on this time much better than they did on first starting from Madras; besides that, the thoughts of home, and seeing once more those so dear to them, buoyed them up, and kept them all in high spirits and on good behaviour. We managed admirably in every way; the captain, officers, and crew trying all they could to make every one of us happy and comfortable, and I was delighted to see that our men appreciated their efforts, and demeaned themselves remarkably well towards them.

We had the misfortune to lose one of our sepoys overboard. It was a melancholy occurrence indeed, for I do believe the poor man was carried down by a shark. He happened to go out into the fore-chains, and by some mischance tumbled into the water. I was standing on the poop when he fell, and as he dropped astern, I leaned over the tafferel and told him not to be frightened, but to swim quietly as the ship was not going fast, and we would soon lower a boat and pick him up. The force of habit never forsook the unfortunate soldier even in his perilous situation, for leaving off swimming, he brought his right hand up to the salute and said, '*Bhote khoob, sahib,*' (very good, sir) in reply to my suggestion. The boat was promptly lowered, and pulled straight up to the spot where the man was seen. The bow-man stood up with a coil of rope in his hand ready to fling it to him, when suddenly he sank to rise no more; he must either have gone down from exhaustion, or cramp, or he must have been seized by a shark; I should say the latter, as he was known to be a first-rate swimmer.

On our arrival in the Madras roads, the worthy skipper of our ship fired a salute in honour of our colonel and the regiment he commanded, a compliment which was duly appreciated by us, the party for whom it was intended. The good folks on shore, however, thinking that the salute was meant for the fort, returned a similar number of guns, in regular style, but were much disappointed when informed that the firing was in honour of the colours of the 40th, then but just arrived from the Tenasserim Provinces. I heard something said about bills being sent to Captain H——for the powder expended at the saluting battery on the occasion, but whether that is true or not I am not quite certain.

We landed late in the evening, and marched into tents pitched for our accommodation on the beach; and after making every necessary arrangement for the proper keeping of our camp, we all met at the club, and finished the night with a capital dinner, and as much iced champagne as it was correct for us to expend on such an occasion, probably too much. What a delicious treat is iced champagne after a month's hot work on board a transport!

About a week after our landing, we marched up to Palaveram, and became there located with the other detachments of the regiment already there arrived. I remember the morning of our march up. We had all gone to a grand ball at Government House, where we had enjoyed ourselves, dancing until a late hour, leaving the festive scene just in time to repair to our tents.

I left the ball-room, and arrived in camp just as the first tap of the *générale* had commenced to beat. I had barely sufficient time to change my full-dress for the more comfortable costume of heavy marching order, and to mount my horse, when *the assembly* was beaten, and the men fell in. I happened to have charge of the regiment; the colonel having ordered the adjutant to march it up to its new station.

On passing Government House we saw that the dancing was still going on, and I made the band thunder out our regimental quick march, 'Rule Britannia', which, with our small drums rolling made a rattling noise among the buildings, and attracted the attention of the people assembled at the ball, and many a fair lady, as they passed us in their carriages, muffled up for fear of the morning air, looked out of their windows to see us as we tramped together to that heart-stirring tune, the favourite of the sea. What Englishman is there whose heart does not leap within him when 'Rule Britannia' rings in his ears?

The regiment had been stationed at Palaveram for about a month or so, when it was overwhelmed with a host of griffins posted to do duty in the same manner as I was in the old ——th, as related at the commencement of this my narrative. There were among them one or two well brought-up lads, but taking them altogether in a body, I never met with such an unruly set of young untaught cubs during the whole course of my experience.

There was not one among the whole set who could be brought to comprehend the absolute necessity of attending to orders, and, as to their showing any respect to their superiors, that was quite out of the question, their argument being that they were as good as their neighbours, and they did not see why they should be in any way subject to older officers.

Learning their duty was matter of secondary consideration; and, as to appearing in time for drill-parades, they came early or late, just as it suited their convenience. Talking to them and pointing out in a quiet way their errors, was like preaching to mud walls and wooden posts; they minded neither commanding officer, adjutant nor anybody else and snapped their fingers at the regulations of the service.

We were consequently under the necessity of adopting measures which very soon brought our young friends to their bearings, and taught them that they could not do as they liked in the army. The tricks which these lads played became so frequent as to give cause to serious animadversion. One night a set of them sallied from the mess-house, bent upon the destruction of the flag-staff in the brigadier's compound, an appendage of which the old gentleman was very proud; and had it not been for the timely interference of one of our officers then present, they most certainly would have carried their intentions into execution.

Another set sallied out and amused themselves by unhinging people's gates and putting them into other people's gardens. One young scamp would take the bugle and sound the alarm and assembly when everybody was asleep, thereby rousing and turning out the troops to the no small annoyance of the slumbering brigadier and commandants of regiments; and many other pranks too numerous for me to enter upon; suffice it to say, they played the deuce, did these self-same young men. The reader may from the above specimens come to the same conclusion, and readily coincide with me in opinion, that the griffins attached to the 40th were the most unruly set of ruffians that ever put on red coats. Glad indeed was I when they were all posted, and the regiment well rid of them.

Consequent on the number of casualties in the ranks of the regiment during the three years that we were at Moulmein, and subsequently to our return to the coast, by invaliding and pensioning, we had a great many vacancies to complete our establishment to the requisite total of one thousand bayonets. Our situation at Palaveram was by no means a favourable one for filling up the gap by recruits, and we did not like to pick up all the wretched beings who swarmed to headquarters from the purlieus of Black Town and Triplicane.

Immediately on our return from Burmah the regiment was broken up, and the usual leave granted to a certain proportion of all ranks, to visit their native villages and homes. Each individual previously to starting, was made to understand that the commanding officer expected him, on his return from furlough, to bring with him an eligible lad for the ranks, near relations, such as brothers and cousins, being preferable. By these means, we succeeded in obtaining some excellent recruits, and the older soldiers were thereby satisfied that many of their sons and other connexions were provided for, and in the same regiment with themselves.

Again, we were not idle at other quarters. Whenever I heard that there would be any annual festival at the famous temples in different places in our neighbourhood, for instance, Conjeeveram, Triputty, as also at Madura, &c., I always dispatched parties of men with native officers, directing them, on arrival, to assume their uniforms and go about nicely dressed, so as to attract attention; and select the finest young men they could possibly procure, never failing to inform them to what corps they belonged, and what lots of promotion was always given to well-behaved men, to which was to be added all the *blarney* and fine talk that the powers of language could command, to induce recruits to enlist.

We thus procured very good recruits with little or no difficulty; the consequences were, that before we had been long at Palaveram, we very nearly filled up our vacancies.

We remained stationed at Palaveram for about two years, and after having been inspected and reviewed by the general commanding the division, received orders to march early the following year to Masulipa-tam, a famous station up the eastern coast, in the northern division of our army. After all due preparations, we quitted Palaveram. The whole corps rejoiced at the idea of leaving the neighbourhood of the Presidency, and of going to a country which is so well known to be a cheap one to the native soldier and his family in all the necessaries of life.

Little did the gallant fellows think, as when the *quick march* was sounded, they rent the air with their shouts of '*Dheen! dheen!*' that dire disease in its most dreadful form would so soon attack them and carry off many a brave heart which now bounded with joy! Alas! alas! The third day after quitting, cholera broke out among the followers and men and did not

Cadets from the East India Company's Addiscombe College in full dress and undress uniform; aquatint from Costumes of the Indian Army

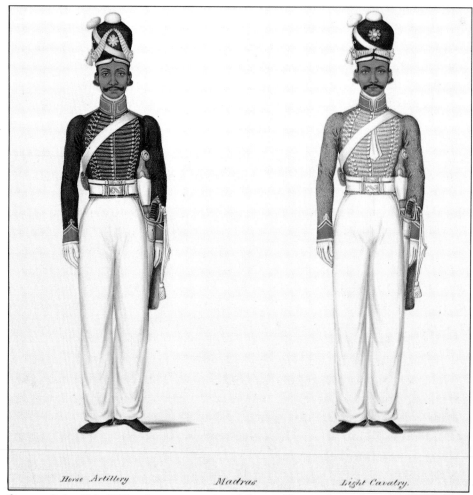

Horse Artillery   *Madras*   *Light Cavalry.*

Sepoys of the 40th MNI, all contemporaries of Ensign Hervey; drawn by an Indian artist in 'Company' style in 1835

leave them until they arrived at Masulipatam, after one of the most disastrous marches which the regiment had made since it was first raised. The havoc among the host of camp-followers was awful; upwards of five hundred fell victims to the scourge, and of the fighting men, upwards of fifty were carried off. Two European officers also died from the complaint.

Never shall I forget the horrors of that dreadful period, the sorrows I experienced, and how my heart bled when I read the various accounts which reached me from the afflicted camp, every letter making mention of some brave soldier with whom I had been associated for years.

There were many strange circumstances connected with the disease during the time it continued its havoc among the ranks of our regiment.

The first and last men who were attacked and died were both *havildars* of grenadiers; the finest and stoutest men; this company I believe suffered more than any other in the regiment, though the generality of those who perished were men of sickly constitutions, which, added to the fatigues and horrors of the march, rendered them easy victims to the disease.

The corps arrived at Masulipatam about the middle of April, and on its marching in, the one which we had come to relieve marched out, leaving all their guards standing so as to avoid contact, and contamination, which was fortunate, for they reached their next station without any symptom of sickness, and without the loss of a man, woman, or child.

But we know not what things will happen to us. My stay with the regiment was but of short duration, as will appear by the sequel. Circumstances obliged me to quit, but I did so with reluctance, since my whole heart and soul were attached to my regiment, and nothing but absolute necessity would ever have induced me to leave it. Having served my ten years, I sent in my application and obtained leave to proceed to Madras, preparatory to quitting the country on a furlough to Old Engand.

I had had little or no recreation since I first entered the service, and I longed once more to visit a land and scenes which I had left as a boy, as well as to see those dear to me, from whom I had been separated for a lengthened period. I therefore broke up my establishment, sold all my kit, scraped together what little money I had, and made preparations for a start. I think I may as well here mention, *en passant*, that I had become a Benedict some two years previously to this period of my life, so that, independently of my single self, I had the welfare and convenience of another, whom it was deemed necessary I should take to England in consequence of continued ill-health.

I must also add, that shortly after the return of the troops from China, I was agreeably surprised at the receipt of a letter advising me of the near approach of a brother, whom I had not seen for a number of years, and who had served in the China campaign. The long expected visitor arrived, but the effects of the climate of China, which had told so fearfully upon many, very soon became visible in his health, and he was, shortly after our becoming settled in our house, attacked with the dreadful fever of which he had several bouts before joining us. The disease affected him to such a degree as to prostrate both mind and body to so low an ebb of debility as to threaten his life; his medical adviser, therefore, deemed it absolutely necessary that he should quit the country without any delay, and seek a restoration to health by a visit to England.

Such being, then, the state of affairs, and having myself, as before stated, a wish to quit, we soon made up our minds to go home together. After due preparation, we started ourselves from Masulipatam in *palankeens*, hoping to reach Madras in about twelve or thirteen days' time.

These conveyances, or temporary dormitories, in addition to holding our respective persons, contained a variety of things, in the way of creature comforts and requisites; clothes, medicines, liquor, coffee, tea, and sugar; arrow-root, spice-box, lucifer-matches, candles, and books, *cum multis aliis*; outside, again, on the roof, was an imperial full of clothes; and at each end was a basket holding goglets of water, bottles of beer and soda, oranges, and so forth; all these addenda supernumeraries to the main establishment of *palkee* bedding and traveller, rendered the burthens rather heavier than the bearers seemed to relish; however, that was of the less consequence, because our temporary abodes became lighter each day, as the good things contained in them were expended.

In addition to supplies carried in and on our *palankeens*, we had three coolies (called 'Cavary-coolies'), each man with two tin boxes, of a peculiar pyramidical shape; in one of these pairs were stowed away, plates and dishes, cups and saucers, and cooking utensils, with odds and ends appertaining to Mr Cook (who accompanies 'muster and missus' riding on a tattoo, or bullock). Another pair contained extra supplies of beer, wine, and brandy (the latter about a dozen bottles, not only because of the spirits being anti-cholera, but to give to the bearers and servants by way of a treat, after a good run or soaking in the rain) and the third pair crammed full of eatables, in the shape of ham, tongue, hunter's beef, sausages of different kinds, pickles, sauces, jams and jellies, butter and cheese, bread and biscuits, and so on.

The tea-pot, kettle, and a bundle of firewood, are fastened to one of the *palankeens*, to be at hand should we stop anywhere for a short while, on which occasion we light a fire, warm some water, and enjoy a dish of tea, or a bowl of arrow-root with port wine in it, both delicious suppers, the reader may be assured, halting of a dark night in the jungle, or on the *maidan* (plain).

To each *palkee* is attached a man called a *mussaulchee*, or, to be more plain, a torch-bearer. His duty is to hold his flambeau, which is supplied at every fresh stage with a certain quantum of oil, contained in a primitive kind of a tin vessel, with a long narrow neck to it; these torches are lighted a little before dark, and afford great assistance and comfort to the bearers in finding their way in the night; a matter of no small difficulty, as the reader will understand, when I say, that at times they have to traverse miles of road completely under water, and so heavy with thick black mud, that it is really wonderful how they can contrive to get on without letting their load fall off their shoulders.

At length we arrived at the Presidency, and took up our abode at St Thomas's Mount, as a temporary arrangement, preparatory to a fresh start for Old England. Here we resided until the month of November, and finally embarked in the *H——*, one of the most beautiful vessels of her description I ever saw.

A period of ten years has been embraced in this narrative, from the first day of my landing on the shores of India, to that of my embarking for England. To detail the reminiscences and occurrences of that time, in which I have been principally concerned, has occupied a space of forty chapters, some of them longer than others, from unavoidable circumstances, and I have confined myself to that number, because it is one which is as familiar to me as mine own name, as dear to me as life itself, and which I shall ever cherish with the proudest feelings of a soldier.

Night travel by dawk; from Robert Thompson's albums of sketches, painted during his time in the 43rd MNI 1850–9

'Tis a number engraven on my heart, to be removed only by the hand of death, when its pulsation will have ceased for ever, and the hand that wields the sword which is ready to flash forth in the defence of that number shall lie cold in the lowly grave.

'Tis a number emblazoned on the colours of my regiment, which is so justly deserving; and 'tis a number which will ever be foremost in the cause of its country, whenever the standard which bears it, and the gallant *sepahees* who own it, may be called upon to maintain its honour, or defend its rights.

I trust that what I have penned may be useful to all whose lot is cast in India, conducive to the preservation of their health, and to the maintenance of that respectability of character, both public and private, so essential to their own welfare, and so requisite for the path of life which they have to follow, in the career they have chosen.

If such should prove the fruits of my experience, I shall indeed feel happy in having presented these volumes to the world.

GLOSSARY

arrak	–	distilled palm sap
batta	–	field allowance
Black Town	–	native town of Madras outside Fort St George
bushed	–	tent pegs strengthened with branches
Cantonment	–	military camp or quarter
cheroot	–	South Indian cigar
chee-chee	–	supposed mincing speech of Eurasians
Choutry	–	plain outside Madras, Army HQ
chunam	–	prepared lime plaster
Company	–	East India Company
Court of Directors	–	Board of Directors of EICo.
cuddy	–	public cabin of an Indiaman
cutwal	–	police officer
dawk	–	post provided by relays of men or horses
doolie	–	simple covered litter
dubashee	–	servant or interpreter
Duck	–	gentleman in the Bombay Service
Ensign	–	juniormost commissioned officer of foot
goglet	–	earthenware bottle
griff, griffin	–	newcomer to India
havildar	–	sepoy NCO equivalent to corporal
hookha	–	pipe smoked through water
Indiaman	–	EICo ship
Indian	–	term appropriated by British in India in early nineteenth century to describe themselves
jemadar	–	sepoy NCO equivalent to sergeant
King's Officer	–	British officer holding King's commission
massulah	–	surf boat of Coromandel coast
miasma	–	noxious vapour responsible for fevers etc
moonshee	–	language teacher or interpreter
Mull	–	gentleman in the Madras Service
naique	–	sepoy NCO equivalent to lance corporal
native	–	term employed by British to describe Indians (see Indians)
pagoda tree	–	source of wealth, from pagoda gold coin of S. India
pal	–	basic ridge tent
palankeen	–	box-litter, from palanquin
parriah	–	common yellow dog, also lowest caste of Hindu
pawnee	–	water, thus brandy-*pawnee*
Presidency	–	three governments of Madras, Calcutta and Bombay, also Madras Fort and town
putrid fever	–	typhus fever
Qui Hai	–	gentleman in the Bengal Service
sepoy	–	native soldier
sepahee	–	see *sepoy*
sub, subaltern	–	junior commissioned officer
tank	–	artificial reservoir
toddy	–	coco-palm wine
tope	–	grove of trees
wallah	–	person
writer	–	junior EICo civil servant

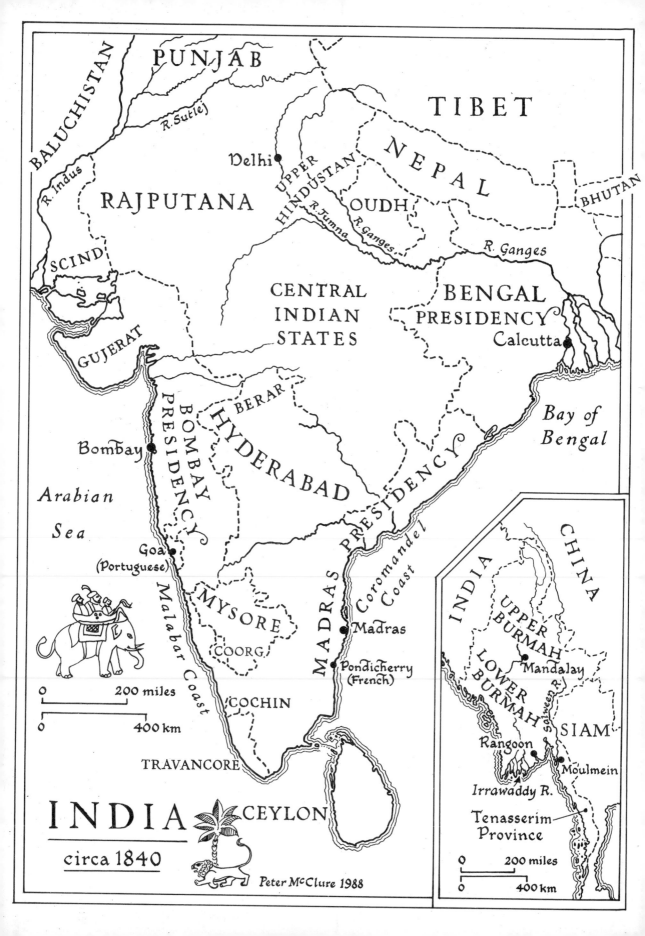

BALUCHISTAN

PUNJAB

TIBET

R. Sutlej

R. Indus

Delhi

UPPER
HINDUSTAN

NEPAL

BHUTAN

RAJPUTANA

OUDH

R. Jumna

R. Ganges

R. Ganges

SCIND

CENTRAL
INDIAN
STATES

BENGAL
PRESIDENCY

Calcutta

GUJERAT

BERAR

Bay of
Bengal

BOMBAY PRESIDENCY

HYDERABAD

Bombay

Arabian
Sea

MADRAS PRESIDENCY

Goa
(Portuguese)

Coromandel
Coast

CHINA

INDIA

UPPER
BURMAH

MYSORE

Malabar Coast

Madras

Mandalay

COORG.

Pondicherry
(French)

LOWER
BURMAH

Salween R.

200 miles

SIAM

0

COCHIN

Rangoon

0

400 km

Moulmein

TRAVANCORE

Irrawaddy R.

INDIA

CEYLON

Tenasserim
Province

circa 1840

0   200 miles

Peter McClure 1988

0   400 km